"THIS IS HARD FOR ME TO SAY."

Jody could barely get the words out.
"I . . . well . . . do you like my dress?" she blurted, realizing how stupid she must sound.

Clif was clearly puzzled. "It's perfect for you. Any man would love it. But did you really want to talk about clothes?"

"No. I'm sorry to be circling the issue but . . . It has to do with my morals—I mean my integrity. Oh, I don't know what I mean except will you please make love to me?"

Joyous astonishment flickered across Clif's face.

"If you laugh at me, Clif McClelland, I'll . . . I'll . . ."

Jody's stammered threat was silenced as Clif gently pulled her to him and whispered tenderly, "I would never laugh at you, Jody. Never."

ABOUT THE AUTHOR

Judith Bolander loves words. Fascinated by etymology, she's always been a voracious reader and now, at fifty-four, a writer. So what better setting for her first Superromance than a bookstore! To this Midwesterner, now residing in northern California, the solid traditions upheld in *The Best of Yesterday* are invaluable. Judith is proud to be publishing her first novel at this stage in her life and hopes her achievement will be an inspiration to other mature writers.

Judith Bolander

THE BEST OF YESTERDAY

Harlequin Books

TORONTO • NEW YORK • LONDON
AMSTERDAM • PARIS • SYDNEY • HAMBURG
STOCKHOLM • ATHENS • TOKYO • MILAN

Published June 1987

First printing April 1987

ISBN 0-373-70264-7

To Ame, Katie and Jeff, who were my motivation and cheering section, and to John for showing me the capabilities of mind and will.

To my Mom and Dad who equipped me to survive, to Alice Regina who made this book possible and to Lucy and Bill who said "Go for it!"

And to Sam, Carolyn and John who were always there....

CHAPTER ONE

HER SLIM BODY tensed in fury, Jody all but threw the telephone receiver into its cradle. "They've done it," she fumed to herself. "They've actually decided to betray me. My own uncles are selling my store right out from under me!"

She pounded her clenched fists on the arms of her chair, then stopped suddenly as another thought surfaced. *What am I thinking of? Betraying me? It's the whole family, not just me. It's Grandpa and Daddy— and every relative who ever loved this place, which means almost every Jenson who ever drew breath.*

Jody's gaze swept her office. It had been a mere four months since she'd redecorated it, a mere four months since her father had died and she'd become part owner and sole manager of Alferic's, the Jenson family's bookstore. A brief proprietorship, but Jody had been well schooled for it. As a toddler she had tagged her father's heels, and it had become a pattern that continued into adulthood. She had gone with him to estate sales, auctions and publishing houses. She had accompanied him on buying trips, and she had worked at his side in Alferic's every chance she got. The bookseller's trade permeated her very fiber.

Glancing around at the grass-cloth-covered walls, the matching cream carpet and the handwoven upholstery in warm earth tones, Jody wondered how much longer she would be able to call this office her own. Tears rose to mist her vision, brimmed, and tracked slowly down her cheeks.

"The whole idea is simply inconceivable," she announced to her desk. "Inconceivable that a Jenson would even contemplate selling Alferic's, let alone do it. Why, the store was even named after Grandpa. What sort of Jenson would want to sell Grandpa's namesake? Well, that's easy enough—a financially distressed sort would. My uncles have gotten our mills into horrendous debt, and now they want to sacrifice the bookstore, too. At this rate, we'll lose every business we own!"

Dragging her eyes from the desk top, she focused on the window to her left. The large oblong of glass overlooked the selling floor of Alferic's and provided a crow's nest view from her second-floor office. As she gazed down at the bustling crowds of holiday shoppers, she remembered another unpalatable fact: the entire Jenson building would be in outside hands if the corporate stock was sold. Not only the ground-floor bookstore, but the three floors of rentals as well.

Fresh anger swamped her sadness and a violent shove at the edge of her desk sent her chair flying backward on its casters. She shot to her feet, lowered the window blind and began pacing the floor.

"Think, Jody," she commanded. "Weeping and wailing never solved one single problem. What you've got here is just that, a problem. Problems have solutions, ergo this problem has a solution. There is a way to keep both building and store in the family. All you have to do is come up with the solution. So get busy and find it!"

Words of strength, but nothing presented itself. No matter how many thoughts ricocheted about in her head, no matter how many times she raked her fingers through her hair, she kept slamming into a solid wall that refused to be breached: uncles versus niece meant two to one. Majority rule would do her in. She couldn't help thinking how much easier things would be if her grandfather had bequeathed the store to her father alone. He was the only son who felt that a fine book was more to be treasured than a rare gem. Instead, the store had been left to all three sons, and now the family was facing the first disruption in its tight-knit history.

No doubt there would be a battle. She wasn't about to submit meekly to the dictates of any of the Jenson-clan males, no matter how ''elder'' they might be. But her chances of winning such a battle were slim. Jody admitted that her knowledge of corporations, the legal intricacies of buying and selling, and the business world in general would all fit neatly into a demitasse, with room to spare, probably. She needed help.

Instinctively she reached for the telephone to dial her brother and then she groaned. Carl wasn't in Minneapolis anymore, wasn't even in Minnesota, and there wasn't much he could do from Seattle at the moment. Who then? Alf, of course, her favorite cousin, whose office was just down the hall. Praying he wasn't with a client, she pressed the intercom.

Alf sounded relaxed and happy when he answered. And, as usual, he was ready to banter with her. ''I'm free as the proverbial bird, kiddo. About to head over to the exchange and make sure the old pork bellies are fattening nicely. Got some hot futures riding on those hogs." He paused expectantly. "Hey, no chuckles? No smart cracks? Jody, are you comatose?"

"No, let's just say, as long as we're into farm animals, that I'm madder than a wet hen. Alf, they've decided to sell their shares after all. That blasted chain, whatever it's called, is going to control the store and the building unless I can come up with a way to stop them. Having come to the conclusion that you're just the man to guide me, I'm counting on instant brilliance in the solution department, mister."

A short silence followed, then Alf let loose with a few expletives, ending on a relatively mild, "Damnation! My own father! Hard to believe. Okay, give me a chance to nudge the old gray matter while trotting down to your office. Something's bound to pop up."

He started to hang up, thought better of it and said, "Wait! Is it safe?"

"Safe? Is what safe?"

"Walking through your office door. I mean, I really don't need to get bopped on the head with a flying coffee cup today."

"Alfred Eric Jenson, that was completely uncalled for. I stopped throwing the crockery around when I was ten—well, twelve, maybe. Anyway, your temper is every bit as bad as mine and you know it. Now, start trotting." Laughing as she ended the conversation, Jody realized how very fortunate she was to have her fun-loving cousin so close by.

A few minutes later, Alf breezed in. "Drew a blank in the instant solution department, I'm sorry to say." He dropped into a comfortable chair in front of her desk and started filling his pipe. "But let me go over some things with you. As I recall, Grandpa's will made express provisions for the setting up of a privately held corporation to control Alferic's and the building. The stock was to be divided equally among the three sons. In addition, he specified that should one or two of them want to sell, the remaining shareholder or shareholders had to be given the right to buy before anyone else. That means—''

"Alf!" Jody leaned forward in excitement. "Excuse me for interrupting, but I'd forgotten that last part. You're saying they have to give me—oh, what's it called—right of first refusal, or something?"

"That's correct. You get a chance to make an offer and, if it's at fair market value, they have to take it."

"Voila! You have just solved the problem." She fairly beamed at him and then frowned. "Unless...Alf, what's 'fair market value'?"

"You've got me there. Except for some vague idea that it's based on recent sales in like locations, I'm at a loss. We'll be dealing with a precise legal definition, Jody, and apropos of that, our next step should be to call Warren. We need a lawyer."

She sighed and slumped back in her chair. "I suppose you're right. Glory, how I hate the thought of getting into some legal tangle, especially with the family. We've always pulled together on everything, not pushed apart."

"Don't start stewing yet, kiddo. It may not come to that. We need Warren just for the groundwork—get the shares assessed, clarify the will, determine fair market value, draw up contracts—all that kind of stuff. Who knows, the whole business may be over and done with in a couple of weeks, all parties wreathed in smiles and popping the Dom Perignon corks."

A chime sounded from above the office door.

"Sounds as though they want you on the floor, boss." Alf unfolded himself and got to his feet. "I'm going to call Dad, just to make sure we've got our facts straight, and then I'll give Warren a jingle and sound him out. Assuming he's not in court for the day, I should have something for you by lunchtime. When you've done racking up profits for yourself, why don't you grab your brown bag and come join me in my lair for lunch?"

Jody had already opened the door of her small washroom and was starting to make repairs to her hair and makeup. "Will do," she said over the sound of running water. "And thanks a million for all the help."

"My pleasure, kiddo." The office door banged shut behind him.

She smiled, then focused her attention on her image in the full-length mirror. "Nuts! I'm a mess—obviously been bawling and trying to tear my hair out."

She yanked the red ribbon from her heavy, honey-colored hair, dashed a comb through it and retied the ribbon. The splash of water had cleared her eyes of redness, so a whisk of powder and a touch of lipstick were enough to make her presentable.

Heading downstairs, she stopped midway, snapped her fingers and retraced her steps. She'd neglected to don "seasonal uniform." The scarlet smock was still half unbuttoned when she reached the bottom step and was instantly accosted; her hurrying feet brought to an abrupt halt by a man's strong grip.

"Excuse me, miss. I see by the smock that you work here. Great color for you, by the way—and I'm in a hurry. My father's hobby is etymology. That means the derivation of words, where they come from, root words, et cetera. Do you have anything along that line that I could get for him? Very expressive face you have," he added as he grinned down at her. "What are you doing in a musty old bookstore?"

Jody's face had, indeed, provided a kaleidoscope of expressions during this breezy speech. Astonishment at his comment on the color of her smock was followed quickly by annoyance at the definition of the word *etymology*, then replaced by amusement at his frank stare of admiration and his final sally. Threaded through these varying reactions was her awareness of the man's vital masculinity, of a power and strength so utterly male that a wild thrill darted through her. It was as quickly gone, leaving her puzzled and every bit as annoyed with herself as with him.

"For a man in a hurry, you certainly are long-winded. We have a fine selection on etymology, this is most emphatically not a musty bookstore, and I wear red quite often. If you will just come this way, please..." She led him swiftly across the floor, smiling and nodding at acquaintances and longtime customers as they went. Stopping in front of a recessed section, she rested a hand on a shelf and turned to face him.

"Here is what we have available. I would suggest the *Partridge*, if your father doesn't already have it. My family finds it invaluable in pursuing one of *our* favorite hobbies—etymology." A pleasant smile, a smothered chuckle at his startled expression, and she was off to open another cash register.

Jody's line moved at a leisurely pace, but no one waiting appeared to mind. They could see that she took time to chat with each person, comment on their purchases and, in many cases, greet them as old friends. Service and personal attention were hall-marks of Alferic's—a very important component of their success story and one of the reasons she loved her work.

"Mrs. Burnell, it's good to see you." Jody's sincerity was evident as she greeted the elderly lady who proffered her purchase. "Some very fortunate young person has a spot on your Christmas list, I see."

"My oldest great-grandson, Jody. He's five now—a perfect age for his first meeting with *Winnie the Pooh*." Her time-seamed face took on an anxious expression as she continued. "Do you think this edition, leather bound, gold tooled—it's so elegant—do you think I'm being foolish? He's so young..."

Jody held on to the change she was about to give her. "I don't know if you're being foolish or not. Does he have many books that he has to be careful with?"

"None that I've seen. He seems to really live with his stories. Even takes them to bed and falls fast asleep on top of the jumble."

"Well, in that case, wouldn't it be extra special to have this lovely volume? A treasure from his great-grandmother? Treating one book differently from his others wouldn't be hard, I don't think."

Mrs. Burnell brightened. "I see what you mean. If too many of his books were the handle-with-care type, he'd stop enjoying them. But one—well, he can respect that. Put it in a bag, dear. My mind is quite at rest. Such a lovely place to shop, Alferic's. Tell me, is Britta here for the gift wrapping again this Christmas?"

"She wouldn't miss it. Same old place and same beautiful papers. She'll be glad to see you."

As a contented Mrs. Burnell walked away, Jody took a quick look at her line of customers. It was quite short, and standing at the end of it was a certain gentleman whose father enjoyed etymology as a pastime. He sent her a knowing, self-satisfied smile, and even from a distance, Jody was aware of his dynamic aura.

The exasperated voice of her next customer precluded any thoughts on the meaning of that smug smile. "Miss! If you don't mind too much, I've been standing here for fifteen minutes now and I'd like to be on my way. We ordinary folks have just as many appointments to keep as anyone else," he complained.

"I know you do and I *am* sorry," Jody apologized as she zipped the entries into her register. "I've worked here for so long that I know many of the customers and it's hard not to chat a bit. Sorry for the delay." She handed him his bagged purchase with a warm smile. "Do come in again. We truly wish to please you."

"Well, the help's certainly nice," he conceded with a reluctant smile. "So's the atmosphere, and I found just what I wanted. My Aunt Agnes, now—" he assumed a relaxed stance "—she loves Sir Walter Scott. Romantic claptrap, if you ask me. But, it's Christmas, so why not make her happy? Now, I like hard covers—for gifts, that is. And where can you find any these days? Why, I've looked—"

"I'm so pleased you gave us a try," Jody interrupted, patting his arm. "We'll look forward to seeing you again. There's some spiced tea over there, if you'd care for a cup on your way out." Good heavens, he was more talkative than Mrs. Burnell! She reached for the next customer's purchase, effectively sending Aunt Agnes's nephew on his happy way toward the tea trolley.

Ringing up a routine sale of Michener's latest novel gave her a second chance to check the number of customers waiting. To her surprise, Mr. Satisfied Smile was still the last one in her line. Why had no one come to stand behind him? And why was his left hand behind his back when he could surely have used its help in supporting the heavy *Partridge*?

Another glance and the mystery deepened.

A middle-aged man approached her line, paused to stare at the broad, Oxford gray back that brought up the rear, smiled and left for another register. What on earth was going on? One patron later, Jody turned to look up into a pair of twinkling eyes the color of a summer sky, accentuated by straight, dark brows and crisp, black hair. Unaccountably, her heart proceeded to do a quickstep.

"We meet again, Miss Jenson. You'll be pleased to note that I took your advice." He plunked down the thick volume, his free hand still hidden from view.

"I'm sure your father will be happy with your choice. And now, would you mind telling me just how you happen to know my name and why your hand is behind your back?"

"I asked one of the salespeople for your name and this is why..." His arm swung forward to reveal the piece of cardboard he was holding, obviously retrieved from some wastebasket. Bold lettering proclaimed, "This line closes after me because I'm taking the lovely lady at the register to lunch."

Jody gaped at the sign. Then, realizing she must look like a beached fish, she promptly snapped her jaw shut.

"Why of all the arrogant, brazen . . ." she fumed with rising indignation. "How dare you turn customers away."

"Hey, they loved it. Understood immediately. Fascinating lawyer meets gorgeous clerk and abducts her for lunch. Who wouldn't fall in with that? Encourage it, even? Especially at this time of year."

"I'll tell you who—me. I wouldn't fall in with that or encourage it, no matter what the time of year." She flipped the book cover open to expose the flap and began punching register keys. "A lawyer. I might have guessed—all those glib words. Typical. How did you wish to pay for your purchase, Mr. Fascinating Lawyer?"

"Clifton F. McClelland, known to my friends as Clif, at your service, ma'am." He handed her a credit card. "Where would you like to eat?"

"Right here, enjoying the lunch I brought with me."

"Seriously? You'd settle for brown bagging it when you could eat in luxury at The Orion?" He shrugged good-naturedly. "Dinner sounds better, anyway. What time should I pick you up?"

"What?" Jody could hardly believe what she was hearing. "Mr. McClelland, you are the most—oh, nuts! Now you've made me enter the wrong digits with your crazy babbling."

"My mistake, only right that I correct it." He stepped behind her and put a hand on her shoulder as he peered at the offensive, demanding flashes on the screen.

Jody was instantly aware of shivers running up and down her arm. His touch had triggered a delightful, trembling sensation that was rapidly spreading through her body. Good heavens! Had Clif noticed it? She pulled away from his hand and turned in anger.

"Mr. McClelland, I will make the correction, whereupon you will accept your receipt, pick up your package and exit this store. Is that clear?"

"Quite. My only question is, when shall I return to pick you up for dinner?" The picture of decorum, Clif stood aside, face set in a pleasant, accommodating expression. "I'll bring character references when I come," he added.

"You're impossible!"

"No, persistent. I know what I want, and I don't give up until I've got it."

"But otherwise perfectly easy to get along with, I presume." She locked her register and put the book into a bag before continuing. "Look, I'll be blunt. I don't like your battering-ram approach. I have not been, nor will I ever be, picked up by a strange man. I detest lawyers and I am not going to dinner with you tonight, or any other night. Now, before I have to call security, here is your father's gift, your receipt, your credit card, and good—"

"Clifton, dear boy! How splendid to see you!" A beaming, stout matron swathed in silver fox clapped Clif on the back. "I saw your dear mama just this morning in Dayton's, buying the most extravagant gift for some lucky young man. And Jody," she exclaimed, navigating a quarter turn to give her a whack, too, which nearly knocked the wind from her. "Dear child, you're looking marvelous. Such color in your cheeks and light in your eyes. You must have just come in from a brisk walk.''

Jody heard Clif's low laugh at this explanation of her fury-flushed cheeks and sparking eyes. Damn! Leave it to old Mrs. Fenton to charge about like the proverbial bull. And she was still rattling on.

''To think you two know each other. Splendid. Just splendid. Perfectly suited. I've known you both from the cradle, so you can take my word for it. Now, a kiss for both of you and I must be on my way. So much shopping to do. Jody, do give my love to your dear mama. This will be a sad Christmas for you all, I know. Fine man, your dear papa was. We shall all miss him dreadfully.'' A damp smack for each of them and she sailed away, leaving in her wake a dismayed Jody and a grinning Clif.

''Well, so much for the 'strange man' excuse, Miss Jenson. The necessary character reference popped up like a genie from a lamp. What time would you like me to pop up this evening?''

''Never,'' she grumbled, walking to one of the store's comfortable seating arrangements and sinking into a leather club chair.

Clif followed suit.

''I thought you were in a hurry,'' she said.

''My priorities changed.''

''Mr. McClelland, I simply can't—''

''In that case,'' he interrupted with a deep sigh, ''you have just succeeded in shattering my afternoon. Now I will have to dash over here between each appointment, stopping first at the handy flower shop next door for large bouquets . . .''

Jody's helpless laughter ran over his words. "You are crazy. Absolutely crazy. You don't even know me!"

"Precisely. A situation I intend to remedy forthwith. So, what time, lovely lady?"

She rested her forehead in her hand and tried to think. She really couldn't have him barging into the store every hour. But surely he wouldn't do such a ridiculous thing. It must all be blustery show.

"Would you really come over here all afternoon?" Jody asked, looking up.

"Scout's honor."

Jody groaned and returned her forehead to its resting place. He had to be some kind of nut. But Mrs. Fenton knew him, knew his family. It wasn't fair to hold his career against him. There had to be some decent attorneys, like Warren, and this Clif had to at least be intelligent, or he'd never have passed the bar exams. Might be an interesting conversationalist, or monologist, as the case would doubtless be. Probably loved the sound of his own voice and, devastatingly apparent, he certainly thought he was God's gift to women. All right, lunch then. Shorter and less resemblance to a date.

Suddenly Jody remembered promising Britta she'd fill in at the Will Call desk and wrapping counter at one o'clock. Judging from the stack of orders waiting to be picked up by customers, Will Call alone would keep her hopping.

"Dinner will be fine," she said, sitting up straight and extracting a pencil and notebook from her pocket. "Seven o'clock, this address." Jody started to get up. "Wait. I have to take my mother to my cousin's for dinner. You can pick me up there." She scribbled down another address and tore the first one up. "And I have to be back there to take her home by eleven." Without giving Clif an opportunity to object, she headed for the stairs to her office.

Irritated with herself, Jody grabbed her lunch bag and headed down the hall to Alf's office, mumbling as she went. "A lawyer. Of all the sorts I could have picked to get mixed up with, I have to pick the most detestable. Words, words, words. By the time we get to the coffee, my eardrums will be numb. Well, no point in stewing about it, I said I'd go and that's that. Maybe he'll turn out to be 'fascinating'—conceited self-assessment! All I can do is hope."

Alf's door was closed, so Jody sat down in the reception area until he was finished with his client. Rummaging through her bag for an apple, she began musing over the latest crisis in her life—the possible loss of Alferic's. The very thought constricted her throat and brought the threat of tears. The store had become her rock in life, a foundation to rebuild on after eight months of little but misfortune and grief.

Since terminating her engagement in the spring, Jody had spent the past few months feeling as though she was dwelling on quicksand. Shortly after her breakup with Rich, she'd lost her beloved father in a car accident that had also left her mother an invalid. To help and comfort her mother on the road to adjustment, Jody had locked up the old Victorian she was renovating at Lake of the Isles and moved back home for a few months. This latest upheaval had caused her to cling more tenaciously than ever to her manager's desk at Alferic's. It seemed the only firm ground in her life. Now that was about to slither out from under her, too.

Maybe I should just give it all up, she thought. *Find a cave for sale in the Himalayas, wrap myself up in saffron robes, sit cross-legged on the dirt floor and chant mantras.* It was the ultimate cop-out, and not without appeal, but definitely just a momentary flight of fancy. Jody was not a quitter.

Despite a sheltered, lavish upbringing, there was steel in her nature, drive and determination in her acute mind. The wealth of the Jenson family had not produced a weakling in Jody. Because it was "old" money, the novelty of acquisition had long since palled. The clan elders demanded character in their young and frowned upon any showy or frivolous spending.

Keeping a close eye on the upcoming generation was not a difficult task. Most of the family lived in one spot, on a peninsula jutting into Lake Minnetonka.

This sizable spur of land belonged solely to the Jenson family. It had been purchased in the early 1900s as a summer refuge from the city heat and, over the decades, cottages had given way to large, permanent homes. By the time Jody was born, the grassy center of the land sported tennis courts, a softball diamond and a volleyball court. What with the lake for boating, fishing and swimming, plus a glorious assortment of tadpoles, ducks, otters and other wonders of nature, it was a children's paradise. They had named it Sanctuary Point, and so it was. The Jenson young met the world, armored in the knowledge that they had a safe house. The Point was always waiting.

Jody had grown up there surrounded by love and care, as well as material plenty. To ease her way still further, she had inherited her mother's Swedish beauty. She was blessed with the candid, wholesome appearance of the finest Nordics, a lithe build and hair the color of corn silk. At age twenty-five, endowed so abundantly, the world was filled with open doors inviting her exploration. However, as she waited for Alf, it wasn't opening doors that furrowed her brow; it was the possibility of a closing door—the loss of Alferic's.

There was a measure of frustration in her thoughts, frustration over her failure to convince her uncles of the store's importance in her life. No matter what she told them, they insisted upon regarding it as a hobby for their young niece. Along with their brother, Jody's late father, the uncles had been raised with old country standards, as were most children of immigrants. In Swedish homes this meant male domination, female acquiescence; males handled the outside world, females handled the homes. Unfortunately, they had gone on to raise their own children the same way while, paradoxically, instilling self-sufficiency in them regardless of sex. The contradiction had presented the female children, like Jody, with a dilemma that was only resolved by trusting their own judgment and acting upon it. However, the uncles were persistent in acting as if they were still in the old country. Despite the upbringing Jody had received, and the ample proof of her dedication and capabilities, they refused to believe that the store had real meaning in their niece's life. Therefore, what difference would it make to her in the long run if they sold it?

Dearest Jody, they would say with paternal condescension and pats on the head. *How wonderful to have something to keep you busy until you get married, as all lovely, delightful young ladies such as yourself do.*

They get married and have babies, they guard home and hearth, they do not run businesses. But it will do until your prince comes along. These words would invariably be followed by more fond chuckles and pats on the head.

Just thinking about their jocular chiding caused Jody to nearly choke on her apple. As if the store were a toy she was simply marking time with until some white charger galloped into view bearing a gallant knight. As if she would ever permit some big chain operation to traduce the quality and tradition that was Alferic's. How would they feel if a huge conglomerate wanted to absorb Jenson and Sons Milling? Why, they'd fight it tooth and nail. They'd be shouting, shaking fists and hiring batteries of high-powered lawyers. And so would she before she'd betray Grandpa, her father and herself by selling their bookstore.

Two shadows appeared behind the glass lettered Alfred E. Jenson, Investment Counselor. Jody dropped her apple core into the bag and stood to smile and nod at the departing client.

"Entrez, mademoiselle." With a bow, Alf ushered her into his business domain.

"Merci, monsieur. Are you free now? Or should I head back to my own office?"

"Free and starving. Here, have a seat." He pulled up a chair for her, leaned back in his own, feet propped on the desk, and bit into a huge roast beef sandwich.

"Did you get hold of your dad and Warren?"

"Yes, to both, and you had it right this morning. They are planning to sell. The offer he and Uncle Nils have gotten is from some New York outfit called Renard Books. It's a discount chain...."

"Discount!" Jody could hardly believe she'd heard correctly. "But, Alf, that means some assembly line operation, fluorescent lights, functional everything—metal everything—cold impersonal service. How could they?"

"Money, honey. The offer this Renard is making is outrageously exorbitant. According to Warren, it's absurd and senseless. Moreover, it'll be all cash, for the whole building."

"The whole building? Cash for the whole building?" Jody could hardly swallow the bite of sandwich in her mouth, and she tossed the bag with her uneaten food into the wastebasket.

"How much are they offering?" she asked.

"Half again the value of the shares, no matter what they're assessed at."

In a voice that caught on rising tears, she said, "Alf, I have a horrible premonition that Mom's not going to be able to meet that offer—certainly not in cash—and Lord knows, I don't have any money."

"I know. The old salary is fine for living on, but skinny as a toothpick otherwise. But don't give up hope, Jody. Be thankful that your dad left the trust fund. Aunt Ingrid can use that and, besides, Warren was encouraging. Here, have a Kleenex and I'll just jabber on while you mop up. Warren remembers Grandpa's will very well, and he claims that no one can doubt the clear intent to keep everything in the family. 'Intent,' apparently, is an extremely strong force in the law. You do have right of first refusal, but you must offer a figure that constitutes fair market value. As we surmised earlier, there is a legal definition of that phrase. Unfortunately, it's a definition open to interpretation.''

Jody sighed in exasperation. ''Naturally—gives the lawyers something to write fifty-page briefs about and spend hours dickering over. Honestly, that word *brief* has to be the misnomer of the century when lawyers use it. Remember that fraud case Dad helped the museum with? Never saw so much wasted paper, time and verbiage in my life, and I've hated—no, that's not fair—disliked lawyers ever since. Well, you said Warren was encouraging?''

''More or less. It's going to take some research but, off the top of his head, he felt that the outcome would hinge on whether the court interpreted 'fair market value' to mean, that which has been paid recently for like properties in similar locations, or the highest offer made. The cash angle will figure, too, but you have the 'intent' of the will to weight your side. He's going to arrange for the assessment of share value—wouldn't hurt to have that done even if nothing comes of this—and he'll get back to us tomorrow.''

''At which point, Mom will no doubt start directing you to begin evaluating her securities so that I can come up with a counteroffer. Damn, damn, damn!'' She punctuated each cuss word with a slap on the desk. ''Just when I thought my life was wending its way toward sanity, this has to happen. And, wait till you hear what else happened today. Alf, I should have just canceled today. Slashed a red pencil through December fourteenth and crawled back into bed.''

''We have another calamity on our hands?''

''Would you believe I'm having dinner with a lawyer?''

''With some difficulty. Who is he?''

"A lawyer who just picked me up. Down on the floor. No, no, idiot, I wasn't *lying* on the floor, I was working a register. Pick up as in unknown man asks unknown lady for a date. Blackmails her, I mean."

Her recount of the episode caused Alf to remove his feet from the desk and frown.

"Jody, I don't like the sound of this guy. Must run a steamroller in his off hours. I'm going to call Mom and have her check him out."

"Alf, don't be silly." She waved her hand in dismissal. "I can take care of myself. Anyway, I told you, Mrs. Fenton knows him."

"Mrs. Fenton," he snorted. "What does that tell me? She knows everyone who ever crawled across the county line. Nope, this McClelland character gets checked out before you go out. Sorry about that."

"Alf Jenson, you sound just like your father—and mine." Jody was torn between exasperation and amusement. "I thought I'd heard the end of all that now that Dad's gone and Carl's moved to Seattle. Don't your own sisters keep you busy enough?"

"Never mind how busy they keep me, I'm still acting *in loco parentis* and *in loco brotheris*, or whatever, for you."

"Fratris," she commented rather absentmindedly, thinking that it really wouldn't be such a bad idea to have Aunt Kirsten, as the family's resident socialite and gossip, find out a bit about Clif. He had come on as some sort of big-time operator, and even though her instincts said yes to him, learning as much as she could beforehand could only add to the evening. The reason for learning it didn't really matter.

"Okay, you win," she said. "You'll be meeting him, by the way. Mom's coming to your house for dinner, so I told him to pick me up there."

"Aha! And, have I got the test for him. Wait till I drop the twins in his lap," he chortled in anticipation.

"Alf, you wouldn't."

"Yes, if Mom hangs a red flag on him. No, if he gets her stamp of approval. Given the latter, I'll be only too pleased that you're going out with a man who isn't just some good-buddy sort."

Jody held up her hand to fend off any further remarks. "We are not going to resurrect the subject of me and men. Understood?"

"Understood. My lips are sealed—for the moment. About tonight's dinner, though, can you get your mother into the van by yourself? I'd be glad to drive over and help if you need me."

"No need, but thanks anyway. Now that she's finally let me move home for a while, I've been able to get that ramp business fixed up and do some practicing. Simple as one-two-three. Just leave her in her chair, zip it into the back, lock it in place and shut the door. She sits back there bowing and waving at the neighbors and passersby like a queen on progress through her domain. Claims it's great fun."

"Great fun?" He shook his head in wonder. "Amazing lady, Aunt Ingrid. A broken body and severe pain, yet she still has great fun."

"I know. 'As long as my brain's in proper gear, I'll do just fine' is what she always says." Jody dusted off her hands and skirt. "Well, back to the old grindstone."

With a light hug she left him. The moment she'd gone, Alf called his mother to check out "this Mc-Clelland character."

CHAPTER TWO

JODY STOOD in front of her closet, debating. What should she wear for dinner with a "fascinating lawyer" who, it had turned out, was one of Minneapolis's most popular playboys? Aunt Kirsten had called her, not at all pleased that her niece was going to spend an evening with Clif McClelland.

"Jody, he has a different beautiful woman on his arm every other week. Tosses them aside like day-old bread. I don't like this one bit. Can you plead a headache or something?"

"Not very well, not without lying. I said I'd go, so I really have to. Aunt Kirsten, I'm not sixteen, you know. I'll be fine."

"Humph! You may be twenty-five, extremely levelheaded and capable, but you are not, thank the Lord, a party girl, or whatever it is they call themselves these days. Don't stand for any nonsense, Jody."

"I won't. I have to pick Mom up at Alf's anyway, so you can stop worrying. What can happen before eleven o'clock? Don't answer that," she added, hearing her aunt's quick intake of breath, preparatory to a lecture. "By the way, is there anything good about the man? Mrs. Fenton likes him."

"Geraldine Fenton is a consummate ass, excuse me, and a busybody. Pay no attention to her ravings. However..."

"Yes?" Jody had prompted, hoping her aunt had heard something positive about the man.

"Well, I suppose it can't hurt your judgment to know a few nice things about him, but don't be lulled by the good news. I called a couple of my friends who know the McClellands better than I do and it seems that young Clif is a brilliant attorney, with a second degree in business. He's apparently a dashing, handsome, charming fellow, who plays several sets of excellent tennis every weekend and skis in the winter."

Another pause. Jody had prompted once again. "But his reputation is still 'love 'em and leave 'em'?"

"Yes. But, interestingly enough, he seems to have not only the respect of his colleagues, but also of the women he squires around. I can't imagine how. I should think respecting a man who treats women like playthings would be impossible. Would you respect such a man?"

"It would be hard," Jody had admitted. "But then, we don't know his side of the story. It might be worth finding out."

"Now listen, miss, don't you be letting him get around you with some tale of woes. You've got a heart like a marshmallow. To think I'm going to be a nervous wreck all evening because of some suave playboy. You mind my words, Jody Jenson, and be picking your mother up at eleven sharp."

"Yes, ma'am!" Her verbal salute to her commanding officer had them both laughing as they hung up the phone.

That conversation had taken place an hour ago, and now Jody had to get dressed and get her mother over to Alf's by seven. In a quandary, she pulled one garment after another out for inspection. Stupid, she thought. What difference did it make? One short dinner. Who cared? Never mind the sensations of the morning. Some kind of fluke. He probably ran on batteries and had sent out electric charges. A mere matter of physics.

Cross with her indecision, she yanked a navy blue, tailored, raw silk suit from the closet and tossed it on her bed. A light-blue silk blouse with a bow at the high neck flew across the room, and navy pumps landed with a thump on the carpet. There! Severe, almost masculine. Approximately as appealing to a playboy as a porcupine. No jewelry, she decided. Certainly no perfume and she would wind her luxuriant hair into a bun. Less than minimal makeup and a severe expression should complete the picture of an old-maid bookworm with no interest in fascinating lawyer types.

Jody grimaced as she made a last-minute check in the mirror. "Yuck!" she said aloud. "I've never looked so unfeminine. Too bad I don't need glasses. Well." She sighed. "It's what I wanted and I've certainly succeeded."

"Jody, luv?" Mrs. Jenson propelled herself into the room. "Anna has me ready. Shall we ... What in the world? I thought this was a date, honey. Is it a business meeting?"

"Not exactly, Mom. Come on, I'll tell you on the way."

BRITTA AND ALF teased Jody about her appearance as they sat around over predinner drinks. And when Clif arrived a short while later, he took one look at her and burst into laughter. Stifling it quickly, he extended his arm to shake her hand.

"I had planned to take you to The Mai Tai, but I think something along German lines would be more appropriate," he informed her as he followed her into the living room to meet her family.

Good glory, Wiener schnitzel, Jody thought. *Things like dumplings, noodles, a zillion potatoes and onions—I'll gain five pounds! Serves me right, I suppose.*

"I'll get my coat," she began after making the introductions, but no one was listening. Clif had seated himself next to Mrs. Jenson, accepted a Scotch on the rocks and seemed prepared to converse. Interesting. Rather out of character for a man-about-town to visit with an invalid, Jody noted. That charm Aunt Kirsten had mentioned, no doubt.

Picking up her half-finished glass of wine, she resumed her seat and listened to their conversation. They were talking about gardening—her mother's special joy and, apparently, his mother's also. Jody hadn't seen her mother so animated since the accident. How very curious. What would a man with Clif's reputation know about a homey topic like growing flowers and herbs? Perhaps he did have a gentle and tender side. After all, one could hardly storm one's way through a garden with any success. But none of that mattered. It would be just this one date. Clif stood and she went to get her coat.

"It was good of you to chat with my mother," she commented as they sped out of the driveway. Jody clutched the armrest. "Do you make a habit of driving this fast?"

"Yes, to the latter," Clif replied, skillfully executing a turn. "But I'm an expert driver, so not to worry. About your mother, she's a charming and delightful lady. It was a pleasure talking with her. What happened to put her in the wheelchair?"

"An auto accident last summer." She decided to leave it at that. No need to mention her father, if he hadn't caught Mrs. Fenton's remarks.

"I see." His tone told her that he had remembered Mrs. Fenton's words and, to her surprise, he slowed down immediately. He must have realized, correctly, that speed had made her nervous since that tragic summer day.

"No hurry," he said easily. "How does The Black Forest sound? You'll fit right in, dressed in that outfit."

"Sounds great. Very Teutonic. Perfect for an icy, stiff Swede."

"Oh?" He glanced in her direction, obviously amused. "I could have sworn I saw some heat in those eyes and cheeks this morning, a bit of suppleness in movement. Ah well, we all make the occasional mistake. Occasional, mind you."

"It may be that this little excursion will increase your list of mistakes for today, Mr. McClelland," she said, trying very hard not to respond to his banter.

A passing streetlight illuminated the teasing twinkle in his eyes. "No way. I met your mother, Alf and his wife seem quite special, the kids smiled at me, and I made friends with the dog. The evening won't be a total loss."

Irrepressibly, her laughter bubbled free. "Plus, of course, an excellent meal. As you say, the evening won't be a total loss. I hope you like German food, Clif. It's a far cry from The Mai Tai.''

He shrugged. ''It's not my favorite, but once in a while it's okay. Oriental, Polynesian, they're more to my liking. We'll try that next time around.''

Jody opened her mouth to protest, but they were pulling into the parking lot and the valet was reaching for her door. She let the ''next time'' hang in the air.

The host seated them in a secluded corner under the predictable Black Forest cuckoo clock. It was ticking merrily. *Perfect,* thought Jody. *A little bird will dart out at frequent intervals and remind me how cuckoo I am!*

Clif ordered a German white wine, with her nod of approval, and then sat back to fix her with a penetrating stare. ''Flaming red is better than somber blue,'' he announced.

''My suit is still bothering you?''

''It's great for the board room. Disastrous for dinner with me.''

''Perhaps blackmailing women into having dates with you doesn't make for happy results. The fact is, I dressed this way to underscore my feelings about this dinner. To me, it's simply a meeting, to be gotten through as amiably as possible, and that will be the end of it.''

The cuckoo chose that moment to pop out and chirp loudly over her head. Clif watched the little bird, then cocked an inquisitive eyebrow at Jody. She nearly looked up at the offender to demand, ''Whose side are you on, anyway?'' Fortunately, the waiter came into view and the ceremony of opening the wine bottle forestalled the need for any response at all.

"So, a meeting is what we're having," he said, once the wine was poured. "In that case, prior to any business negotiations, I always like to know something about the person I'm dealing with. Tell me about yourself, Miss Jenson."

"Born and raised in Minneapolis. Close, happy family life, one brother. A Wellesley graduate, M.A. in English literature. I'm a bibliophile, also a lover of long walks, ideas, music and good conversation, and I make my living as manager and part owner of Alferic's." She sat back, solemnly sipping her wine, eyeing him over the rim of her glass.

Clif's eyebrows rose. "Manager and part owner...I'm not surprised. You fit the part. Is that it?"

"That's it," she nodded.

"A fulsome review. Tells me everything I need to know."

"Very businesslike, I thought. Meetinglike, you might say. And it does tell you everything you need to know. After all, you really don't have to know a single thing about me."

"Hmm." Clif drummed his fingers on the table, a frown making creases between his dark brows. "Why so difficult, Jody? Okay, so I came on a bit strong; I always do. It's just the way I am when I see something I want. No woman's ever objected before, or wrapped herself up like an armadillo to go out with me. Good Lord, you act as if I were a pariah of some sort, a menace to helpless maidens, the villain on some stage—"

"Clif, I'm sorry," she interrupted. "I don't mean to be rude. I know you're not a menace to anyone. It's just that—well, this whole evening is stupid. We have nothing in common. I only came because I couldn't have you charging into the store every hour or so bearing armloads of flowers. Still, that's no excuse for being unpleasant now that we're together. I'll be on my best behavior from now on."

"How do you know that we have nothing in common?" he challenged, ignoring the rest of her comments.

Jody played with the stem of her wineglass. "I don't know, except through hearsay, and that's not really a fair basis for judgment."

"Hearsay? What are you talking about? What have you he—"

"Hello, Clif," a sultry voice broke into his words.

Jody glanced up to see a striking, raven-haired beauty looking at Clif with undisguised pleasure in her eyes.

"Laura! Hello yourself." He stood to make introductions, a noncommittal smile on his face.

Laura's gaze shifted to Jody. "A business associate, I presume?"

Jody patted her severely coiffed hair, primmed her mouth and gave a curt nod of, assent. "That's correct. Mr. McClelland called a board meeting for this evening."

Clif choked, then quickly regained his composure.

"Clif, if a business conference is the best you can come up with for a night out, you've certainly changed your style. If you decide to take up the old ways, I still have the occasional free evening. Why don't you give me a call?"

It would have been Jody's turn to choke over a laugh if she hadn't suddenly felt a pang of sorrow for Laura. It seemed pitiful, somehow, that this beautiful woman should be offering herself so blatantly. Her thoughts must have been evident in her voice when she said goodbye, because Laura seemed startled briefly, though not enough to keep her from sending a dazzling smile in Clif's direction before sauntering back to her own date.

"Don't feel sorry for her, Jody." Clif smiled and winked at Jody as he sat down. "Yes, I got that. You'd make the lousiest poker player around. But, I repeat, don't feel sorry for her. She knows where she stands with me, and she's the type who's just been out for a good time from way back. That's why I dated her a few times, as I did the dozens of others like her."

"So I've heard." She said it lightly, but there was an inexplicable heaviness in her chest at hearing him confirm the image she'd been given.

He looked at her sharply. "Aha! So, that's it. My reputation precedes me."

"It does."

"Okay, let me hail the waiter before he despairs of our ever eating, and then we'll talk about it."

She and Clif both ordered the only fish dish on the menu—baked and stuffed with onion something or other. But it would be easy enough to eat around the stuffing.

"Tell me what you've heard that bothers you," he said, refilling their wineglasses.

"Nothing bothers me, Clif. I've heard about your dating habits, and that simply tells me that we're not the same sort of people. I—"

Interrupted by the repeated notes of "cuckoo, cuckoo" flying over her head, she glared up at the intruder. "Bird, your days are numbered!"

Clif threw back his head in laughter. "That bird is more sensible than you, Jody. You should pay attention to him."

"Don't be silly. Now, where was I?"

"Embroiled in some nonsense about our not being the same sort of people, I believe."

"It's not nonsense, Clif. I am, emphatically, not like Laura, and she's the kind of woman you choose to be with. But, look, this is an inane topic of discussion. There's absolutely no need to pursue it at all. We're only having this one date or, rather, meeting. Tell me about your serious side," Jody asked in an attempt to swing the conversation around. "Do you have one?"

"Definitely. But, first, Jody, listen to me for a minute. I am a thirty-one-year-old bachelor. Expecting a monk is totally unrealistic. At the risk of boring you, I'm going to repeat myself once again. Just as Laura knows exactly where she stands with me, so does any woman I date. I'm up-front with my intentions. I don't play games, and I don't go around breaking anyone's heart. What more could you ask?"

"Nothing. And I think more highly of you for being so direct and honest with people. The point is, however, that I'm not asking anything of you, Clif. You don't need to justify a single action of your life to me. Your life-style doesn't need to be subjected to any microscope of mine—oh, this looks delicious." She thanked the beaming waiter who had placed the dishes ceremoniously before them. "Smells delicious, too." And, after one bite, tasted appreciatively with eyes closed, Jody announced, "It *is* delicious. We did a perfect job of ordering, Clif."

"There, you see? We both like stuffed, baked fish. Who could ask for more? Too many similarities and you'd be bored to tears," Clif concluded, looking absurdly proud of himself.

Jody shook her head, chuckling at his sally. "Mr. McClelland, you are certainly most persistent. Do let's drop the subject."

"One more thing. I submit that it is unfair, illogical and irrational to make a final judgment on the basis of the circumstantial evidence thus far presented."

"Delivered like a true barrister. I'm not quite sure of the precise meaning of 'circumstantial,' but I get the general idea. No proof, no corpus delicti, or whatever, behind my 'evidence,' so I'll let the rest of the evening speak for itself—though I'd better warn you that I'm not always rational and logical. But, I do try to be fair."

"Well, that's 'fair' enough, I'd say. After all, logic and rationality are pretty rare commodities in the human race, especially in females. Ah yes, I think by the look on your face that it would be the better part of discretion if I just let that one go." He grinned at her indignant expression.

"A wise decision on your part, very wise. How about substituting your own biographical sketch?"

"Right, defuse the situation, so to speak. Born and raised in St. Paul; close happy family—there, two similarities right in a row—two brothers, U of M, then Yale Law School. My chief interests are law, ideas—there's another one, this relationship's getting dull already—tennis, skiing, stimulating discussions—might be one there—and women. The latter only on a casual basis. So what do you think?"

"Very interesting." Jody was still laughing at his 'dull already' remark. She suspected that, whatever else life might be around Clif, *dull* was an adjective that would seldom come to mind. "Your dinner's getting cold and, really, it's too good to let that happen. I'm beginning to think that I've never properly appreciated German food. Eat and enjoy while I explore these similarities of ours, or possible similarities. Sports. Let's take sports. How do you feel about badminton and croquet?" Clif nearly choked on his food.

"I knew it." She sighed. "How about Ping-Pong?"

"Possible," he managed.

"Well, that's the extent of my proficiency in that field. A hopeless combination as you can readily see."

"No, I don't see. You're just being perverse. And, after promising to be on your best behavior, too. Ought to be ashamed of yourself, Miss Jenson."

"Oh, I am." She sat back, a suitably contrite expression on her face. Toying idly with a spoon, she wondered about the inconsistencies she detected in Clif.

"Clif? You seem like someone solid, serious even. Why the superficial social life?" She was immediately appalled at the pain that filled his eyes and reached across the table to cover his hand with hers. "I'm so sorry. I've barged into your private life like a clumsy busybody. Please forgive me. It's none of my business."

"It's nothing for you to bother about, Jody. I was just thinking about some nieces and nephews of mine, my older brother's children, and one in particular I'm trying to shepherd along. My irresponsible older brother, I might add. He's still reeling from his third divorce after blithely siring . . . but, why am I boring you with all this?"

His pain receded and he looked at her tenderly. "You're so lovely, Jody, inside and out. I knew it the minute I saw that expressive face of yours." He caressed her soft cheek with his fingertips, bringing a thrill that immobilized her. Swiftly and deftly he pulled the pins from her chignon and let the tawny sheen cascade around her shoulders.

Why can't I move? she wondered. *Why are cartwheels turning in my chest? Oh, glory, he feels something, too. He's staring at me in disbelief. I don't believe this, either.* She wanted him to hold her, kiss her. Suddenly she realized that the cash register incident wasn't a fluke. And if it was, she now had two flukes to deal with. Abruptly she sat back again, yanking her hand from his as if it had been resting on a hot griddle. Two flukes. She wouldn't touch him again, just in case.

"Jody? Don't you see it? Don't you feel it?"

"See what? Feel what?" she parried. "I'd like some coffee please, and then I'd best be going. I have to get Mom home by eleven, you know. She needs..." She heard herself rattling on like some demented...

"Cuckoo, cuckoo," the clock sang out above her.

"That damn bird," she mumbled. "Clif. For heaven's sake, it's not *that* funny." Jody tried to remain stern as he nearly rolled off his chair in hearty laughter. Finally, she gave in and joined him.

"It's only ten o'clock. Plenty of time." He signaled the busboy for coffee. "But we'll call it a night if you're in a hurry."

In the foyer, Clif helped her on with her coat, lifting her hair free and smoothing her coat across her shoulders. Then he pulled her lightly back against him to brush a kiss on the top of her head. Nerve ends tingling at his touch, she resisted the impulse to lean against him. Three flukes? She was glad that the silly clock was too far away to hear her thoughts.

Jody asked Clif about skiing as soon as they got into the car, effectively setting him off on a recitation of his plans for the holidays. His family owned a condo at Vail, and since she knew next to nothing about either the sport or the place, she was able to keep him busy with explanations all the way to Alf's house. She heaved a sigh of relief when he cut the engine.

"A delightful board meeting, Mr. McClelland." She assumed what she supposed was Teutonic reserve. "Thank you for a wonderful dinner. I'd ask you in, but . . ." Her aloof pose wasn't selling.

"I'm not going to close the evening on that note, Jody. I'm going to call you tomorrow, and I'm going to kiss you good-night."

Before she could do more than send a startled glance his way, he had tipped her face up and covered her lips with his. Warm and loving, his lips gently caressed hers in a way that demanded nothing. Such a simple thing, a kiss; but the car rocked beneath her.

To her surprise, he raised his head without asking for more, gave her an appraising look, touched a forefinger lightly to her nose and got out of the car to open her door. He escorted her to the house and only stayed long enough to make sure she was safely inside.

How very different he is from what I expected, she thought. Busy with her musings, she said very little to anyone, even to her mother on the way home.

Instead of getting into bed when she was ready, Jody sat on her window seat hugging her knees and watching clouds scud past a near-full moon, wishing that she could be watching it all with Clif. The fluke notion was crazy, she thought. She was attracted to him like a moth to a flame. And as overused as that phrase was, she could not have found a more apt analogy. He was loving and tender, funny and thoughtful. But he was an avowed playboy, casual when it came to women. And that's where she'd succumb to the flame. She'd fall in love and he would respond casually, putting her smack dab where she was last spring, stuck with the unpleasant task of ending a relationship. So, no more Clif McClelland.

The words seemed to lack conviction, so she repeated them aloud. "No more Clif McClelland."

The firmness she'd tried for had wavered a bit, so she added another sentence. "It's the intelligent thing to do, and you do want to be intelligent, don't you?"

Even that didn't come off in very convincing tones and she was afraid that the mere sight of Clif could erase all this intelligent business. Her heart might very well take over. She'd simply have to concentrate on what her head was saying and learn to squash her feelings. That shouldn't be too hard now that she was aware of the problem.

CHAPTER THREE

IN A ROUTINE GLANCE through her office window the next morning, Jody spotted Clif wandering around the store, obviously in search of someone. Feeling like a teenager, she closed the blinds slightly and peeked through the slats to watch his progress. Just seeing him quickened her pulse. Now he was speaking to one of the clerks, and she couldn't help wishing that she was the one being regarded by his sapphire eyes. He was such a magnificent man—tall, bronzed from the ski slopes...

"I am certifiably crazy," she announced to the window, just as Clif raised those blue eyes to range the upper walls. She released the blind with a snap, realizing immediately the mistake she'd made. "Damn. What if he saw...?"

Risking another peek, she discovered that he had indeed seen the motion she'd made. He was staring directly at her. A grin split his face as she got her wish—their eyes met. And then he was striding purposefully toward the stairs.

"Good show, Jody," she said in disgust. "Moon over him like the rest of his harem, or stable, or whatever." Tightening the belt around her lemon-yellow, light wool dress, Jody walked toward the door and opened it just as Clif bounded up the final two steps. When he caught sight of her, his grin faded into a look of admiration, only to be replaced by frank yearning as he focused on her slightly parted lips.

Jody backed up, distressed by the sensations coursing through her, the mad desire she had to press against him and pull his head down to hers. Controlling her emotions and reactions was proving all together too difficult. She'd never experienced an attraction like this. She was cross with herself and at the same time, confused. It seemed absurd to have to avoid him, yet if she couldn't rein in these exciting responses to his presence, she would have to do just that—avoid him. No matter what her feelings, Clif was dangerous.

"Come in," she said, astounded to find that her voice sounded normal. "What a surprise. Is that my lunch you're carrying?" Jody nodded toward the brown bag he was holding.

"Negative. Coffee-break time. This is some sort of surprise for me, too." He gestured around the comfortable room, pointing at the carpet, upholstered furniture and lamps. "I never expected such an elegant layout in a bookstore."

"In keeping with the elegance of Alferic's, of course."

"And the elegance of its manager/part owner," Clif added, sweeping an exaggerated bow.

"Why, aren't you gallant! Compliments with the morning coffee, yet. What more could a woman ask for?"

"Me, naturally." He flashed a winning smile and flung his arms wide.

Jody laughed at the pose but turned away from his invitation. To busy herself, she began clearing papers from the couch. She loved his teasing repartee and wanted to be close to him, but she was firm in her decision to steer clear of involvement.

"Come on, Mr. Modesty," she coaxed, "your treat smells much too heavenly to wait any longer. What did you bring?"

"Ah, well." He shrugged good-naturedly and sat down. "Win some, lose some. I brought croissants, hot from the oven, jam and butter. I was hoping you could supply the brew."

"Coming up." Jody brought steaming mugs of coffee to the table, along with a plate for the pastries, and paper towels for napkins. Then she curled up against the corner cushions beside him.

"Raspberry! My favorite jam." She put a liberal dollop on her croissant. "Mmm, wonderful. A great idea, Clif. Thanks." She closed her eyes to savor each bite.

"My pleasure, Jody."

"Mmm," she said again, and opened her eyes to find him staring at her mouth.

"Did you know that it's entrancing to watch you eat? Mesmerizing, in fact." He chuckled at her astonishment. "Noticed it last night. It's like an experience for you—savoring each mouthful slowly, thoroughly. And every once in a while, your tongue slips out to catch a wayward crumb. Gives me all kinds of ideas."

"Ideas? What ideas?"

Clif picked up the remaining bit of roll on her plate, rested an arm along the back of the couch behind her head and grazed her lips with the jam-covered morsel.

"Go ahead, Jody, eat it."

She opened her mouth obediently, this time keeping her eyes open and locked with his. His finger traced her lips, then moved to his own tongue. Slowly he licked the jam from the tip of his finger and Jody felt her pulse rate quicken. It intensified as she noticed his eyes, fixed now on her mouth, deepening from sapphire to indigo. A telltale throbbing in his throat matched her own.

She swallowed and began to lick the jam from her lower lip. Clif met her tongue with his. Her head fell back against his arm, his mouth still holding hers, his tongue gently probing for admission. Parting her lips for him, Jody found herself experiencing an awareness of her body that was unknown to her, felt a rising ache of wanting that she knew could consume her.

To be kissed languidly and thoroughly, eloquently and completely, was so very new. Anyone else she had been with had seemed to think that kissing was simply the first step on the road to somewhere else, to be dispensed with as quickly as possible. Clif, with his tender, leisurely exploring of her mouth, was acting as if a kiss could be an end in itself, that it was of the utmost importance that he learn every nuance possible before moving any further.

Sensations that reached her very toes quivered through her at the caressing of his tongue. Tentatively, she began her own probing, feeling a new surge of passion as his mouth welcomed her, permitting her own eager tasting, tasting that made her never want to leave his arms. Clif suddenly groaned and pulled her against him, cradling her head with his hand. His lips were hard, his mouth demanding, as if he wanted to possess every surface he could reach. She felt bereft when he finally lifted his head.

"Dear God," he murmured, his hand very slowly and lightly outlining her cheeks and chin, his fingers sifting through her hair. "Jody, what is it with us?"

"I don't know," Jody replied absently, wondering when her breathing might return to normal, wondering how she was going to stand it when he left—and wondering what her life might be like if she followed the desires within her. "Something," she supplied lamely.

Clif's laugh resembled a croak. "Something is right. Something like unbelievable."

Jody forced herself to sit up, slip off the couch. The thought of losing control with a man like Clif had served to gather her scattered wits and return her to the real world. She was sure that once she truly had her thoughts in order, her brain would discover some rationale for turning into Jell-O over a simple kiss. But simple was hardly an adequate word to describe the thrill, the desire, the response she'd just known. Despite her shaky knees, she managed to stand up and walk to her desk.

"Hey! What made you go and do that?" Clif protested, sounding indignant and distraught at the same time.

"End of coffee-break time, I'm afraid."

"Can't be." He looked at his watch and grimaced. "You're right. Damn it. Never occurred to me to get more than one appointment rescheduled. Listen, Jody," Clif began as she pointed him in the direction of the mirror on the washroom door, "I've got a meeting with my partners this afternoon—probably last until five-thirty or so—how about I pick you up around seven again? This time we'll . . ."

"Clif, no. Thanks, but no thanks. I—I can't get any more involved with you," she blurted. It was the truth, but she couldn't elaborate without going into a history of her engagement and she wasn't about to do that. If only she could react to him in some neutral way, just enjoy his company without all the fireworks.

"Jody! You're not even giving us a chance. It's been twenty-four hours since we met, on the dot, by the way. We've spent approximately five of those hours together, laughing and talking. And we've shared a kiss that left you breathless and me in agony. Good Lord, we want each other madly and you want to drop it. I suspect because of some ill-timed, foolish gossip. You're not being reasonable."

Resting against her hands on the edge of the desk, Jody stared at her foot, pointlessly drawing circles on the carpet. A smile curved her lips as she realized Clif was right. With all her heart she wanted to see him again—despite all her rationalizations.

"What's so funny?" He grinned at her, pocketing his comb and coming to stand in front of her.

"My mental gyrations," she answered. "Clif, don't worry about the gossip thing, that's not the primary reason. After all, I'm not the least bit hesitant about saying no to a man when I want to. One can hardly arrive at the age of twenty-five these days without learning at least that much."

He took her gently by the shoulders, though holding her at arm's length. "What is the primary reason then, Jody?"

"Me," she answered directly. "My reactions, my past . . . don't ask me about it, please."

"I wouldn't dream of it. I only hope you'll tell me of your own volition one day."

He looked at her speculatively, aimlessly moving a few things around on her desk. "Suppose I assure you that I will not put you in the position of having to say no. Would that change your mind about seeing me?"

"Yes, but . . ."

"No buts, Jody. I'll see you at seven."

"Not tonight, Clif. I promised my mother I'd make chili for dinner. For some reason or other, she's had a yen for something spicy."

"What a coincidence, so do I. But I suppose she'd be more comfortable without company?"

"No, it wouldn't matter at all. You'd be game to try my cooking? Are you angling for an invitation, Mr. McClelland?"

"Sure am," he replied, grinning boldly at her.

"Please be my guest. Much better than going out." Then she added, her eyes sparkling with mischief, "No cuckoo clocks."

He pulled her lightly to him. "I'll miss that little bird—no one to tell you when your thinking's gone off the rail. Except me, of course. Until seven, then." A soft kiss and he was gone.

From the moment Clif left, Jody found herself too distracted to accomplish anything. Her thoughts kept drifting back to the feel of his hands caressing her, the look of his passion-darkened eyes above her and the touch of his mouth, both tender and ardent. A stern lecture to her emotions was required before she was ready to greet the staff members she had summoned to her office for a noon hour meeting.

Jody had hired the three young people for the Christmas season. There had been a few customer complaints against them, and it was up to her to straighten things out, as well as to apologize to the trio for the inadequate training she had given them.

The two men and one woman were graduate students at the university. It had been Jody's brilliant, or so she'd thought, idea to bring this bright, knowledgeable threesome into the store over the holidays to help out in the sections dealing with their fields of expertise. The regular staff, freed to some extent from their regular duties, would then be available to man extra registers and assist in the Rare Books room. That particular room, where the volumes were kept under lock and key behind glass doors, generated an increased amount of interest at gift-giving time and demanded far more knowledge on the part of the sales personnel than straight subject sections.

Jody's reasoning up to that point had been sound and had proved successful. However, she had neglected one of her father's firm dictums: no member of the staff on the floor without extensive training in Alferic's concept of bookselling. She had told them to be attentive to customers, but not emphatically enough to counter today's prevalent attitude toward selling in general—total self-service.

Such a view was at complete variance with Alferic's philosophy of warm, personalized contact between buyer and seller. It had simply not occurred to her that the students would not physically help customers find what they wanted, that they would merely point a finger vaguely and say, "over there," or that they would scribble illegible sales slips and gesture toward a register when a purchase had been selected. Longtime customers had been grumbling and new customers, who had been told what to expect in the line of service, were disappointed. Jody was thoroughly annoyed with herself. Her store was treating customers just as Renard's would.

As if that weren't enough, one of the young men had insulted an overbearing lady requesting a work by Rousseau, telling her she was more the Nietzsche type. Jody had soothed the ruffled feelings of this particular patron herself, even as she felt an amused understanding for the clerk. The woman had been built along the lines of a female Russian shot-putter, and had been belligerent to boot. One couldn't help but feel that Nietzsche might have been the better choice. However, that was hardly the prerogative of a salesperson to point out.

She sat the young people in comfortable chairs and set a coffeepot and cups on the table. Being of an age with them, Jody opted for a seat above their eye level so they would have to look up to her, in a visual sense, whatever predilections they might have toward treating her with the familiarity of a contemporary. The corner of her desk was the spot she chose, hoping to appear as a friendly authority figure akin to a professor in an informal seminar grouping.

"First of all, I want to thank all of you for the work you've done during these hectic weeks. It's tiring and often frustrating, I know. Unfortunately, along with the help you've given us, I've received a few complaints about the service, or rather, the lack of it. I lay the blame for this situation at my own doorstep. It is due to an oversight of mine. I failed to stress sufficiently our credo here at Alferic's, and I would like to remedy that now. It won't take long and you may add the time to your lunch hours.

"It is our belief that the purpose of a bookseller is to bring customer and book together in rewarding pleasure. To that end, my grandfather and my father created a personal bookshop where browser or buyer will find unusual books and warm, individual attention from a knowledgeable, trained staff. For the length of time that you will be with us, there is no need for in-depth training in the mechanics of running the store. There is ample personnel on the floor to answer any questions you might have along those lines. But— and this is where the customer complaints apply—you must supply the warm, individual attention. It is Alferic's specialty. Our patrons depend upon it.

"Despite the difficulties inherent at this busy time of year, I expect you to take your customers to the shelves they are seeking, make a couple of suggestions if they ask or you think it might be useful, and try to keep an eye on them in case further help seems appropriate. If they find what they want and wish to make a purchase, you take them to a register and mention the name of the person operating it as the one who will complete the sale for them, then you thank them for coming to Alferic's. This may be the last sort of business where customers don't rush in and rush out, grabbing a purchase en route. We intend to keep it that way, and we are willing to take whatever time is necessary to do so!

"Obviously, happy customers are what we're after and I expect it to be what you're after, too. We are not going to achieve that goal by treating their requests with disdain, or laughter. For example, if someone who operates a pneumatic drill for a living comes in and asks for a volume of Wordsworth, you take him to the poetry section and get Wordsworth out. Never mind if, to your way of thinking, Whitman or Ogden Nash would be more suitable. How do you know? Maybe it isn't a celebration of self, or laughter, that's missing in their lives. Maybe it's communion with nature, dreams and sensitivity.

"Don't presume! Fulfill their desires and suggest that, if they are not happy with their choice, will they please come back and you'll help them find something else. At the same time, I do expect you to use your own judgment, especially if someone has told you what he or she wants the book for and has clearly made an inappropriate choice.

"End of spiel. Any questions?"

To her amazement, they were all grinning widely and nodding in appreciation. The young woman actually applauded.

"No wonder everyone likes this store so much," she exclaimed. "Giving service like that. Not like I remember when I used to go shopping with my mother. I suppose that's why you make so much money."

"What makes you think we make lots of money?" Jody poured herself some coffee and sat down with the group.

"Why, it's obvious—Oriental rugs and leather chairs in alcoves, antiques scattered around, shelves that look like bookcases in somebody's home. I don't know, the whole atmosphere just says 'plush.'"

"You're right, and I'm glad you noticed it, but the money it took to create that atmosphere did not come from profits on this store. I had a very shrewd great-grandfather and grandfather who bought acres of land around here when the Twin Cities were young and growing. There is money in the family, but Alferic's has been a labor of love for us. For the interested family members, this is where our hearts are, as far as the business world is concerned. Believe me, if making money is what you are after, do not choose to be a bookseller. You can make a very adequate living, if you are good, but the solid rewards are in the joy of the books themselves and bringing them together with appreciative, fascinating people. If that doesn't compensate for lack of riches, don't do it. There may be money to be made in the paperback trade, or selling texts and technological books. I wouldn't know about those.''

Glancing at her watch, Jody stood up and laughingly shooed them out, saying that the store would be closing before they finished their lunches and the rest of the staff would be after her with a noose. She extended an invitation to come and talk to her anytime they had questions, suggestions or anything they felt like discussing. Jody closed the door feeling that the meeting had been successful and that she'd be hearing no more customer complaints about the ''rude young people these days.''

CHAPTER FOUR

JODY SURVEYED the kitchen and was satisfied. It was her special place in the house, and she wanted Clif to appreciate its warmth and comfort as she did. The room was a statement of the way she liked to live, and if he didn't feel at home here, she would never feel at home with him. It seemed a far cry from the world of any playboy, but she could still hope.

Large, yet cozy, the country-style kitchen held happy memories for Jody. She had spent many hours of her childhood curled up in front of the hearth, listening to her mother read stories aloud. The aroma of homemade breads and soups had filled the room as their lifetime housekeeper-cum-companion, Anna, presided over preparations for the evening meal. Rosy, mellow brick walls, rag rugs on the plank floor, gaily patterned chintz in blues and soft reds on the chairs and couch all provided an aura of welcome. In a bay window beneath hanging plants was a scarred, round oak table, and herbs from her mother's garden hung from beams to dry, lending a faint scent of mystery to the air. It was a room that proclaimed occupancy by a family, one that enjoyed convivial mealtimes together and after-meal relaxation by the fire. Including perhaps, to judge from the books and magazines scattered about, a good read thrown in.

Pretty casual, Jody thought, as she looked around. If Clif was the type who demanded formal dining, complete with damask, crystal, sterling and china, he was going to be disappointed. Tonight he was getting red-and-white checks, geraniums, pottery, tumblers and stainless steel—and his hostess in pants and a sweater. "Well," she murmured, "take it or leave it, mister. Tonight I'm going to learn a bit more about you. That is, we are going to learn a bit more about you," Jody added as she moved toward her mother, seated by the hearth in her wheelchair.

"Mom, how are you doing?" Jody tucked a lap robe more securely around Mrs. Jenson's legs. "You've got yourself parked awfully close to the fire here, aren't you hot? Do you want this off your lap?"

"No, dear, the heat feels good, and so does being downstairs. I'm glad I decided to come. Jody, I love this room. Full of memories as it is, I love it."

"I'm right with you there, and I'm hoping Clif will be, too."

"He will." Mrs. Jenson's serene confidence brought a laugh from her daughter.

"My mother now has ESP?"

"That's right. You'd be surprised at all the esoteric brilliance I'm developing from this wheelchair. Why, I'll soon be a regular psychic."

"Just as long as you stop short of mind reading. I'd hate to be monitoring my thoughts every time I'm with you."

"Well, dear, if I ever find myself reading your mind, I won't let on. Seriously though, I like Clif very much. Liked him the minute I saw him, and I wouldn't have if he weren't going to love our kitchen."

Jody got them each a glass of wine and sat down at her mother's feet. "Why did you like him right away?"

"No particular reason I can put my finger on, just an instinctual liking." When Jody didn't comment, Mrs. Jenson continued. "A much-abused word, *like*. A limp word, some would say, but to me it means an easy compatibility, companionship even in silences, pleasure in hour after hour, day after day...a lifetime of being together."

"I know what you mean, Mom. My instincts are saying the same things, and my senses are rejoicing in a physical attraction I can't believe."

"Add respect to liking and passion and you've got a rare combination."

Jody shifted impatiently. "Do you realize that I've only known this man for some thirty-six hours? How can I be talking this way?"

Mrs. Jenson chuckled and patted the blond head at her knees. "In my experience, when the right man came along—namely your father—there was an instant zing. No thinking, just—zing."

Jody joined in her mother's laughter. "Well, I know what you mean there, too. In fact, *zing* is just the right word." And then she turned pensive, swirling the wine around in her glass as she thought. "But I don't know if he's the right man for me."

"His life-style? Is that what's bothering you?"

"Yes, and I sure wish I knew what was behind it. His shallow existence seems out of character somehow."

"I expect it is. But don't fret over it. You'll soon know the reason. People generally give themselves away, if one is alert enough to pick up the clues."

Jody returned to her former lighthearted mood. "Here I am, acting like a hound hot on the trail, sniffing out the quarry."

The doorbell sounded over their fresh merriment. Jody opened the door to see Clif smiling at her through the leaves and blossoms of a huge, creamy poinsettia plant.

"Our first Christmas decoration," she exclaimed as she led the way to the kitchen. "Clif, it's gorgeous."

He let out a whistle of admiration when they walked into the kitchen. "What a great room! What a great smell! And, Mrs. Jenson!" Genuine pleasure lighting his face, he handed the plant to Jody and went over to shake hands with Jody's mother. "Does this mean that I'm going to be lucky enough to have dinner with two lovely ladies?"

"Only one of us will be enjoying your company, Clif, but I do thank you for the wonderful compliment." She patted the couch next to her wheelchair. "Come sit beside me for the few minutes I'm going to stay. Unfortunately, my back has a disappointing habit of saying 'I quit' about seven-thirty, so I'll content myself with having a drink with you and then get comfortable in bed. What a lovely poinsettia you've brought us."

Jody set the plant on the hearth and stepped back to assess the effect. "Perfect," she said. "Clif, I just love the color. You couldn't have pleased us more."

"I quite agree," added Mrs. Jenson. "And now, Clif, what can we offer you to drink?"

Jody got the Scotch on the rocks he requested and resumed her seat on the rug in front of the fire. She was delighted to see that Clif had removed his jacket and stretched his feet out in front of him. He seemed thoroughly relaxed and quite at home.

"Just what a man needs after a hard day's work," he said. "Beautiful women, soft couch, fire, a drink and good hearty food. You were right, Jody, this sure does beat a restaurant. Except in the clock department, of course."

Mrs. Jenson chuckled. "The clock department...hmm...now what could that mean? An inside joke already?"

"Absolutely right." Clif laughed over Jody's groan.

"A portent, I'm sure," said Mrs. Jenson. "But, enough of that for now. Clif, last night we talked about your mother. How is she managing with the holiday bustle?"

"Just fine, though it's hectic. She's all excited about the arrival of her grandchildren for Christmas. My younger brother, Rob, and his wife will be here next week with their two boys. Pandemonium from start to finish. But Mom loves it, obstreperous boys and all. The racket about does my father in, but he grins and bears it, and checks the days off on the calendar."

"Like many a grandpa before him." Mrs. Jenson smiled in recollection. "Jody's father thought one child at a time was just right, but all together they were too much for him to handle. I'm like your mother—I can't wait for mine to get here, also next week."

Clif got up and began searching his pockets. "I have a message for you from a fellow herb gardener. Mom wanted me to ask you if you'd like a...slip? cutting? I can't remember...of costmary, whatever that is."

"Costmary! Why, I'd love it. What a perfect thought on your mother's part. It's an herb you hardly ever hear of anymore. The leaves are marvelous for tea. Clif, I wonder if she'd like some of my . . . never mind, I'll call her myself. Who knows, we may find all kinds of things to share.''

Jody gestured at the herb-bedecked rafters. "Does your parents' kitchen look like this?''

"No, but the attic does. I used to go up there when I was a kid, just for the smell. I'd sit there imagining myself in all sorts of exotic places. Like Zanzibar—that word used to fascinate me. Good Lord, what made me remember that? Haven't thought of it in years.''

"You sound like a romantic," Mrs. Jenson remarked.

Clif shook his head rather vehemently. "Not me. Maybe when I was five or six, but not anymore.''

"Well, the world isn't too kind to romantics these days, so I'm not surprised that you've buried that side of yourself. My family—parents, brothers and sisters—were little else. It made for a dreamy, leisurely sort of life, but somewhat short of the practical.''

"I wouldn't trade it for anything, though," Jody responded firmly.

"Not trade, no, but I expect a healthy dose of each is the best arrangement one could have. It certainly worked for me and your father. And, now, will you call Anna for me, luv? It's time for me to get in bed.''

Jody jumped up. "I'll take you, Mom—save Anna the trip on the stairs.''

Clif stood, wanting to help, but Mrs. Jenson declined his offer. "I appreciate that," she said, "but we've got the routine down pat. It will only be a couple of minutes before Jody's back. I'll give your mother a call, and again, thank you for bringing the lovely poinsettia. We'll all enjoy it.''

When she returned, Jody found Clif on the couch, his long legs stretched toward the fire. He seemed as content as a cat.

"How about a refill?" she asked.

"If you'll sit down here with me and not be bustling around with the food, I'd love one."

"Drink and a nonbustling me, coming up." She got seconds for both of them, kicked off her shoes and sat down on the couch next to him, feet tucked under her.

He draped an arm over her bent knees and sighed happily. Jody didn't disturb his tranquility with words. She was more than satisfied with the smiles he sent her, the pressure of his hand on her legs. Contemplating her mother's belief that the best relationships were a rare combination of liking, respect and physical attraction, Jody couldn't help but think of Clif. The more she saw of him, the less she could imagine not always respecting him, not always liking him. And as for the physical attraction, she dared not move lest he lift his arm and take away the delicious tremors his touch was causing.

"Interesting meeting I had today with my partners at the law firm," he finally commented. "Your name was brought up, to my astonishment."

"Mine? You're joking!"

"No joke. Yours. One of the senior partners has just acquired a client from a New York firm, a client who needs counsel here. Renard Books."

Jody's eyes widened, first in disbelief, then in growing dismay. "I don't want to believe you. Clif, I don't want you representing Renard. They want my store. You can't—"

"Whoa. Slow down a minute. *I'm* not representing them." Clif gripped her knee tightly. "It's got nothing to do with me, or us. Really, Jody, I'm not involved.''

"But you must be, or will be. You want your partner to win the case, don't you?''

"Not necessarily. I don't know enough about it yet. But I do know that I don't want you upset, so what say we drop the subject? For now, anyway.''

Jody hesitated. "Clif, are you sure you won't be involved? This suit is just about the most important thing in my life right now and, well, I would hate it if you were on Renard's side.''

"Maybe you *would* like to talk about it now?''

Jody bit her lip in thought, then nodded. "Yes, I would. I don't like putting off difficult things. I keep right on thinking about them until they're confronted and resolved. Let me put the bread in the oven, then I'll tell you about Alferic's. Unless you'd rather I didn't?''

"Jody, I want to hear about everything to do with you. I just don't want you upset, that's all.''

"I'm not.'' She smiled reassuringly, but she knew she would be upset if he disagreed with her refusal to sell. Such a response would send her flying away from him again, just when she was beginning to have some hopes of a possible relationship.

Jody began by telling him about her grandfather and the history of the store, and repeated the essence of what she had told the students that noon hour. She mentioned the part her parents had played in expanding Alferic's services, how her father had been an expert in appraisals, and in rare and antiquarian bookselling, and how her mother had added antiques and plants to the setting, as well as the lithographs and woodcuts that adorned the wall space in the alcoves.

"And now there's me, Clif. I've worked there all my life. It's my turn to add something to my heritage, not turn it over to some discount chain that sells on an assembly line basis with no personal service."

"Some would call that progress, Jody."

"I wouldn't," she replied with an emphatic shake of the head. "Progress, by my definition, makes life better. How would selling to Renard make anyone's life better?"

"It would save your uncles' business."

"You've got a point, and I am sorry about their plight. I'd do most anything to help them, but their business reversal—well, as far as I know, they caused it themselves with poor planning for that expansion. I just can't believe that selling Alferic's and the Jenson Building to outsiders is justified. My offer will be perfectly fair, and it will fulfill the terms of Grandpa's will."

"Okay. You have other reasons?"

Jody had the distinct impression that she was not going to like his attitude. Now it was her turn to want the subject changed. "Yes, personal ones, but they can wait. It's time to get some of that good, hearty food into the working man's stomach."

Clif claimed the chili was the best he'd ever eaten. He had consumed three helpings as proof, and had done ample justice to the salad that Jody had served with the meal. The bread basket yawned empty, except for a few crumbs at the bottom. Jody felt sure that his appreciation was sincere and that she couldn't have pleased him more.

"Last night you assured me that we couldn't have ordered more perfectly." He put down his napkin and sighed in satisfaction. "Tonight was perfection plus, and the credit is all yours."

"I'm glad you think so. That's exactly what I was trying for. Coffee here, or back by the fire? You choose."

"The fire. I think I can just about manage to haul myself over to the couch without staggering." He effected an exaggerated wobbly walk before plopping down on the sofa and stretching out full length. His eyes were closed when Jody set the steaming mugs of coffee on the table. But her hands were no sooner empty than he pulled her down to sit alongside him.

"Big phony," she teased, punching his shoulder playfully.

He chuckled, drew her head nearer for a kiss and then settled her against his chest, tucking her head between his cheek and shoulder. "I may be the most contented man in captivity right this minute—full stomach, comfy couch, warm fire and the loveliest lady I know in my arms. Comfortable?"

Jody closed her eyes, reveling in the feel of Clif's hard muscles beneath her, the strength of his fingers weaving through her hair, the softness of his lips against her forehead. She, too, felt utterly content, until sharper sensations began pushing contentment aside. Her body responded to the touch of his hands with an inner trembling of longing. Her pulse raced to keep time with the rapidly increasing rhythm of Clif's heart, pounding against her ear. His fingers slowed and stilled and, coffee forgotten, they lay there and let their mutual desire build. Jody's one fleeting thought of danger was quickly buried by her clamoring senses.

When Clif lifted her chin to bring their mouths together, she welcomed his fervent lips and tongue with avid longing. He turned her easily to rest their lengths together, and Jody felt herself wanting the caress of his hands, now exploring gently beneath her sweater. He was so tender, so unhurried. Then his kiss deepened to complete possession, and his touch grew demanding.

Jody tensed and something of her tension must have been transmitted to him. His touch reverted to a languid coaxing that, while it grew stronger, did so without hurt. When she was ready to surrender completely, alarm bells sounded again in her head. She was not yet sure of this relationship. But, having let their intimacy progress this far, she didn't want to stop, didn't know how to without being a tease....

Clif slid her sweater down, taking the responsibility upon himself, and held her close. "After telling you you'd be safe with me, I seem to be going back on my word. I think I am only now learning the meaning of the word *irresistible*. There must be magic in that touch of yours."

"No," she murmured, the tremor in her voice matching the catch in his. "It's just us—something about us—I don't know.... Let's give the coffee a try."

She got up to dump the cold contents of the cups, thinking that it was little short of incredible the way his nearness and caressing affected her.

Clif sat up, swiping the back of his hand across his forehead. "I wouldn't mind a little brandy, too, if you have it."

She did, and she poured them each a bit in crystal snifters before sitting down—in a chair a few feet away! For reasons she was hesitant to probe, she felt irritable. A coiled spring in need of release. She guessed maybe Clif felt edgy, too. He'd gotten up to pace the floor and seemed more than a little distracted.

"So," he said. "Let's carry on with our discussion of you and Alferic's. Should be a good topic, approximately as romantic as a bath in the North Atlantic." He grinned ruefully at her and cocked an eyebrow. "Come to think of it, that wouldn't be a bad idea right now." He swallowed a hefty gulp of his brandy and continued. "The personal reasons for your wanting to keep Alferic's. That's where you stopped before dinner."

"Yes, well, I've had some losses in my life over the past few months, and I need the store as an anchor, stability—something like that, I suppose."

"Your father, your mother's invalidism, I know about those. What else, Jody?"

Jody watched the amber swirl of brandy in her glass for a moment. "A broken engagement," she finally confessed.

"Ah! The something I hoped you'd tell me about of your volition one day. A traumatic break, from the sound of your voice. Is now the time? The 'one day'?"

She shook her head in the negative, too private a person to be comfortable divulging matters so close to her heart. "For now, it's enough to say that I misread him . . . as a man. I saw things that weren't there and it was disillusioning. Taught me a bit of caution, if nothing else. Anyway, back to Alferic's. For me, it's not just a piece of real estate to trade in the marketplace; it's an integral part of my life. Actually, the Jenson Building could never be just a piece of real estate to any of us. Most of us, anyway. It's as much a part of the family as our name, or our heritage, or our dreams. Hanging in the library is one of our most

treasured possessions—a picture of Grandpa standing in front of the building, his chest all puffed out, an
arm around Grandma. The baby she's holding is my
father, and above them all, the stonemason had just
finished carving Jenson Building. It's part of us, Clif.''

"Yes, I see that. And, right now, it's of special importance in your life. I see that, too. What I don't see
is why your uncles want to sell it to Renard, and why
Renard is offering such an exorbitant price.''

"That's been bothering Alf and me, too, the
amount of money they're willing to pay, I mean. As
for my uncles, they never have been interested in the
store. It *is* just a piece of real estate for them.''

Clif got up, tossed a fresh log on the fire and poured
himself another brandy. "If I've got this straight, your
grandfather's will stipulates that any shareholder de-
siring to sell must first offer the sale to the other
shareholders at fair market value. Is that correct?''
She nodded and he continued. "You will make such
an offer, based on recent sales of similar properties in
like locations. At the same time, we have Renard, with
his outrageous offer, in cash. Must have underworld
connections. Anyway, the case will hinge on a definition of 'fair market value.' Very interesting.'' Clif
stared thoughtfully into the fire.

"And, the intent of grandpa's will—to keep the
building in the family—will be a factor, too. Or, so
Warren claims.''

Clif merely nodded, preoccupied with his own
thoughts. "Jody, you seem like a realist to me. But it
seems unrealistic to me to become so attached to a pile
of steel and cement when circumstances would dic-
tate otherwise. Life, after all, is about change and
movement, buying and selling, and business is about

making profits. You don't run a business on senti-
ment. You run it on profit-and-loss statements. Your
profits must be downright negligible and your over-
head astronomical—the wasted space, all the time you
take with customers. Jody, your operation would drive
any businessman crazy. That kind of service is passé.
Alferic's is passé. Seems to me that the sensible thing
to do is sell to Renard, make yourself a tidy bundle
and, if you want a little bookshop, well, you could
work something out.''

''That may sound sensible to you, Clif,'' Jody re-
butted, anger causing a hardness in her voice. ''But it
sure doesn't to me. I don't need the money, I don't
want to relocate—for reasons I just gave you—Alferic's is not a 'little bookshop,' and what do you mean,
'passé'?''

''No need to get excited. I'm just trying to be real-
istic and help you. Why passé?'' He shrugged. ''I can't
say I paid a great deal of attention to the actual store
on my two visits. My thoughts were zeroed in on a
certain gorgeous clerk. But my recollection is of a
pretty inefficient layout. Upholstered furniture set off
in various nooks, antiques sitting around like in some
private club library—''

''That's it!'' she broke in, enthusiastic over his per-
ception. ''You caught it right away. You see, Clif, our
store is the sort people browse in. Not right now,
everyone's in a hurry at Christmas time, but during the
rest of the year they do. And the layout is very efficient for that goal. Our customers love it. They can
pick up a book, sit down in comfort and examine the
artwork, the paper, bindings, typeface—Clif, a book
can be an experience. Hand-cut pages feel rough,
leather bindings creak delightfully, fine laid paper has

a special scent and, every once in a while, there's the thrill of discovery—anything from the contents bringing new insights to an original manuscript.''

Clif chuckled and blew her a kiss. ''Never knew anyone could get all wound up over a few dusty books. They really have a special smell?''

''Definitely. A wonderful one. You'd notice it right away if you went into an antiquarian bookshop, and you will if you go into our Rare Books room.''

''Okay, I'll try that sometime. But, Jody, no one browses anymore.'' His tone implied that the thought was too absurd for consideration. ''We lead a fast-paced life. Who has time to poke around looking at typeface? You must get about one-third the business you could if you had a brightly lit place, things like central registers and functional shelving. Forget the comforts and go after the profits.''

''Who has time? Lots and lots of people do. Minneapolis and St. Paul aren't hick towns, for heaven's sake. There's lots of sophistication here, to say nothing of a rather well-known institution we have called the University of Minnesota.'' She paused to squelch the sarcasm that was creeping into her voice, and then went on. ''Faculty members from the 'U' are in the store constantly. The department heads and the librarians are forever wanting us to locate something. Alferic's is a busy place. Busy with book lovers, busy with people who want much more than the latest paperback espionage novel or a cheap edition of a classic. And they love our atmosphere, with the comfort and obvious invitation to indulge their tastes. Really, you're quite wrong to think we don't serve many, many people.''

Clif nodded his head in a way that made light of her comments. "So okay, I'll grant you that there's a call for your merchandise and services. But right at Nicollet Mall? Jody, that's a poor return on investment. You've got a spot that could turn a real profit, could be used for something essential...."

The coiled spring jumped free. She set her glass down with a thump. "Something essential," she snapped. "Comfort isn't essential to you? Quality isn't essential? Leisure, savoring, browsing—not essential? What are you? A robot beeping your way through life, crunching over everything gracious, munching dollars?"

"No, I'm not a robot." His voice was low and stiff with control. "I'm a practical, no-nonsense businessman. If I want a book, I don't want to have to waste time digging around some archive, weaving around lamps and planters and squinting at section designations in Old English script as if I were in 'Ye Olde Book Shoppe.'"

Jody jumped to her feet. "And, if Renard's had been on that corner yesterday morning, you'd never have found the *Partridge*, either." Her voice was almost shrill. "Nor would you have found anything at all on etymology, except some thin, trite paperback for the novice. *If* you happened to be lucky," she ended.

"I'd have been lucky enough not to meet with Minneapolis's hottest temper!" he countered, standing up, grabbing his sports coat and striding toward the front door.

"I'm not done," Jody said to his retreating back.

He stopped and turned to face her. "I'm listening."

"I do have a quick temper, Clif, though not a vicious one. You are proud to say that you go after what you want. I am proud to say that I am passionately devoted to whom and what I love. And more than willing to fight for them!"

"My error—" he inclined his head "—please accept my apologies. Anything else?"

"Yes. You, quite clearly, think I'm a fool to go to such lengths for a 'little book shop.' Passé, you call it. Why don't you find out just how passé Alferic's is to the Twin Cities and its surroundings? Why don't you spend some time talking to our customers? Spend an hour or two asking them how they would feel if we weren't there. Or would the time spent not be practical?"

Though his mouth was still grim, Jody thought she saw the glimmerings of a twinkle in his eyes.

"All right," he said. "You're on. I'm not in the habit of walking out on controversy, but my own temper seems to be pretty fragile at the moment and the argument can't be resolved at this point anyway. Not until I've met your challenge. After that? You'd better be ready to resume the…ah…discussion." He winked at her and was gone.

To her disgust, he closed the door softly. "I'd have slammed it," she said.

To her further disgust, there were tears slipping down her cheeks. She sank onto the couch, wondering if they could ever agree. Clif was a practical, functional, efficiency-oriented man. Dollars, dollars, dollars dominated a life that marched in straight lines. All they seemed to have going for them was some weird chemistry. Weird? *Glorious*, was more like it.

She began reliving the sensations his mouth and hands had brought her, and suddenly she sat up straight. "That's it," she announced to the empty room. "Of course! We started loving and never got anywhere, so he was frustrated. He disagreed just because he was on edge."

No, that was not it. She picked up her brandy snifter and sat back once more. Clif had been cool and rational. She had been the first to lose her temper. And now she had challenged him to come back to the store. Two days ago she had been leading a quiet, patterned life. Now she was mixed up with one suave, chemically bubbling lawyer who was bound to get mixed up in the Renard case. If she ever saw him again, she would have to use her head—and keep her cool. And if she couldn't manage that, she could at least make sure she wasn't available when he—if he—met her challenge. Maybe she could be in Africa.

Staring into the fire, she had a better idea. She would be in Cob Center, Iowa. Rich still wanted her, and the only thing that ever bubbled in Cob Center was a teakettle. Probably never even heard of chemistry, except from some old stick of a teacher. That's what she needed, a safe, sane existence as a minister's wife, doing good works with the Ladies' Aid, putting on ice-cream socials and serving lemonade.

The thought brought a smile to her lips, and she realized that she was finally ready to laugh over the incidents leading to the breaking of her engagement with Rich. She was ready to stop calling herself stupid and foolish for misjudging the man. She had, after all, been very naive, and the situation had assuredly held some humorous moments.

She and Rich had met in Jody's senior year of undergraduate study, during a weekend party at Yale, where Rich was a divinity student. There had been no great attraction on her part; he was just another friend of the young man she'd been with. They'd chatted some and she'd accepted his invitation to a football weekend a couple of weeks later, not so much because of any promise she saw in him, but simply because football weekends were such fun.

As it turned out, they hadn't even bothered with the game. Instead, they had taken advantage of the picture-postcard New England fall to ramble for hours through woods glowing in brilliant scarlets, golds and oranges. They had discovered so many mutual interests during their walk, even to favorite authors and composers, that Jody was sure she had never met a more compatible man. For her, mental congeniality was the extent of any attraction.

Rich apparently felt more than that, but he was so circumspect in his wooing—his kisses were chaste, his hands never left her shoulders—that letting him express any physical desires was as easy as shaking hands. And just as exciting. Jody had been fed up with the slobbering and pawing she'd endured on most of her dates, so she was secretly relieved, and content with his shy advances.

They had dated all that year and the next, while she was getting her master's. Everyone said what a perfect couple they were, not just in intellectual pursuits, but also in appearance. Rich's dark Celtic heritage was a perfect foil for Jody's fair Viking blood.

He'd proposed at Christmas and she'd accepted. It then developed that he expected to sleep with her, and she'd thought, why not? They were going to be married, after all. She hadn't enjoyed the experience particularly. Rich was always in a rush and rather furtive about the whole thing. But it hadn't hurt much after a while, and he had claimed he needed it. So she had obliged.

The only real effect on Jody had been to leave her wondering if she was destined to miss all the thrills she'd read and heard about. Though she and Rich made "beautiful music together" in a multitude of ways, it had never been the case in bed. She had hoped that they both just needed the security of marriage to relax and enjoy. Ecstasy was out there somewhere, and she had definitely balked at the thought of missing it.

During the spring break, Rich had taken her home with him to meet his parents, the Reverend and Mrs. McNab. Home was a strict Calvinistic farming community in Iowa—Cob Center by name. It might as well have been on another planet as far as Jody was concerned. She, who among her own friends was considered a near specimen morally, to be stuffed and sent to the Smithsonian upon her death, was thought to be fast and loose in grim-faced Cob Center. Her thinking on the subject was that the Smithsonian was welcome to Rich's entire town—that it should be walled in as a museum and admission charged to view an otherwise extinct species. Jody could not have imagined a more appropriate fate for a group of people who thought dancing, singing, cards, laughter, bright colors and sex—unmentionable—were sinful. To this community, life was a serious, hardworking, sin-laden vale of tears. When Jody, in her innocence, had suggested that God had created laughter, that the birds sang and danced, at least during the mating season, Rich's mother had nearly swooned. A gloomy Rich had later told her that words like mating were not used in polite company, and would she please mind her tongue.

He had been further distressed when, the next day, she had come downstairs in an electric-blue afternoon dress to accompany his mother to a Ladies' Aid meeting. She had protested that it was one of his favorite colors on her. It was high necked and long sleeved, and anyway, she didn't have any dun-colored clothes. Mrs. McNab forbore any comments. She merely spent the afternoon bearing this burden the Lord had sent her, while looking as though someone had popped a lemon slice in her mouth and sat her on a thistle.

All this had been as nothing, given the final explosion. One evening Mrs. McNab had surprised them in the haymow, Jody's scarlet blouse open, her poppy-printed skirt rucked up. Rich was in the position he routinely assumed—mouth clamped to her breast and hips pumping frantically. Some miracle had prevented the woman from tumbling right back down the ladder as she gobbled like a turkey cock and got out words like "harlot" and "Jezebel."

"Mother!" Rich had scrambled up, hands flapping to shield his embarrassment. "I can't help it. She tempts me. Flaunts herself. I can't help it...."

"The devil's mistress," his mother had hissed. "I knew it. My husband will put you on the next train. You blaspheme our God-fearing home. Richard, you get down this ladder at once!"

A wounded and raging Jody had been left all askew on the floor of the loft as Rich hastened to obey his mother, still muttering about temptation. Jody had marched into the house, hay sprouting from hair and clothes, walked up to a cowering Rich and slapped him. Hard. Then she yanked off her engagement ring and handed it to Mrs. McNab with the words, "Why don't *you* put it on the next candidate for him." Facing Rich once more, she had spat the word "hypocrite" at him and sped upstairs to pack.

She had gone on to finish her master's program, deaf to Rich's pleas for reconciliation, his protestations of regret over his behavior and his avowals of strict loyalty in the future. For Jody, his betrayal had destroyed any possibility of trust or respect on her part. In addition, she had been utterly dismayed that she could have misjudged his character so. She had thought him strong, and he was weak; she had thought him a man with ambitions and goals, and he was a boy afraid of his mother; she had thought him deeply in love with her, and he had failed her at the first provocation. The experience had shaken her faith in her own ability to assess character and had, also, left her wary and disinclined toward commitment to a man.

And now she had met Clif—a man whose complexities intrigued her, and with whom she felt fully alive. Clif, with a tenderness that set her senses humming and held such promise. Here, at last, was the man she'd been dubious of finding. The man with whom she could become one and reach the fulfilling culmination she'd been led to believe was possible. But Clif was a playboy, a love 'em and leave 'em sort. The type of casual relationship he indulged in would be impossible for her to bear.

"My world turned inside out for a man I've known a grand total of two days," she grumbled. "No, that's not true." A sudden thought surprising her. "I've known him since before I was born."

Jody had to chuckle at her fanciful notion. Still the words held a ring of truth for her. Somehow, some way, it felt right to think of them together, as if their paths were intended to cross and become one path. Foolish? Possibly, but the thought satisfied her heart.

CHAPTER FIVE

JODY SENSED Clif's presence in the store just after they opened the next morning. On this busy Saturday she was, of course, nowhere near Africa or Cob Center, Iowa. She was manning a register. Forcing herself not to whip her head around to search for him, she completed a sale and then made what she hoped would appear to be a casual perusal of the floor, an owner-checking-up-on-things sort of survey. Clif's hard blue eyes riveted hers from across the floor. He sent her a curt nod and turned to chat with a customer. She hoped he wasn't telling anyone why he happened to be spending his time observing the activities in Alferic's.

With her mind only partially focused on her customers, Jody made more errors during the next hour than she usually made in a month. Her disgust with herself reached a peak when Clif's laughter at some response resounded over the floor and distracted her, a distraction that had her fingers rambling over the keys in directionless abandon. The register promptly objected.

"Are you sure you want to do this?" it inquired in eye-wrenching chartreuse.

"What? Why of all . . . you impudent thing." Jody exclaimed.

Her startled customer's eyebrows shot toward his hairline. "I beg your pardon?"

"Oh, not you . . . I didn't mean you, not for a minute. It's this . . . this . . . look at that! An ignorant machine is asking me insulting questions."

The gentleman chuckled and his brows dropped into place. "Your first day on the job?"

Jody had to smile at the mild and fully justifiable question. "No, far from it, but I do seem to have some kind of thing about computers. I'm forever doing battle with them. Please forgive me for taking so long."

The gentleman shrugged good-naturedly. "I'm in no hurry. Go ahead with the corrections."

Wishing briefly that Carl hadn't been so successful in persuading their father to put in computerized registers, and vowing that these would be the last such nuisances in the store, she voided out her errors. By the time she had it all right, the sales tape was six inches long—for one book! Happily, the patron wore a large grin as he left. No harm was done, but she welcomed a reprieve from the register in the form of a distress call from Britta.

The problem was at the Will Call desk and concerned an elderly man, a professor at the university, who was all but wringing his hands in agitation. It seemed that he, through Alferic's, had ordered a rare edition of Burns's poetry from Edinburgh some months earlier and had received a call the previous day telling him that the book had arrived. Now it could not be found.

"Miss Jenson," the professor began nervously. "The faculty Christmas party is tonight and I simply must have the book. The lady I purchased it for is expecting something special from me and I simply must—really, I must—oh dear, I don't know when

I've been so distressed. It *has* to be here." He peered distractedly at the shelves behind Britta's back.

"I'm sure it is, Dr. Withers," Jody soothed. "As you said, it has to be, and I'll find it if I have to turn the place upside down. Won't you please browse around a bit? Have some coffee or tea? I'll bring the book to you the minute I find it. Being such a small volume, it probably just slipped behind one of the others. Now, you just enjoy yourself."

Jody turned him gently by the shoulders and started him off toward the poetry section before helping Britta make a thorough search of the orders awaiting pickup. "It's not here," she concluded. "How can that be? He got a phone call. It's got to be here, it's just *got* to be."

"I know." Britta began scrabbling through drawers and clearing the surface of the counter.

Jody got down on hands and knees, poked through the wastebasket, felt beneath shelves, then sat back on her heels, frowning in consternation. "Are the calls to customers about orders still made by whoever happens to be available at the time?" she asked.

"Yes, from one of the stockroom phones. I remember Inga calling Dr. Withers. I was in there unpacking a carton from Rodale at the time. The Burns came by mail and Inga had just gotten the delivery. She was all excited since she'd taken the order from Dr. Withers in the first place. After she called him, she set it down for me to bring out here, and I can't remember what I did with it, if anything. Oh, Lord, how could I be so dumb?"

"You're not dumb, Brit. Alf would never have married a dumb woman." Jody gave her a quick hug. "If anything's dumb around here, it's our system—or lack of it, I mean. Glory, I'll bet Inga even forgot to enter it in the receiving log. Well, we can't worry about that now. I'll check the stockroom, by the phones, the desk top—the obvious places, and if it's not right there, I'll have to confront the good professor and stall for time.''

Five minutes later she was admitting momentary defeat to a distraught Dr. Withers.

"Miss Jenson, this cannot be. Alferic's was most highly recommended to me for excellence and dependability, and now you've lost an early edition, a collector's . . . What will I tell Lenore? Oh, dear . . .''

"Dr. Withers, please,'' Jody interrupted, resting a placating hand on his sleeve. "It is not lost, and I will locate it. However, I do not want you to waste your valuable time standing around waiting while I search. Would it be all right with you if I took your address and delivered the book to you? By twelve o'clock at the latest?''

"Deliver it? But, Miss Jenson, I live in St. Paul.''

"That doesn't matter. What does matter is that you've made a trip over here only to find that we've failed you. It's important to me that we make up for your inconvenience, that we convince you that we deserve our reputation for excellence and dependability. Does my delivering it meet with your approval?''

His pale eyes blinked at her from behind his wire-rimmed glasses, and his formerly pursed lips became a tentative smile. "Why yes, the dinner isn't until seven. Yes, it most certainly does.''

"It most certainly does *not* meet with mine,'' a resonant, male voice announced. Jody whirled to meet Clif's frowning face. "Excuse me, Doctor. I'm a family friend—Clif McClelland.'' They shook hands. "Would you mind telling me where in St. Paul you live? I know some parts of the city are safer than others, even in broad daylight.''

"Clif! What do you think you're—''

"Please, Jody, bear with me. It's quite likely that I'll be taking you over. For your own safety.''

Jody tightened her lips against the angry words that wanted to escape. How dare he simply march up and take over? As if she couldn't handle the situation herself. If Dr. Withers weren't standing there she'd . . . But, instead of venting her anger, Jody decided to drop that line of thought and focus on the professor.

"Pardon me, Miss Jenson, but the young man is entirely correct. You do need an escort. My neighborhood was a fine one when I was growing up. But now, as with so many old neighborhoods, it's deteriorated. I stay on because it's my home, even though I have to caution ladies to be careful. Do accept his offer, Miss Jenson.''

Jody had to smile at his choice of words. "It sounded more like a command to me, Dr. Withers, but you needn't worry, I promise I won't come alone, and I will find your book.''

"Professor—'' Clif gestured toward the closest alcove "—why don't you have a seat over there. I'll join you in a minute to get directions from you.''

Then he looked at Jody. The stern expression on his face was belied by the laughter tugging at the corners of his mouth. "And I will find you, Miss Jenson, so you can just drop that plan you're cooking up to find another driver.''

Jody watched him sit down with Dr. Withers, conscious of a suspicious tugging at the corners of her own mouth. Her crossness had been dissipated by mirth, but she still thought she'd ask someone else to take her. However, the first order of business was to find the missing volume.

She was on her hands and knees once more, this time in the dust, flashlight focused beneath the shelving, when Clif swung the stockroom door open and joined her.

"Need some help?" he inquired, obviously trying to stifle a smile as he looked down at her.

"Not from you. Just give me the directions, please. I'll get someone from the store to escort me to St. Paul."

"Nope." He started to poke about in the next section of supplies and stock. "You're stuck with me. I'm the only one with the address and the directions for how to get there. Just what is it we're looking for, anyway?"

"A slim, small package, rewrapped in the original mailing paper from Edinburgh. That's in Scotland," she added, remembering his insulting explanation for the word *etymology*, and also deciding she'd get the phone number from the order and call Dr. Withers for the address.

"Talked to Britta at the Will Call desk on the way in," he said, rummaging through a lower shelf. "Enjoyed seeing her again."

"Hmm." Jody flicked some dirt from her smock and then straightened suddenly. Dear heaven, the orders were on Britta's counter. She glanced at Clif, suspicious of his nonchalant, innocent expression. "Did she give you anything?"

Clif merely patted his pocket and grinned in reply.

"You are the most exasperating man—person—I've ever had the misfortune to meet. I'd very much appreciate it if you would simply leave the premises and let me handle this. I have a job to do."

Britta leaned in around the door. "Any luck?"

"I haven't had a chance to really get started. This— this—" The door swung closed before Jody could get the words out. Britta had gone back to her post.

"Okay, Jody," Clif announced, taking advantage of the interruption to take charge. "You start here, at this end, and I'll begin at the other. Do you have another flashlight?"

"I asked you to leave."

"I heard you. Now, let's get busy, this is one helluva long wall of shelving."

"There's another flashlight in the desk drawer," Jody offered. She turned her back to him and began emptying a shelf. *I give up*, she thought. *He's impossible and it's just a waste of time to wrangle with him. Without a squabble, his way seems to be the only way.* She played a beam of light under, over and around the empty bookcase. Nothing. Merchandise replaced, she moved on to the next section.

"Good Lord, Jody, some of this stuff must have been here since the turn of the century. I've never seen so much dust, boxes of junk, odds and ends of paper. No wonder you lost the book. Haven't you folks ever thought of devising a system? Streamlining this operation? So you've got a dinosaur in front. Might be some sense in that, but it makes no sense whatsoever to have one back here, too." He sneezed, then continued grumbling under his breath about dusty inefficiency.

A sharp retort rose in Jody's throat and just as quickly died. He was right, absolutely correct. Pausing to study the room, the validity of his accusation hit her with a jolt. The place looked like the attic of a secondhand book and junk dealer.

It was a long and rather narrow room, with a freight door at one end that opened onto an alley. The door into the store itself was at the other end. One of the long walls was solid shelving. The original and now somewhat sagging lumber was packed with books. Against the opposite wall, boxes of paper and business supplies were stacked helter-skelter, with broken fixtures, the odd lamp shade, a chair minus one leg and other castoffs thrown in for good measure. Slightly off center, parallel to the long walls, was the series of freestanding shelving units upon which she and Clif were focusing their search. These held a mélange of items ranging from boxes of old papers to current material that needed attention, adjustment or repair. Only the huge rolltop desk was miraculously uncluttered.

The whole arrangement reflected the way in which the stock was handled—sloppily. Clif had said, ''No wonder you lost the book.'' There was no possible way to contradict him, and Jody came to a swift decision. Her next order of business would be to revamp the room, establishing an up-to-date system to better serve their customers, and make life easier for the personnel.

''Here's something.'' Brushing at his knees, Clif handed her a slim volume. ''Thought I'd found the missing book for a moment there, but it seems to be some old diary.''

Jody flipped back the cover. ''It's Grandpa's! This is his writing. Look, Clif. It's like some copybook exercise, all spidery and precise.'' With great care she turned brittle pages the color of rich cream. ''His journal. Oh, Clif, what a find. It starts when he and Grandma were married, their first house, furniture, 'the finest horsehair sofa for the front parlor.' Think of the secrets that might be in here, the fun it will be to read.'' She raised sparkling eyes to his.

Clif touched a finger to the tip of her nose, and he brushed her cheek and chin lightly. ''You look so beautiful right now . . .''

''But, hot-tempered,'' she finished for him.

''No, not necessarily. Feisty, maybe—under certain circumstances.'' He moved the ladder and climbed up. ''There was a bit of tension flying around last night, but I've decided to give you the benefit of the doubt.''

''Generous of you,'' she countered sarcastically, venting her anger with a semisatisfactory slam of the desk drawer she had laid the journal in.

''I rather thought so myself.''

Jody thumped some books on the floor. Smug, too. On top of everything else, he was smug. Not that it mattered right now, she thought. What did matter was the sound of his random humming coming closer. That meant they had almost covered the entire row of shelving with no success. The book *had* to be here, somewhere.

After some five minutes of tuneless crooning, Clif proclaimed, ''That does it. No Burns.''

He helped Jody to her feet, one arm encircling her waist, his other hand brushing strands of hair from her face. ''No need to scowl, I'll think of something.''

She accepted his tightening arms, welcoming the secure strength of him, the assurance of his confident words. At the same time, she was baffled over why this closeness didn't feel strange. After all, they had been antagonists last night and most of this morning. Now the sheltering circle of his arms and his lips against her hair felt so right. Surely she wasn't becoming so confused as to be more than simply interested in this impossible, dictatorial playboy. And yet she just plain never wanted to move.

The sound of voices and laughter through the door brought her back to the immediate problem.

"Have you thought of anything?" she asked.

"Sure have," he said, sliding his hands down her hips before stepping back. "Not a syllable of it has to do with books, though."

She answered his low laugh. "It must be after eleven, Clif. I've got to find the Burns. People are going to be coming for their lunches, sitting around. It'll be impossible. Let's try the trash barrels. They're next to the phones, so maybe it got pushed into one of them."

Dumping the contents of the two containers produced nothing but a grand mess.

"Jody, what about those boxes stacked up in the corner by the freight door?"

"Empties, from deliveries, waiting for the collector tomorrow. It's a good thought but the particular order we're looking for came by itself, in the mail. It couldn't very well be in one of them. I'm about to give up and go home for my father's edition. Use it for a substitute. It may not be rare, but it's quite early."

"Wait a minute. Those boxes probably sit over here for a while, being unpacked, before they're stacked up. Let's look. What have we got to lose?" With that, he walked over, yanked a box from the middle of the nearest stack, bringing the rest tumbling down.

The first thing to catch Jody's eye was a label with the words Rodale Press. That's what Britta had been unpacking.

"Clif, that one, the Rodale carton. Is there anything in it?"

Clif delved in. "Some old notepads, broken pencils—looks like someone swept a cluttered desk top into—voila!" Triumphantly he held up a slim package wrapped in brown paper covered with foreign postage.

"Clif, you're a genius." Jody hugged the little book to her chest.

"About time you noticed that. You're a bit slow on the uptake, but I forgive you. Fortunately you've got a few other attributes. Now, run up for a coat while I get my car. I'll have you there on time, if we get moving." With a quick kiss and a playful swat on the derriere, Clif sent her on her way.

JODY DIDN'T BOTHER HIM with conversation while he was preoccupied with the multiple distractions of heavy noon-hour traffic in the city streets. Instead she found herself admiring the skill with which he maneuvered through crowds of scurrying pedestrians, horn-blaring cabbies and heedless, careless motorists. She noticed he was never cross and even smiled occasionally at some inanity of his fellow man. Masterful and competent, she thought. Rational and clearheaded. She felt safe here beside him. That is, if she ignored the silly chemistry business. That was certainly dangerous.

But Clif was so determined in his own way of doing things that they could never get along anyway, and his casual attitude toward women made it that much easier to say no. Jody frowned as a sudden thought occurred to her. Could it be that his supreme self-confidence quite naturally accompanied strength, competence and capability? That loving Clif—which she most assuredly did not, this was mere idle speculation—would mean accepting his attitude as a natural offshoot of the qualities she admired? Actually he was very much like the men in her own family. They, too, were strong, competent, and capable—definitely autocratic. Yet, underneath, they were caring, loving, and essentially gentle people. It was an interesting concept but of no practical concern to her. What was of practical concern was Alferic's.

"Time for a report on your morning survey, I believe," she said as they crossed the river and headed into St. Paul.

"You're sure I shouldn't save it for the return trip, as insurance that you won't stomp off in a huff and get a taxi," he teased.

"Beast!" She clipped him on the shoulder, half serious, but smiling at the same time. "I'm sure, but I'll wait anyway because there's something else I'd rather talk about. Clif, it seems that I have to thank you for coming into the stockroom today. That's right, thank you. And not just for the obvious—finding the Burns. I'm thanking you just as much for your comments on our nonexistent system. There's simply no justifying the inefficiency. It's bad for the customers and hard on us. First thing Monday morning I'm going to get on it. Any suggestions?"

"But, of course. Did you doubt it?"

She answered his grin with a sigh of resignation. "Not for a second. Carry on, I'm listening."

Before actually offering any advice, Clif quizzed her about current procedures. Questions that, as she answered them, made her more and more exasperated with herself.

"Clif," she interrupted, "excuse me for breaking in, but I'm saying 'I don't know,' or 'I'm not sure' to every other thing you ask about. I'm disgusted with myself—terrible management. I've been plain negligent about everything but the actual selling floor, counting on our faithful staff to keep everything glued together. They're not going to be with us forever."

Clif sent her a look of surprised admiration. "First of all, I want to say I'm impressed. A woman in this day and age who admits to needing a man's help is a rare find."

Jody thought that was a pretty farfetched opinion and sadly cynical, but she bowed a thank-you. "I'd ask for a gold star, but the fact is that I'd ask the man in the moon if I thought he had the advice I needed."

"I'm doubly impressed," he said, and then went on to present a veritable armada of ideas on the stockroom.

They had reached Dr. Withers's neighborhood by the time Clif had finished reorganizing all the procedural business of Alferic's. He'd covered everything from bills of lading to inventory management; use of floor space to designs for shelving; ordering to accounting systems. Almost every department needed to be computerized.

"I hate computers," she protested.

"Jody, that's like saying you hate today."

"Sometimes I do," she admitted. "But I can see that sometimes I need the new technology, too, and I'd best get used to the idea." She began hunting for house numbers. "There he is, on the right up there, waiting for us. Correction, coming to meet us."

His expression anxious, the professor trotted along his walkway. Jody waved the package reassuringly as they pulled up.

"I'm so relieved," he said, beaming, and opened the car door for her. "You've no idea how upset I've been. Gift wrapped, too. You are a marvelous lady, Miss Jenson."

"Thank you, Dr. Withers, all part of Alferic's tradition. Except that it was Mr. McClelland who actually found it for you, and he's not part of the store at all. However, Britta did wrap it. She sends her apologies for the hasty job—she did it in a rush while I got my coat. The original mailing paper from Edinburgh is still very much intact. Your Lenore will know the effort you made to get her something special."

"Perfect, just perfect. And here I stand talking when I should be offering you both a cup of tea. Won't you come in?"

One look at the refusal beginning to shape Clif's lips, and Jody hastened to step in ahead of him with an acceptance. "Although," she added, "I do have an appointment at two, so one cup will have to be our limit."

"Splendid." Dr. Withers turned and walked toward the house.

Clif took Jody's elbow and bent to say in a grumpy voice, "I hate tea. Of all the insipid drinks..."

"Maybe he has some sherry," she whispered back.

"That's an improvement? Ugh!"

"That's what you get for inviting yourself along."

By this time they were being ushered through the door. Clif's only response was a mumbled, "I shall endure."

The professor led them down a rather dreary hallway to the kitchen. Jody took a quick glimpse of the living room and dining room as they passed. Both looked dim and unlived in. She didn't spot a single lighthearted or personal touch. But the kitchen was a different story. Books and papers were everywhere. Photographs of three young children decorated the refrigerator, and several ceramic figurines sat on the counters, clearly the projects of preschoolers. The windowsill was lined with pots of violets, but most surprising of all, the professor was now relaxed, all traces of agitation and fussiness gone.

"I hope you don't mind sitting in here," he said, quickly clearing the plain wooden table and chairs. "When I'm home, this is where I spend my time since my wife passed away."

Clif had been examining the photos on the refrigerator, his puzzled expression saying that he found it hard to reconcile children with his image of Dr. Withers. "I'm certainly sorry to hear that, Professor," he sympathized, "but it looks as though you've got some cheerful young ones to keep you company. Your grandchildren?"

"Yes, and what a help they are. Wonderful children. The joy of my life. I'd be one of those well-known 'basket cases' if it weren't for them and my daughters, I'm afraid. And now, the tea."

He led Jody over to a cupboard, swung the cupboard doors wide and pointed to an array of teas, the likes of which she'd never seen outside a specialty shop. "Now, my dear, why don't you make a selection for us?"

Jody glanced over the bewildering display. "Good heavens! How can I possibly choose? I've never even heard of most of them. Are you a connoisseur?"

Dr. Withers chuckled at her dismay. "No, but my students seem to think I'm the tea-drinking type, whatever that might be, and I've been inundated with it every Christmas for years. Frankly, I don't know a thing about most of them, either."

Jody shifted the tins about looking in vain for something that said orange pekoe or English breakfast tea.

"I give up," she finally admitted. "Why don't we just settle for your favorite?"

"That would be Glenlivet," he answered in a solemn voice.

Jody's questioning repetition of the name was met by a roar of laughter from Clif. "Professor, that's a winning selection if I ever heard one," he declared, "especially if you'll add some ice."

Jody looked at him in surprise. "Iced tea on a cold day like this?" And then she noticed a wide grin on Dr. Withers's face, too. "Okay, you two, what's going on here? Where's this Glenlivet you both want? I didn't see it in here."

"My dear, I was just testing the waters, so to speak. If neither of you had reacted, I'd have picked something on the shelves. However, the instant recognition by Mr. McClelland permits me to walk over here, where I keep the Glenlivet, and offer you this."

He flourished a bottle of Scotch with another label Jody had never seen.

"Miss Jenson, if you'd prefer tea, I'd suggest..."

"Not on your life, Doctor. Just make mine with both water and ice cubes. And please tell me why I've never heard of this Glenlivet."

"Gladly. My name is Jack, by the way, and I'd like you to call me that. Let's dispense with all this formality, or the first thing you know, I'll be treating you as students and start giving you a lecture on Chaucer."

Jody said first names were fine by her, but Clif was more expansive. "That clinches it—first names only. Not that Chaucer doesn't sound uplifting, but I don't seem to be in just the right mood."

Jack's eyes twinkled merrily behind his glasses. "My students would empathize with your sentiments every time they sit down in my classroom. Lecturing on medieval writers these days is an exercise in futility. But, enough of that—try this, Jody. Tell us what you think."

She sniffed it and rolled the first sip around on her tongue before swallowing. "Unusual," she said. "Not at all like any other Scotch I've ever had. More flavor...there's a substance to it...body...depth...smoky maybe?"

"Excellent." Jack fairly beamed at her. "This is the real stuff, as you young people might say. Straight malt whisky from Scotland, mellowed by long aging in oak casks. The smoky hint comes from the way the malt is dried. What we get over here is a poor, blended imitation. So, Jody, while I may not be a connoisseur of tea, I know a good Scotch when I taste one."

Clif had stretched out comfortably in his chair and was clearly enjoying himself. "Jack, I think you are a man of many surprises."

"Having some trouble fitting me neatly into the stuffy, professorial mold?" Jack smiled at them, completely at ease. "Especially after the incident this morning, when I'm sure you thought I'd be a perfect fit. The fact is, I'm rather uncomfortable outside of the university atmosphere, or my own home and stamping grounds, so I tend to get nervous—always in a hurry to finish up whatever errand I'm on, the way I was in Alferic's. Although I have to tell you, Jody, I was most comfortable in your absolutely delightful store—a perfect bookstore, and I wish we had more like it. No, it wasn't the store that disconcerted me, it was the missing Burns."

"It will never happen again," Jody promised. "Clif has plans to modernize our clumsy system—behind the scenes, that is."

"I'm certainly glad you added that qualification." Jack sighed in relief. "I'd have gotten upset all over again if you'd meant the part I saw this morning. As far as I'm concerned, you've got a treasure there, young lady. I've heard about Alferic's for years, but until recently, we had a fine bookstore in St. Paul, so I'd never gone over. Now it's gone. The proprietor died, the children aren't interested—an all-too-frequent story. It seems as though, little by little, all the service and quality is vanishing from our society."

Clif cleared his throat. Jody swallowed a smile, and Jack glanced speculatively at both of them. "Bit of a contretemps going on, I gather. So, enough of that. My daughters are going to be so pleased that I stepped out of my rut, as they call it, and ventured into some place new. Astounding how prickly one's children can be when they've decided on precisely the right thing for you to do."

"They're giving you a hard time, Jack?" Clif asked, more than happy to pursue this new line of conversation.

"Not really too hard. They just keep up a steady, 'Dad, you must get out more. See something new. Meet somebody new.' That sort of thing. I expect I should, but the rut is mighty comfortable."

Clif leaned forward and rested his arms on the table. "Jack, I just happen to know a man who's a connoisseur of Scotch, a Dickens buff—hardly medieval, but at least it's literature—and is fascinated with etymology. Think you'd have anything in common with such a man?"

"I most certainly would. Who is this man?"

"My father. And I know just the place to get the two of you together—Alferic's. One of those alcoves would be perfect for a good confab on the world of books."

Well, well, Jody thought. A few cracks seemed to be developing in Clif's defenses. Hallelujah!

Jack looked a little nonplussed, but also interested. "Your father, you say. Why, I suppose…that is, if he wouldn't mind . . . although I hadn't intended . . ."

"Jack," Clif interrupted, "if you want to get someplace, you have to dive right in. Take the first step, the second will be easier, and by God, before you know it, you're there. Creeping is a waste of time. Nope, I'll give you two days to cogitate and then we act."

Chuckling as he had earlier, Jack addressed Jody. "This young man doesn't have a single blade of grass under his feet, does he?"

"Not even a sprout. The pace can be downright dizzying at times, but I can honestly say that his ideas are good ones, and this is one of the best. Anyway, what have you got to lose by agreeing?''

"Nothing. Though I might lose by turning down such an offer. Clif, you're most thoughtful, and I will think on it.''

Clif gave him the benefit of two full days for the process, saying as they left that Jack could expect a call in forty-eight hours on the nose reminding him that, if nothing else, he could enjoy some more time in Alferic's.

Driving away from the house, Jody posed a question that had occurred to her during their visit. "That was a great thing to do, Clif, really great. But tell me, would you have made the same offer if Jack's favorite brand had been Lapsang Souchong instead of Glenlivet?''

"No, probably not.''

"Why?''

"Because I doubt that we'd have seen a man who would enjoy my father, and vice versa. What brought the idea to mind was Jack's obvious humor—the way he brought the Scotch up in the first place, the fun in his eyes. And then there was his openness with us, the way he told us about his nervousness and his daughters' concern in a matter-of-fact way, nothing drippy or maudlin, no poor-me trips over his wife's death. Good Lord, to think I'd shunted him aside as a fussy little man not worth bothering about.''

"Maybe you're beginning to think that full service isn't such a total loss?'' A touch of mischief was evident in Jody's voice.

Clif ignored her teasing. "I never said that it was, Jody. I appreciate it myself, as do quite a few others. I discovered this morning. Jack sounded like an echo from some of my interviews. No, it's not that. My objection was, and is, that it's just not a profitable way to conduct business today. Frankly, I don't see any other reason for being in business, especially in the most valuable section of downtown Minneapolis.''

She was sorely tempted to challenge him, but thought she'd leave it alone for the time being. After all, progress had been made today, and pushing people often resulted in more resistance than before. "Okay, I'll let that pass for now. I have another question for you. Would you put Jack in the profit or loss column?''

Clif sent her a sour look and then laughed. "You're a clever woman, Jody Jenson. How am I supposed to answer that?''

"Aha!'' she crowed triumphantly. "I now take great pleasure in saying 'gotcha.' ''

Clif reached over to ruffle her hair. "You're fun to talk to, did you know that? However, I want it known that I have no intention of leaving you one up on me. I'll think of an answer before long.''

"I'll be waiting. And Clif... you're fun to talk to, too.''

Clif's expression was serious, but he opted for words of seeming lightness. "Regular mutual admiration society around here. Now, a question for you. Do you really have an appointment at two, or was that just a way to keep the visit brief?''

"No, I don't have an appointment exactly. We're just going to get our Christmas tree, that's all.''

"Sounds like fun. Who's 'we'?''

"A bunch of us who make the circuit of tree farms and end up worn out and soaked in St. Cloud for pizza. The group started years ago and it was small then. Now it's darn near unwieldy.''

"A long-standing tradition, I gather,'' Clif commented.

"Right. My parents and two other couples started it when I was about two, but the parents are glad to leave it up to the kids these days. Not surprisingly, some of 'the kids' now have husbands and wives and kids of their own. Must be three dozen of us going today. Mass confusion, probably.''

Clif smiled at the vision of thirty-six people attacking a tree farm. "You'll strip the countryside bare like a plague of locusts.''

"You sound like Alf.'' She laughed. "He keeps threatening to buy a forest just for us, so the rest of the population has a chance to cut down their own trees.''

"Not a bad idea. Might even be a good investment. So, do Alf and Britta go on this little adventure?''

"Thanks to me, they do. I'll have you know that I'm an absolute star in the role of Cupid. Britta's parents were one of the original couples, and I introduced their daughter to Alf. Neither Britta nor Alf ever looked at anyone else again.''

"Hmm…never looked at anyone else?'' He shook his head impatiently. "Well, would thirty-seven be more unwieldy than thirty-six? I could fend off the crowds while you decide, maybe even help you.''

"You're on,'' Jody declared. Having Clif along would make the afternoon much more exciting, as well as give her a perfect excuse for not riding with Tommy Fairfield. He was the son of the other "original'' couple, a longtime friend and a nice fellow, but about as stimulating as a bowl of Pablum. Worse yet, he was convinced that he was the perfect man for Jody.

They arrived at Alf's as arranged, and Jody changed into the ski pants and jacket she had dropped off on her way to work. Clif was soon outfitted by his host, and with the exception of the infant twins who were left with a baby-sitter, they all piled into Britta's station wagon.

Before they set out Alf turned to Clif, seated in the back. "Afraid you're getting more than you bargained for, Clif. The kids will drive you crazy before we're halfway there."

"Doesn't bother me a bit," Clif answered, reaching forward to ruffle five-year-old Kirstie's hair as she sat securely between her parents. "I'm partial to female charmers." Kirstie giggled at his remark.

Eight-year-old Ivar, sitting between Clif and his Aunt Jody, snorted in disgust and whispered to her, "He wouldn't think she was so charming if she got in his room and messed his model planes all up."

Having overheard the remark, Clif leaned across Jody. "You're right. Lucky for me that my models are all safe at home, I guess."

Ivar was astonished. "You build models?"

"Not anymore, but I built loads of them when I was your age and I still have them. Cars, though, not planes."

The boy's face lit up. "Say, do you think maybe I could see them someday?"

"Can I come, too?" Kirstie chimed in. "I promise not to mess them up, Mr. 'Clelland, and anyway, it was all an accident. I didn't mean to break his plane, but dumb old Ivar doesn't like accidents, so he got all mad and yelled anyway."

"Kirsten," Britta gently warned.

"Well, he is dumb...okay, I'm sorry, Ivar."

"Now, young lady, you will not interrupt while Mr. McClelland and Ivar are having a discussion. Let's see how many blue cars we can count between here and St. Cloud."

The game effectively erased the suspicion of tears in Kirstie's eyes, and the rest of the trip was smooth and peaceful.

Their destination was the parking lot of the pizza restaurant in St. Cloud, where they would meet the rest of the group and leave some of the cars to be retrieved after supper. Jody had been quiet for most of the ride, fascinated by the rapport Clif had with her young cousins. In the space of a single afternoon, she had learned more about this man than weeks of dinners would have revealed. Everything she discovered was so heartwarming and genuine that his life-style seemed more of an enigma than ever. The clues, she said to herself. These are the clues Mom was talking about, the signposts toward his real character. A character I could so very easily love. She laid a hand on his knee and smiled at him, gestures that surprised Clif, though they clearly pleased him. He covered her hand with his.

They were the last to arrive on the scene, and Tommy was on his way to the car the instant he spotted them.

"Jody! I was afraid you weren't coming!" He opened her door wide and peered in. "Hi there, Ivar. Let me help your cousin here, and then you can hop out."

As Clif climbed from the other side of the car, Tommy suddenly recognized him. "Why, I'll be

damned. McClelland! Haven't seen you since old
Henley's class at the 'U'—an experience best forgot-
ten. The old boy nearly kept me from graduating.
What brings you here?''

Clif chose to ignore the question as he greeted his
fellow alumnus. "Hi, Tommy. I take it you represent
original couple number three?"

"Right you are. And that's my sister over there,
with enough offspring to drive an uncle bananas—
four at last count. Matter of fact, this yearly venture
is beginning to look like a kindergarten field trip. I'd
pass on the whole thing if Jody weren't here."

"Is that so?" Clif sent a quizzical look in her direction.

Fortunately, Alf's rallying call of "Let's get this
show on the road" eliminated the need for her to reply.

Tommy took her elbow. "I've got the truck right
over here, Jody. We might as well head out."

She slipped her arm from his grasp. "Not this year,
Tommy. Clif's here because I invited him, so we'll ride
with Alf and Britta. I'll bet a couple of your nieces or
nephews would just love to ride in one of Grandpa's
company trucks."

"May the Lord deliver me," he groaned. "No, if I
can't have you along, my brother-in-law will jump at
the chance to get away from the squalling kids. He's a
lousy substitute, but *c'est la vie*. See you at the first
farm." Tommy sent a decidedly unfriendly glance
Clif's way before he walked off.

"He looks a bit put out," Britta remarked as they
piled into the station wagon.

Though his eyes remained serious, Clif grinned at her. "You're right. I suspect he's planning to chop a large spruce so it falls on my head."

"Want me to stop and get you a hard hat?" Alf jested.

"Negative. Just cover my back, pal. That should do it."

When they reached the first stop on the itinerary, Britta was insistent that Jody and Clif go off on their own, saying that the car trips would be ample exposure to children for one day. Tommy hadn't appeared yet, so Clif acted with alacrity in picking up a saw and heading toward a path that angled promisingly away from the main lot.

"Something going on between you and Tommy?" Clif asked Jody once they were out of earshot.

"No, nothing's going on. He's just an old friend—been around most of my life. Sometimes we fill in for each other as a handy date for dances or plays, or things like that."

She stopped to look at a tree. "Lopsided," she concluded after a brief perusal.

"Unless there's some sort of time limit here, why don't we walk to the end of the line and work back?" he suggested.

"Good idea. Might be fresh territory out there and less tramped-over slush. My feet already feel wet."

Clif brushed aside her comments. "Tommy's what I think you women call a good catch—wealthy, decent looking, bright enough for a conversation. Of sorts," he amended.

Jody laughed at his judgment of Tommy's intellectual prowess. "You weren't just joking about your persistence, were you? Must come from examining witnesses, ferreting out the ugly facts. Or were you always this way?''

''Diversionary tactics, Miss Jenson?'' He scooped up a handful of untrampled snow. ''I have an answer for those.''

''And I have an answer for you.'' She darted behind a tree to scoop up her own ammunition.

Peeking through the branches, she couldn't see him at all, so she stepped out a little. Splat! A soft snowball hit her in the middle of the back.

''Sneak attacks aren't fair,'' she called out, and ran around to the other side of her pine. She still couldn't spot him, but the tree on her right suddenly shook, dropping its load of snow in a wet thunk. She sent her missile flying toward it and bent quickly to get another ready.

Clif grabbed her from behind, his strong arms imprisoning her own at her sides. ''Give up?''

''Never.'' She giggled as she tried her best to wiggle free, but to no avail.

''Why, I've caught me a spitfire.'' Clif spun her around to face him, laughing at her fruitless efforts to free herself. ''And now it's my turn to say 'gotcha.' ''

She looked up to protest and caught her breath at the nearness of him.

''Jody?'' His laughter slowed, then stopped. ''Jody...'' he whispered against her lips as he bent to kiss her.

There was little tenderness in his claiming and little restraint in her response. Every sensation she felt told her that she wanted this man. She ached for him and it seemed too soon when he pulled away. So much for acting intelligently, Jody chided herself as she rested her head on Clif's shoulder. Chemistry would always win out against logic when they were together.

"I could easily forget the blasted tree," he said at last.

Jody sighed and stepped back. "I'm afraid I did. Let's hope some of the little ones are causing enough hullabaloo to slow up the parade."

She glanced around them while he retrieved his hat and the saw. "Clif, this looks like a good stand of trees right here."

"So it does. Which one do you want me to start whacking at?"

"Patience . . . patience. This takes a bit of time."

"Can't imagine why. Look, over there. Now, there's a perfect tree. Tall, straight . . ."

"Arrogant," she pronounced.

"Arrogant? A tree's arrogant?"

"Naturally. Now look at this one here. Obviously friendly. The top is even tipping its hat to us."

Clif's eyes crinkled in amusement. "My first thought when I saw it. Of course, it will tip its star at you, too, but if it's what you want, here goes."

Jody peered amongst the branches for a minute. "No, this won't do. No bird's nest."

"Bird's nest. Of course. A perfectly sane requirement—if you happen to be a visiting bird."

"No need for teasing, Mr. McClelland. It's an ancient Swedish custom and means good luck for the next year."

"Good Lord! I can see we have our work cut out for us. A friendly tree with a bird's nest in residence ought to keep us here until moonrise."

"One more thing." She tried to appear chagrined despite the laughter bubbling at his bemused expression. "It mustn't mind being cut down."

"Correction, *sun*rise. Tell me, how does one go about probing the wishes of a tree?"

"One asks it."

"Naturally." He took her in his arms once more. "You are some kind of woman, Jody Jenson. Some kind of woman."

This time his kiss was only tender and loving, and when he lifted his head, she said, "And you, Clif McClelland, are some kind of man...."

To Clif's surprise, they found a tree with the proper prerequisites in short order. The perimeters of the tree farm were precisely the place to be because the birds favored that location, and according to Jody, the poor trees were lonely and eager for the hubbub of a holiday living room.

Clif cut down the tree they had chosen with a minimum of epithets. "Never did get too well acquainted with saws," he grumbled in explanation. Jody stifled her laughter, aware that the grumbling and bad language were due to disgust at showing a lack of competence in front of her. For her part, she found his struggles so endearing that she was hard put not to brush the hair from his forehead, as one would a small boy who had touched her heart.

It was the first year Jody had found a tree so early in the day, a feat for which Clif claimed the credit, so the two of them spent the rest of the trip keeping track of and amusing the boisterous youngsters. Thanks to a large number of direct hits during innumerable snowball fights, they were the wettest of the group when they made it back to the pizza parlor. It didn't matter. They'd had a marvelous time.

The restaurant was warm and cozy inside, and the glow of happiness Jody felt was quite enough to dispel any discomfort caused by her damp clothing. Judging from the way Clif kept looking at her, she thought it quite possible that he felt the same inner warmth himself. If only his dating habits weren't so bewildering. If only everything weren't going so fast. If only...

Jody cautioned herself that she could very easily "if only" herself right out of living. She needed to learn to relax and just let things happen. Today had been wonderful, and there was always tomorrow....

CHAPTER SIX

JODY HAD NOT BEEN HOME more than half an hour before she learned that tomorrow would not be a glorious repeat of today. A phone call from Clif gave her the shoulder-drooping news that he wouldn't be able to see her until Monday.

"Rob, the younger brother I mentioned the other night, gets in with his family tomorrow, and Mom wants us to gather round the festive board *en famille*. I'd hate to disappoint her, so we'll have to forget our tentative plans. But I'll call again, and we can work out something for Monday."

"That's fine by me. I don't want your mother disappointed, either." Jody's voice had suddenly gone flat. A long, pallid Sunday loomed ahead without Clif's presence to give it zest. "I have to go to an auction Monday afternoon, but otherwise I'm free, unless something comes up at the store or with Mom."

They left it at that. Jody hung up, still feeling deflated. She was berating herself for giving in to her disappointment when the phone rang once more. It was Alf and he also had something to say about Monday.

"Warren's been trying to get hold of you . . . guess you were still en route. Renard's flying in for a settlement conference on Monday. It's scheduled for one o'clock at his attorney's office, and Warren wants to see you at twelve-thirty to go over his ideas. I'll meet you there and we can all walk to the conference together.''

''A settlement conference? Alf, what's that? I've never even heard of such a thing.''

''Neither had I, but it sounds like a good idea. Warren explained that it's simply an informal meeting of the parties involved, to discuss the problem—hopefully without exchanging blows—and to try to settle out of court.''

''Out of court? No way! Unless it goes our way. Otherwise we're going before a judge.''

''I agree,'' he said in calming tones. ''Don't think I'm going to advise you to give in, Jody. The biggest plus, as I see it, is that this will give us a chance to size up our opponent, find out what's behind his outrageously high offer. That seems worthwhile to me.''

''Hmm...I hadn't thought of that angle. Okay, we'll do it. You know, Alf, I think I might actually look forward to this. Maybe I'll get a chance to tell Renard off.'' And when Alf made a sound of alarm, she added, ''Don't panic, dear cousin, I'll be extremely courteous and eminently ladylike. Yes, yes, I promise. So relax and I'll see you at Warren's.''

JODY WAS CONSCIOUS of anticipation all Monday morning. Despite her preoccupation with arrangements for reorganizing the stockroom, the coming afternoon conference was seldom far from her thoughts. She was quite certain she would be able to convince Mr. Renard of her adamant intent to keep her store, or, better yet, to effect a settlement to her liking right at the conference table.

As the time for the meeting drew near, Jody slipped into the jacket of her turquoise, Chanel-style suit. She hummed contentedly as she added the few simple gold chains she'd brought with her. Changing from her comfortable work shoes into black pumps, she smiled at the result. "Perfect, *mademoiselle*. Feminine, professional and smart, all observable in a single glance. So, best be on your toes, Mr. Renard Books." Saying the words aloud boosted her confidence. She reached for her briefcase and coat and left her office, ready to tackle the enemy.

THE FIRST PERSON Jody saw as they were ushered into the conference room was the last one she'd expected to see—Clif. Her heart went into its customary acrobatic act at the sight of him, throwing her off stride momentarily. He was easily the most vital presence among the men, strikingly handsome in his taupe business suit with barely discernable pinstripes. Face alight with pleasure, he excused himself from the group he was chatting with as soon as she walked in.

"Jody, that's the best board meeting outfit I've ever seen, and you're the most beautiful lady to ever grace this room." Clif delivered the compliment sotto voce before continuing in normal tones. "I'm as surprised to be here as you are to see me."

Her worry plain, Jody asked, "Are you on the case now?"

"No, just sitting in. Clark, he's the senior partner over there talking with Warren, may have to be in Chicago in January, the probable time of your court hearing. He wanted a backup to cover this meeting and I just happened to have a clear calendar. Rob and

I had hoped to spend some time together and I'd rearranged everything. Will it bother you?''

"Yes and no," she hedged. Though happy to see him, she knew his presence would be a distraction. However, Warren was being introduced to Joseph Renard, so she thrust her troublesome reactions aside to focus on the man.

Mr. Renard was of medium height and somewhat stout with good living. His expression was benign—unless you caught his eyes. Peculiarly colorless and cold, a flat wash of pale hazel, they didn't seem to belong on the same face as the smile.

"You're certainly not at all what I expected, Miss Jenson," he said.

Jody acknowledged his banal greeting with a firm handshake and a simple, "Mr. Renard."

"Do you model on the side?" he asked, boorishly looking her up and down.

"No, I do not." Her words were delivered as shards of ice to counter his crude compliment.

Renard's genial expression was instantly replaced by one of malice. Jody almost recoiled from the look. It passed so rapidly that she wondered if she'd imagined it. But Clif's behavior told her that he seconded her observation. Standing at her side, he stiffened to quick alertness.

Baffled by what she considered an overreaction to her rebuff, Jody simply inclined her head in dismissal and turned to give her uncles a hug. Betrayal or not, they were still her loving family and no contretemps, large or small, could change that fact.

To open the conference, Warren and Clark each presented his respective client's case. Jody listened attentively. The offer Warren was making on her behalf was an amount based on recent sales of "like properties in like locations" as opposed to Clark's definition of "the highest offer made, in cash." Both attorneys readily admitted that the other's definition had precedent at law. Both felt that at this point in their research, a judge could hold for either party. These statements comforted Jody, telling her that her mother's money would not be wasted in prolonging a dispute she had no hope of winning. She was not simply a stubborn sentimentalist disrupting the family on flimsy grounds.

Jody was the first to speak when the lawyers were finished.

"Mr. Renard, why are you offering such an excessively high price for our building?"

Clearly caught off guard, the abruptness of the question had precisely the effect on the man that she had wanted—a revealing moment without his mask. For a few seconds his eyes narrowed venomously in her direction and then the pleasant facade was back in place. But not before she had received his message— the man hated her. No, that was crazy. Surely she was imagining things, misreading the signals somehow. He didn't even know her. How could he hate someone he didn't know?

"Miss Jenson—" Renard's voice held none of the malice she'd seen in his face moments before "—I thought I had made that clear to you, by way of your uncles. Apparently, they didn't pass the word along. You see, I've been wanting a Minneapolis outlet for a long time. Your location is ideal, meets my needs in every respect, and the purpose of my high offer was to insure my getting the building promptly and easily.

Obviously I miscalculated your devotion to Alferic's."

"You most certainly did, Mr. Renard. I love our store, as did my father and grandfather before me. It's part of our family heritage and I will fight as hard and effectively as I am able in order to preserve it." Jody sat back, noting that Clif was steadily regarding Renard's affable expression.

"Commendable, Miss Jenson, most commendable. Nothing more important than family loyalty, no siree, nothing more important. I must admit, though, to being surprised that you'd turn down such a tidy sum of money. Seems to me that you're mostly concerned about the bookstore—that the rentals don't matter so much. You could make yourself a bundle *and* keep Alferic's if you'd simply relocate. Why not do that?"

Jody glanced again at Clif, expecting to catch an amused expression as his earlier advice was endorsed. His eyes had not wavered from their study.

"Mr. Renard," she began, "I would choke on money from a sale of the Jenson Building. There is no possible amount that could induce me to sell. As for relocating, the Jenson Building and Alferic's are synonymous and have been for eighty years, an institution in downtown Minneapolis. And if for some unforeseen reason, we should decide to close our store, I would never, ever consider besmirching its fine name by replacing it with a discount outlet. Shall we bring this unconstructive discussion to a close now?" To emphasize her intent, she started gathering her papers into a neat pile.

"Wait just a minute, Miss Jenson. We put more books in the hands of more people in a month than you do in a year. We're the ones making the printed word more available to the common folk, not your sort. After all, isn't that what our business is all about?''

''Yes, it is, and yes, you do have a greater volume than Alferic's,'' Jody replied. A shrewd insight prompted her to add, ''Though I doubt that pleasure in bringing reader and book together weighed very heavily in your decision to sell books. Be that as it may, there is a definite place in the book world for your sort of merchandising, but not at the expense of my sort. That is to say, not at the expense of quality, taste and personalized service. You will please note the fact that I am not suggesting the destruction of your stores, but that is exactly what you desire for mine— destruction. Be warned, Mr. Renard, I will not permit any such destruction without making you wish you had never heard of Joanna Diane Jenson. I intend to fight you with every weapon I can command, including years of appeals all the way to the Supreme Court of the United States, if necessary. Should you emerge victorious, it will be as a maimed conqueror. I'll make very sure of that.''

Before either attorney had gathered his wits enough to speak, Renard jumped to his feet, hand stretched across the table toward Jody. ''Well said, young lady, well said. I admire your spunk, I surely do. Well, I see you won't even shake hands with me, so we'll have to wind this up without the customary courtesies. Since there's no hurry about all this, we can talk again in January—come up with something that will satisfy us both—help your uncles in their trouble. I'm sure you want to help your uncles, Miss Jenson, and just possibly your grandpa and daddy would want exactly that, too. At any rate, you think about it."

He then turned to his astonished lawyer. "Just let things ride for a while, Clark. Let's all take time out to enjoy the holidays."

Joviality dripping, Renard favored each of the uncles with a ham-fisted clap on the shoulder. "How does a drink and a snack sound to you, Eric? Nils? Been hearing about the restaurants in this town for years. It's high time I had a look see. Clark, old boy, I'll get back to you later in the day." And out they trooped.

"Well," Warren said into the silence that followed the click of the closing door. "What happened to all that insistence that we 'get this thing wound up today'? That's all I was hearing before we sat down."

"Beats me," Clark admitted, his hands extended in a palms-up gesture. "I'll let you know what develops. Strange fellow. Meanwhile, have you the time to stop by my office on your way out? Something's come up on that trust matter we've been working on."

Alf left with them, but on his way out he gave Jody a hug. "Bravo, Jody! I think it was the speech of yours that ran him off."

Once they were alone, Jody faced a serious Clif across the table. "Why so grim?" she asked.

"The man's a goon, Jody. Yes, I know, it's a strong word. But that's how I'd call it." He got up to pace the room. "There's evil intent behind that breezy front. Dangerous, very dangerous. It worries me." Clif stopped behind her chair and pulled it out so she could stand. He took her by the shoulders for his next words. "Jody, I want you to promise me that you will never be alone with that man."

"That's an easy promise to make, Clif. I'd never want to be. He makes me uneasy. That dislike, or whatever it was that he flashed at me, was all out of proportion to the situation. I'm only holding up a sale for heaven's sake. He has nothing to lose. If he gets tired of fighting, he can just go buy another building. It's me and my uncles who have something to lose. I really don't understand the man's emotional involvement."

"Neither do I, and I sure as hell wish I knew what was behind that phony smile. That was nothing but drivel about taking our time, enjoying the holidays— all feigned. It's a stall to plan his next move, or so I believe."

"What next move could he make, Clif?"

"Beats me. What beats me even more is trying to associate that crude character with books—unless they're adult books."

Jody smiled at that thought. "Nothing to worry about along those lines, I'm sure of that, at least. Warren had someone look over their stores in New York and my uncles did, too. Believe me, they'd shy away from pornography like they would from Typhoid Mary."

"Pretty straightlaced, are they?"

"Ramrod! You could safely say rigor mortis has set in, so don't bother your head about that one, Clif. Not that I can associate Mr. Renard with books, either. I just think he's making money on them. He'd drop them soon enough if the profits went down."

"Well, I'm sure glad he's not my client, and I doubt that Clark will be firing off any thank-you notes to that New York firm that sent him. Why the furrowed brow?"

"I'm wondering how Mr. Renard got hold of the information on the finances—of Jenson and Sons, I mean. I can't imagine that either of my uncles would tell him."

Clif rubbed his chin thoughtfully. "No...it's hardly the sort of thing you would tell a prospective buyer. But, enough of all that. When's this auction you're going to?"

"It's been going on for a couple of hours already, but the manuscripts I'll be bidding on won't go under the hammer for a while yet."

"Manuscripts?" he asked, pulling her close to weave his fingers through her hair.

"Icelandic sagas—for a client of ours." Her finger outlined his lips and chin.

"Who in his right mind reads Icelandic sagas?" Clif murmured against her brow.

"Scholars of Icelandic literature, of course," she whispered as his mouth found hers. All that mattered now were the tremors of excitement that his tasting and exploring tongue sent through her. She felt his hands press her against him briefly, and then he slowly released her.

Clif stepped back with a sigh. "I'm a glutton for punishment," he admitted. "Be okay if I came along this time, or is Tommy doing the honors again?"

"I will be quite alone, Mr. McClelland, and I'd be delighted to have you accompany me."

Clif chuckled at her playful formality and made no further mention of Tommy.

"So, when do we have to be there?"

"I'd like to head over there right now, if that's all right. Our expert has appraised the manuscripts for me, but I still want to have a look before I bid. But what about Rob, weren't you going to spend the afternoon with him?''

"'Were' is correct. Once my sister-in-law found out about this conference, she packed my poor brother off to the Walker Art Center with the kids for a crash course in twentieth century art, so she could have a few hours of what she termed 'well deserved peace and quiet.'''

The disgust in his voice told her, quite clearly, that his opinion of his sister-in-law was less than high, but Jody didn't pursue it.

"Well, at least he's with his sons and that part will be fun. As for you—" she slipped an arm through his "—you are in for a real treat. Auctions are terrific fun. Come on, I'll fill you in on their mysterious workings on the way over."

JODY AND CLIF took seats toward the front of the auction room. Jody explained that this allowed the auctioneer to easily observe her secret signal. Several regular bidders had such signals, ranging from a nearly imperceptible shrug to the mopping of a brow.

"What's yours?" Clif asked in a whisper.

"This," she answered, extracting a long scarf from her purse, looping it over her neck and slipping the ends into a gold ring. "If I adjust the ring up or down it means I'm upping my bid one hundred dollars."

Clif sent her a wicked grin, accompanied by a suggestive wink. "You just let me handle the signal department. Give my knee a squeeze when you want to bid, and I'll gladly maneuver that ring around for you. Better yet, I think we need a few trial runs, starting now."

"Slight problem, Mr. McClelland. If you start sliding this thing up and down, I'm likely to wind up owning *A General System of Horsemanship in All Its Branches*, and I really don't want it. Otherwise, it's a great idea." She patted his knee consolingly.

"Ah well, win some, lose some, to use one of my favorite phrases." He covered her hand with his and settled back, eyes twinkling as he looked around. "Good Lord, a roomful of agitated, twitching people hopping up and down. How does the auctioneer keep it all straight?"

"With difficulty. Even the experienced ones occasionally knock down lots to the wrong bidder."

"Certainly understandable. Jody, are you all right? You keep tensing your hands."

"I'm a bit nervous," she admitted.

His eyebrows rose in genuine surprise. "You are? Why?"

"This is the first time I've been to one of these without my father, the first time I'll be doing the bidding on my own. Heaven knows I've gotten enough vicarious experience over the years, but that's not the same, and the client is adamant about getting these manuscripts."

"No matter how high you have to go?"

"That's what he said, but our expert said two thousand was what they were worth. I'd hesitate going over that."

"If anybody tries to compete with you, I'll tie him to his chair. Immobilize him so he can't even produce a nervous tic."

She smiled, then tensed anew. Her manuscripts were on the block.

The bidding opened at two hundred dollars and moved rapidly up to five hundred, with Jody sitting motionless. When it appeared that they would go for that price, the gold ring slid up her scarf. Immediately, a gentleman sitting in back upped her bid by two hundred, bringing the price to eight hundred dollars. Again the ring; again his challenge. They were at eleven hundred. She repeated her action and the results were identical. The price was now fourteen hundred dollars. Clif swiveled his head to glare at the man, but to no avail. The price moved up to seventeen hundred.

As the bid reached the two-thousand-dollar mark, Jody did some quick thinking. Her client's chief pleasure in life was his study of Icelandic culture and literature and he had said "any price," presumably in all sincerity. The top value according to Alferic's expert was two thousand dollars, but words such as *value* and *worth* were relative. Given her client's narrow field of interest and the importance of the sagas in his eyes, they would be far more valuable to him than to a general bookseller. Therefore she was justified in spending more than the appraiser advised.

The bidding had moved to twenty-three hundred and, noting the slightest of hesitations on the challenger's last raise of two hundred dollars, she came to a swift decision. "Three thousand dollars," she said calmly, gratified to hear a snort of disgust behind her and then silence. Even more gratifying was the startled glance Clif sent her, followed rapidly by a wide grin and nod of approval.

The hammer fell. Her client would get his Icelandic manuscripts.

CLIF HANDED HER into a taxi, climbed in beside her and demanded enlightenment as to the reasoning behind the sudden jump in her bidding.

"My thinking went like this. First, the fellow had been just the least bit cautious in bringing the bid up to twenty-three hundred dollars. Secondly, I figured that twenty-five hundred was probably the top bid he'd planned on. Third, if I went up to twenty-four hundred, he might very well decide that I was reaching my limit too. He'd go ahead with his two-hundred-dollar increment—what's a hundred over budget at this point—hoping I'd fold. Fourth, there's always the possibility of getting carried away when you're bidding. Then it's easy to be reckless, forget whatever limits you've set for yourself. If he'd reacted that way, I could have been faced with nudging the four-thousand-dollar mark, just out of spite on his part. Therefore, something dramatic on my part was called for, or I would have one very angry client. So, fifth, I decided to make him think in terms of some substantial sum to top me. At three thousand he'd have had to overshoot his mark by five hundred dollars plus, and it worked. It silenced him, and I got what I came for."

"I'm impressed. Yes ma'am, I am impressed. Beneath that glorious mane of honey tresses lies an acute brain."

He regarded her thoughtfully, as if seeing something he hadn't seen before and was not quite sure what to make of it.

"Had you thought I was a bit dense?" she asked, her eyes teasing him.

"No, no, it's not that." Clif looked out the window, his fingers drumming on a knee.

"What then?"

"I had you pegged as intelligent, all right, but as a dreamer sort—not too practical, not given to thinking fast on your feet, not at all aggressive in going after what you want. Now, twice in one day, I find I've got to rethink those ideas." Judging by the scowl on his face, the prospect was none too pleasing.

"Twice?"

"Right. First came the settlement conference. I'd expected Alf to do the 'standing firm' speech. Thought you'd pretty much just sit there looking beautiful, maybe toss out the occasional angry retort. Instead, you were precise, concise and emphatic, calm, cool and collected. Also beautiful. Damn all!"

"Why 'damn all'? All those things would be to my credit, wouldn't they?"

"Yes, that's what's bothering me. How many other assets are lurking around to surprise me?"

"Good heavens," Jody exclaimed in astonishment. "Do you want to find out things about me that belong in the debit column?"

"It would help."

"Help? Help what?"

"Me. My thinking about you." It was a rather uninformative response, but he couldn't very well tell her that being bowled over by a woman was a new and startling experience for him. Nor could he tell her that he thought the only explanation for such an occurrence was that some magic was involved. Not that he'd ever given any credence to such mystical happenings. But what other reason could there be for this woman whom he wanted to be with every minute, who set him afire, and whom he also, wonder of wonders, respected?

Jody waited for some elaboration. None was forthcoming. And they were almost at Nicollet Mall. "We're nearly at the store. No explanations for what I consider a weird remark?"

"Nope, but I do have a question. What are you doing tonight?" He had to laugh at her bemused expression.

"You are some kind of puzzle, Clif."

"I'm some kind of puzzle to myself at the moment." He instructed the cabbie to wait and walked her up to Alferic's door. "So, what's on the agenda?"

"Decorating the tree. Hopefully under Mom's supervision, but she wasn't feeling very good this morning, so it may just be me."

"Would it make your mother uncomfortable if I dropped by for a while? *The Nutcracker* is on the McClelland family agenda for tonight, but I begged off. Rob's boys leave something to be desired in the discipline department. Anyway, I've seen the thing enough times to last me till my grave. What do you think?"

"She'd love it. Mom's convinced that you're a 'fine, wonderful man,' quote unquote. I keep suggesting that her antennae might have been skewed by your charm, but she refuses to listen."

Jody laughingly dodged the light clip he sent to her chin.

"Just for that, I'll come early and stay late."

Nothing could have pleased her more than the prospect of a long evening with Clif. As the taxi bore him away, she was still chuckling, this time over her own thoughts.

She might as well admit it. Hours without him were hours of waiting to see him again. In the space of four

short days, he'd become a very important person in
her life. If she wasn't careful, she would find herself
in love. And then what? One mighty large problem,
that's what. Plus, in all likelihood, heartbreak.

But once again, events in the McClelland household were going to prevent their being together. She
got the news later that evening by telephone. Clif had
made the mistake, as he termed it, of stopping by his
parents' house before going on to his own apartment,
and he'd found himself in the midst of chaos.

Just returning from their museum tour, his brother
was claiming exhaustion and a sudden lack of interest
in *The Nutcracker*. The nephews were cranky and
bawling, and his sister-in-law, Sue, was complaining
loudly about how she wasn't going anyplace without
a stern man to help her with the kids. Grandpa was
useless, and Grandma would never swat them one
when they deserved it. Clif had sent Rob to the den
with a stiff drink, the boys upstairs with the maid for
a bath, and had told the incensed Sue that he would
take Rob's place.

"My God," Clif had concluded. "Sue can be so
selfish at times. And Rob has about as much back-
bone as an amoeba when it comes to handling anything unpleasant. On the domestic front at least."

Jody pondered the comment about Sue for quite a
while after they hung up. Surely no woman would do
less than her best to keep her husband and children
happy. If a woman chose marriage as a career, then
her responsibility to the partnership was the creation
of a harmonious home for her family, a place of understanding, support, and above all, love. At least,
that's what her mother had always taught her, and it
was the way most of the Jenson women felt. Most as-

suredly it was the way Jody felt. Jody only hoped that for the sake of Rob, Sue and their boys, Clif had exaggerated the situation.

CHAPTER SEVEN

BECAUSE HER MOTHER had endured a pain-racked day and had gone to sleep after sedation, Jody was faced with decorating the tree alone. She had decided to cheer herself up by creating a mood of seasonal festivity. A fire crackled merrily in the fireplace, Handel's *Messiah* flowed from corner speakers, the lights were low, and she had on her favorite robe—a wrap of butternut cashmere. Just as she located the box of light strings, Anna provided the finishing touch, a bowl of fragrant, hot glögg, Sweden's traditional Christmas punch.

She was near the top of a wooden stepladder, easing lights into the branches, when the doorbell rang. Who in the world? Jody heard Anna heading for the front entry and she returned her attention to the tree.

"Don't move, darling, I want to drink in this picture of you."

Startled, Jody turned her head toward the doorway. Clif was standing there, his face lit in wonder. She started to say something, but he went on.

"You against the firelight, stretched out like that. God, you are exquisite!" Slowly he began walking toward her, arms raised to lift her down. His cheek stroked the luxury of her sunny hair, his hands caressed the kitten-soft wool of her robe.

When he kissed her, Jody savored the crisp coldness of his skin, fresh from the night air, and she rejoiced in his hunger for her lips and mouth. She felt his passion for her as he pressed her to him, and she was glad.

"Lilacs," he murmured against her throat. "You smell of lilacs in the spring." And then, in the hollow of her throat, he whispered words she didn't quite catch, words that sounded like "want you" and "afraid." Whatever he'd said, he released her after that.

Attempting to lighten the mood, Clif walked over to the punch bowl and inhaled the spicy aroma. The rendezvous appearance of the room must have penetrated his senses at some point, moving him to ask, "Expecting someone? Pretty seductive setting, plus you in that handy robe."

When he turned to meet her gaze, his eyes were heavy with hurt, and Jody stilled the words of annoyance that had been on the tip of her tongue.

"No, Clif. No one. I only created this atmosphere to make myself feel better, to make it seem like other years. I guess I'm trying to recreate a past that can't be recreated. Dad's gone and Mom is an invalid, asleep upstairs. That's the reality and no one is going to be here with me."

Clif rubbed his forehead distractedly. "I'm sorry, Jody. That was a thoughtless thing to say. I seem to be as irritable as hell. Must be the evening's uproar."

"Here. Come sit down and put your feet up." She pushed an ottoman under his legs and laid his jacket on the couch. "Roll up your sleeves if you want to and prepare yourself for some TNT in a cup."

"TNT?"

"Yep." Jody handed him a cup of the warm beverage. "It may look like mostly fruit, and there's plenty of that, but the punch part is brandy, port and aquavit—Scandinavia's answer to vodka."

"Good Lord! Do I dare get on the ladder after that?"

"After one, yes. More than that, no. I need help with the lights, so you'll have to take time out after that glass and work for a while."

From her chair opposite him, Jody kept up a light-hearted patter about the finer points of glögg making, telling him about all the spices, especially cardamom, the fruits and nuts, and the mystique surrounding aquavit. A true aficionado, she told him, would insist upon an aquavit that has been over the equator and back. This information actually appeared on the bottle label, guaranteeing the contents were the real article.

When she saw that he had relaxed, she gave him a chance to vent his anger. "Would it help to talk about what happened at home? Why it is that you're here and not at *The Nutcracker* keeping your nephews in line?"

He was slow to answer her and when he finally did, his response made about as much sense as his puzzling remarks in the taxi.

"This is the strangest thing," he said.

"Pardon me? You seem to be a master of riddles today, Mr. McClelland. What is the strangest thing?"

"My wanting to talk my life over with you. I don't have that urge with other women. Also, I don't use words of endearment. Tonight I called you darling. Either I'm losing my mind or you *are* magical."

"No other explanation possible?"

"None. So you can just banish that imp of mischief from your eyes, Miss Jenson, and listen to my recap of the evening's home scene. I was saved from the Snow Queen and Sugar Plum Fairies, by a virus that has the nephews squalling with earaches. Sue was hysterical. She'd been counting on going out and showing off her new dress."

"Clif, she must have been concerned about the boys—any mother would be."

"You don't know my sister-in-law. When Rob married her, she and Rob were high school sweethearts, survived college apart and decided to get married before Rob started medical school. She was so pretty and shy then—I thought she was wonderful. So off they went in a flurry of rice. The world was their proverbial oyster. Rob had anticipated a few hard years ahead, but then he'd be a wealthy doctor and they'd live happily ever after. Ha! Two babies later they began to really feel the pinch. Limited by Rob's meager allowance and his refusal to let her accept money from her parents, sweet Sue began flying a different set of colors. Grumbling, complaining and a sour face became de rigueur. By the time residency years rolled around, still financially strapped, she decided she'd really gotten a raw deal and she's still bitter—even to this day. If I hadn't already been turned off by the thought of holy matrimony, Rob and Sue's marriage would have done it for sure."

"That's so sad—for all of them. Something's gone terribly wrong somewhere and...well, I'd like to meet Sue someday."

Clif rose, walked toward Jody's chair and helped her to her feet. "Get the other side of the story, you mean? Maybe someday...hmm, you smell so good, feel so good . . ." He covered her mouth with his in a lingering kiss, so warmly tender yet filled with sensual promise that Jody felt wrapped in love. He freed her lips, his eyes intently studying the contours of her face as his fingers softly sketched them. His own face was curiously blank of expression. Suddenly he backed away, his gaze homed in on the tree, and he sighed. "Time for me to get busy, I guess."

While he repositioned the ladder, Jody slipped some lively carols on to replace the majestic Handel. She was delighted to hear him begin singing along at the first notes. What an enigma he was. Adding her voice to his, she began handing him the strings of light and, in no time at all, they had the tree glowing in multi-colored brilliance. Saying she'd take care of the ornaments while he relaxed, she sent him back to his chair and refilled his glögg cup. He still had to help place the decorations on the top of the tree, so Jody teasingly warned him to go slowly with the TNT.

Clif continued to sing, tossing an occasional suggestion her way between carols. He seemed so content, but Jody's thoughts were some distance from the task she was performing and could not be called content.

Clif had commented on the seductive setting. Jody wondered if subconsciously she had created it, hoping he would come. And if she had, what of it? The time had come for her to start enjoying the easy, carefree relationship Clif was offering. Why not express the tumult his touch set off? She had to forget the prissy code of yesterday and move into today. Even if marriage was out of the question from Clif's point of view, his words and actions suggested that he was happy around her. Why couldn't she expand her concept of integrity to include giving herself to a man she was so fond of and who was obviously smitten with her? Life was about growth and change. And if she was given the opportunity, she would marry him. But until then...

"Jody, that ever so expressive face of yours tells me you're having troublesome thoughts."

Startled at the interruption, Jody blurted, "Sorry, Clif. I'm not a very stimulating companion for you, am I?"

"I'm not complaining. As long as I'm in the same room with you, I seem to be inexplicably cheerful. Care to tell me about those thoughts?"

"Only that I was born in the wrong century," she offered, having to laugh at the way he was taken aback.

"Would you run that past me again, please?"

"I just don't fit into today's world very well. Top dollar, efficiency, functional, high tech, pleasure where you find it, instant gratification, that's what 'now' is all about, and not in the least what I'm all about. Everybody else is roaring by in the fast lane while I meander along the shoulder. I was wishing I could be different."

Clif catapulted out of his chair and took her gently but firmly by the shoulders. "No, don't you dare change, or even make the attempt." He pulled her nearer and clasped her in his arms. "Listen to me, Jody. In a world of fractured souls, you're a whole. Your integrity is a gem to be guarded. You're so honest, up-front with your feelings, and you don't play games with people's emotions. Don't ever change. Promise me you won't do anything that isn't right for your soul, or spirit, or whatever term you like best. Promise?''

"I promise," she answered promptly. "I promise not to do anything that doesn't seem right for my soul."

He gave her a quick hug and went back to his chair.

Now Jody was faced with a dilemma. If she was true to herself she had to admit she didn't feel comfortable making love without commitment, but Clif refused to even consider commitment. Now what? Should she accept the differences as irreconcilable and move on before she got hurt?

Jody opted for bringing a few things out in the open before writing finis to their relationship. "Clif, why are you so dead set against marriage? Is it because of your brothers?"

"That, yes, but there are so many other reasons, examples actually, of infidelity among people I know, that it makes me sick. And they can't be so very different from the rest of the population. Contracts are made to be kept, vows are sacred, at least to me, and I couldn't bear it if I felt like straying or if my wife ever... Well, you get the picture."

"Yes, I get the picture and I can understand how you feel, even though I haven't seen that among my friends, and certainly not my family. Sure, some marriages are happier than others, but then some lives are happier than others. Do you know *any* good marriages?"

He shrugged. "My parents and yes, a few others. But I wasn't talking about shallow, flighty people, people you might expect to take vows lightly. I'm talking about my older brother—not Rob, he would never think of it—and would you believe, my closest friend? I was his best man five years ago. Two years after the wedding he was going on business trips with his secretary, and he told me his wife has a lover. Good God, I'd thought she was a wonderful person and my friend an honorable man. Talk about disillusionment!''

''Not surprising. That's too many couples that are close to you. Maybe I've gotten the wrong idea, but it seems to me that you blame the women almost completely. Clif, surely it's a two-way street?''

''It has to be,'' he agreed. ''I tend to zero in on my sisters-in-law because I hate seeing my brothers unhappy. But God knows I can see things they're doing wrong— One quits at the first sign of a problem, the other gives in to keep the peace. And now let's get off this abominable subject. It's one I run from as if a tornado were imminent.''

''And so, being well acquainted with the habits of tornadoes, you are firmly ensconced in the southwest corner of the basement,'' she said in jest, and succeeded in erasing the scowl from his face.

''Right on target, madam, no northeast attic corners for me, thank you. And speaking of targets, looks like it's about time for the job I've been targeted for— decorating the top of the tree. Where are the baubles I'm supposed to use?''

''Right here in this very carefully packed box. These are our most meaningful ornaments. We always try to put them at the top, away from the Jenson toddlers that come visiting, and hang the unimportant ones on the bottom branches, where curious fingers can reach.''

''Why meaningful?'' Clif poked gingerly into the top tray.

"Some are gifts, some show things Carl and I were interested in as kids—like this guitar here—but most of these remind us of vacations. Every place we went, we picked up a souvenir for the tree."

"A canoe." Clif grinned in delight at his find. "Don't tell me you like to paddle around in a canoe, maybe fall asleep by a camp fire?"

"Surprised? Under certain circumstances, I love it."

"I don't believe it. What circumstances?"

"When the family goes to the Boundary Waters."

"The Boundary Waters? You got this up there? Jody, I envy you. That's a trip I've always wanted to make."

"And so you must. It's a glorious place. All that unspoiled wilderness, about a million acres, Dad said. Everything from rapids to placid lakes, no power-boats of any kind, except in a couple of areas. It must be the quietest spot in all of the United States or Canada. Well, the tundra's probably quieter in Canada, but the Quetico will do just fine."

"So, you paddled right on into Canada? No problems with that?"

"No. You have to clear customs, stop at a ranger station, get some permits, but we never had any trouble with it."

"Mmm, no powerboats?"

"Nope, that's why it's called the Boundary Waters Canoe Area, except no one ever uses the full name. There's even a limit as to how low planes are allowed to fly. The only sounds you hear belong there. Fish jumping, birds singing, animals scampering or crashing through the woods. And the loons. Somewhere in this box is a hand-carved loon. It's probably my favorite ornament. Clif, I'd go back just to hear the loons.''

Still toying with the little canoe, he nodded in agreement. "That weird cry, or laugh, or whatever it is, really gets to you. The sound is impossible to describe, but once you've heard it, you never forget.''

"Haunting, yet comforting. I know that seems like a contradiction in terms, but that's how I'd describe it.''

Amused at his continued interest in the memorabilia, Jody began to think he never would get them on the tree. "You sure are intrigued with those bits of our history. Trying to avoid a trip up the ladder? Too much TNT, maybe?''

"Not really, it's just good to think of all the wonderful family times these remind you of. But, it's onward and upward time for yours truly. You keep the baubles coming, and how about a little elaboration on those Quetico trips? For instance, what memories give you the most happiness?''

"That's any easy assignment—the evenings. They were so much fun, Clif. The serenity of twilight, the pristine water. And occasionally a deer or bear would come down to the lake to get a drink. But mostly, I remember the glorious times we had as a family. In case you haven't already figured it out, I'm a sentimental nut.''

"I figured it out. So, what all did you do?''

"We laughed, told stories and sang. Actually, we sang during the day, too, voyageur songs to pace our paddling, and marching songs to make the portaging easier. At night, my guitar came out of its case and I'd plunk out some tunes to wind up the day. First, though, Dad read to us. We went through *The Jungle*

Books and umpteen readings of 'Gunga Din,' and just about everything else Kipling wrote. The same with Longfellow. I had 'Hiawatha' memorized by the time I was four. And then we toasted marshmallows, made 'some mores' and all the usual things you do around a camp fire.''

Abruptly Jody fell silent, overwhelmed by the pictures her words had conjured up—her patient father teaching her to bait a hook, balance a pack for portaging, stroke a paddle. She remembered the gusto in his voice as he sang ''On the Road to Mandalay,'' and the hushed, loving conversations of her parents overheard late at night from the snugly warmth of her sleeping bag.

''What is it, Jody?'' Clif's voice broke softly into her reverie.

She shook her head sharply and smiled up at him. ''Sorry, I was just reminiscing a bit there. How are you doing?''

''Fine, but a little guitar music would help. Perfect accompaniment for the cup of glögg I'm about to indulge in.''

''Amateur Night With Jody! Clif, I'm really not at all skillful, not even very good. My family were gentle critics, thank heaven, but I don't want to subject you to my twanging.''

''Not to worry, I'll be a gentle critic, too, especially after I've downed some more of this fruit concoction.''

''You've got a point. Okay, get comfy and get your critical faculties anesthetized.''

And so Jody played and sang some of the tunes she'd played and sung around the camp fire, familiar mainstays such as ''There's a Long, Long Trail

Awinding,'' ''Beautiful Dreamer,'' and ''Shanty Town.'' Clif asked for more each time she tried to end the impromptu session. She was aware of his steady regard and rather restless shifting about in his chair. Looking up quickly, she was surprised to see an expression of melancholy in his eyes. She decided to bring the recital to a halt with the lullaby carol, ''What Child Is This.'' Written to the plaintive melody of ''Greensleeves,'' it was apparently not to Clif's liking. His restlessness had taken him from his chair to the fireplace, where he was simply staring into the flames.

''Clif? What's wrong? Don't you like that carol?''

He came over to stand in front of her. ''It wasn't the music, Jody. That is, it was the music, with you playing and singing. You're so lovely and true, innocent in the best sense of the word....'' As his voice trailed off, he reached over to twang one discordant note on the guitar.

''You're a mighty confusing man, Mr. McClelland. Here you are again saying terrific things about me and looking miserable about it.''

With a rueful laugh he said, '' 'Confusing' is the right word and it's my problem. No need to subject you to my turmoil. Anything more for the top of the tree?''

''No, the job's done.'' She watched in dismay as he put on his coat.

''Jody,'' he said, ''I need a little thinking space, so I'm going to say goodbye. When I've got my head on straight again, I'll be in touch. Sorry to be so abrupt,'' he added.

Jody's heart lurched and her stomach did a sickening nosedive. His goodbye had sounded so final. But she stuck on a smile as she walked him to the door, and she kept it in place until he got into his car and then drove away.

Goodbye, he'd said. Not good-night, but goodbye. Because he was confused. Over what? Racing through the things he had said, the word *innocent* leaped out at her. Of course! He'd thought she was too innocent for his way of life.

And then she'd brought up marriage, and all that drivel about the happy couples she knew of. No wonder he'd grabbed his ring finger and run. There would be no circlet of gold on *his* hand . . . ever.

She poured herself a cup of glögg and curled up in a chair to think things through. If she had scared him off, where did she go from here? Basically, she had two choices. First, she could do nothing. That way she could go around with her halo blinding the world and her principles intact. Or second, and much to be preferred, she could call him up and tell him she had vacated the Smithsonian forever, and would he please get on with seducing her.

The outrageousness of that thought set her off in a fit of giggles. Glögg sloshed precariously about in the cup as she pictured the scene. She would pick up the telephone, a nervous wreck over being so bold, stumbling and stammering her way along, babbling into the mouthpiece about innocence and integrity and Smithsonians and beds. No, that wouldn't do at all. There were some conversations totally unsuited for the telephone. No, she'd have to see him face-to-face for her revelation. And just where would that be?

"Got it! Mishus Fenton's Open Houshe." She frowned and tried again, "Mrs. Fenton's Open House on New Year'sh Day." That final nightcap of glögg had made her tipsy. She stood up and wove toward the stairs, giggling as she went.

Though she felt absolutely dreadful the next day, Jody's resolve was still intact. She would tell Clif on New Year's Day. Meanwhile, there was Christmas to be gotten through.

CHAPTER EIGHT

CARL AND HIS FAMILY arrived. The house resounded with the sounds of stampeding feet, shouts and yells— all the racket that goes hand in hand with three healthy, curious children under the age of eight. If any of this bothered Mrs. Jenson, she wasn't letting it be known. Her wheelchair was in constant motion as she gaily followed her grandchildren about, usually with one of them on her lap. Anna grumbled about all the work, the sticky hands and the dirty clothes. But her twinkling eyes negated her words as she turned out cookies and pastries by the dozen.

Jody lavished attention on nieces and nephew. She organized the youngsters into a makeshift band to perform for the assembled Jensons on Christmas Eve. Augmented by Alf's oldest two on piano and herself on guitar, the group made a satisfactory effort at harmony, although Jody was secretly cringing during a practice session that Carl chose to interrupt.

"Jody, could I interest you in a quiet, peaceful lunch, somewhere far away? Barb's gone shopping and Mom said she and Anna would be delighted to watch the brood." He removed his youngest from the piano bench, where she had been happily thumping away, "accompanying" her aunt. "I love my children with a passion, but not just before Christmas. It's like living with a passel of jumping beans. Vociferous jumping beans. So what do you say?"

"A resounding yes is what I say." Jody hastily snapped her guitar into its case and swung around to face the disappointed children. "Merely a postponement, folks. Rehearsal at four sharp. Meantime, you can practice by yourselves. Tomorrow's opening night, you know, so you'd better get crackin'!"

Carl blew a sigh of relief as they left the house behind. "That band idea was a lifesaver, Jody. Maybe I should say mother saver. Barb is eternally grateful that the kids are tootling and xylophoning away in the rec room, tunes and squabbles all effectively removed from hearing range. By the way, I'm headed for The Mai Tai, is that okay with you?"

"Only if you'll get me spareribs and one of those mai tais for openers," she teased. He knew full well that she loved the restaurant.

"You got it, little one."

"Little one!" She glared at him, this time only half teasing. "Between you and Alf, I never will be considered a grown woman. To you I'm 'little one' and to him I'm 'kiddo' or 'child.' Revolting!"

Carl met her indignation with a hearty laugh. "Well, from what I've been hearing from Alf, your arrival into adulthood seems to be in question."

"What? Carl, what are you talking about?"

"All in due time. Over the spareribs will do. Right now, I want to find a parking space."

Jody obligingly stilled her curiosity, helped search for a vacant spot and waited for their appetizers to arrive before demanding an explanation.

"Talk, mister," she commanded. "The spareribs are here."

"Well, our cousin, whose perspicacity I respect, claims that your temperament this past week or so has been rather mercurial. Any comments?"

"Damn," she muttered, tracing a circle on the linen cloth.

"Damn what? Or who?"

"Damn all. He's right, Carl. I blow up, spill tears and stomp around, as if I were twelve or thirteen."

"Anything to do with this McClelland guy?"

"What made you ask that?" she replied in surprise.

"Alf tied it in—the timing I mean. Before that fateful day when McClelland 'blackmailed' you into a date, he claims you were just your usual self."

"Another 'bingo' for Alf. It does have to do with Clif, combined with everything else, I suppose. Rich, the accident, the legal mess . . ." She shrugged and her words straggled off.

"Jody, are you mourning Rich?"

"No, not really, just that I was, to say the least, somewhat lacking in that perspicacity you credited to our cousin. I totally misread Rich's character. That's all that nags at me and makes me wonder if I'll do the same stupid thing again."

"You *are* too trusting, Jody. Always thinking everyone's as open as you. And you may be misreading this Clif McClelland. Anyone who's a hockey ace—that's right, he played hockey for the 'U,' I remember reading about him in the papers—has to be happy shoving people all over and bonking their heads on the handiest hard surface. He's probably the sort who would get a date precisely the way he got his first one with you."

"No, Carl, he's not like that at all. He's gentle and tender, cares about people and their feelings. Besides which, he's intelligent, witty, fun, exciting, handsome—"

"Jody, he's swept you off your feet," Carl interrupted. "For God's sake, he's nothing but an opportunistic playboy! Yes, I've heard all about the pretty women he's used and flung aside—"

"No," she broke in hotly. "Those women are just out for a good time, the way Clif is. They know he's not looking for commitment. Carl, he's been disillusioned along the way. He told me about it, told me why he doesn't want permanence."

Carl covered her hand with his. "Jody, we've all been disillusioned along the way. That has to be the oldest line in the book. 'Sleep with me, comfort me, I need you. You understand why I can't stay.'"

"Are you saying that you doubt my judgment? That you think I'm not astute enough to see through a line?"

"No! I'm not saying that at all. You're plenty astute, Jody. It's that I'm not here anymore. I can't keep up, talk things over with you like we used to, plus I don't know the guy and I'm apprehensive about what I'm hearing. You don't like to bother Mom, Dad's gone, I'm in Seattle. Jody, I'm just trying to cram it all into one lunch. Sorry if I come across as pushy."

"You don't really. Guess I'm just touchy. And Carl, there's one slight additional problem—I think I love him."

"I see. Something special is going on. Well, I'm not about to question your decisions and feelings. You're not a youngster dating the likes of Rich anymore and you're plenty sharp. I know that if you give yourself to him you will think of it as a gift, given in love, and signifying a permanent commitment. So please go slowly. Think carefully, and be aware of the possible consequences. End of lecture. Now hoist that menu, my stomach's knocking on my rib cage.''

Carl examined the list of entrées, but Jody couldn't think about food. Her menu remained unopened in front of her. It was great to have a brother who cared and who understood her so well, but she had made up her mind. She would abide by her decision. Clif touched something in the core of her that no one had ever touched before. They were attuned in some way beyond anything she had known, and she meant to give it a chance at fulfillment. If she wound up on the slag heap, well . . . she'd handle that somehow.

THE REST of the afternoon was spent gift wrapping and rehearsing the band. Jody was on her way to her bedroom to change for dinner when a UPS delivery arrived for her. She carried the package upstairs, wondering if she'd ordered a gift for a friend and forgotten all about it.

Flipping open the long, narrow box, Jody stared at the contents. A gold pendant in the shape of a cuckoo clock, bird popped out, beak immobilized in an eternal chirp, was suspended from an exquisite gold chain. The card had fallen to the floor. She stooped to pick it up with trembling fingers. The plain, white enclosure card said only, "Clif." That was it. The boldness of his signature suggested he had been angry when he had signed it. Angry at her, no doubt, for being so "cuckoo" as to be an "innocent." She laughed softly, thinking how surprised and pleased he would be when he learned that she had ceased being "cuckoo."

Impatient though she was, Christmas week sped past, disappearing in a whirl of relatives and visiting. To Jody's delight, New Year's Day and Mrs. Fenton's reception were upon her almost before she had time to catch her breath.

Because of Clif's preference for the color, she decided to wear red. The utter simplicity of her dress was a statement of taste, and the sinuous flow of silk jersey seemed created expressly for Jody's slim figure. The gold cuckoo pendant was her sole jewelry. She felt beautiful and desirable as she set off with Barb and Carl—and near bursting with anticipation.

After an hour of chatting with people she was scarcely aware of, saying words she'd never recall, Jody was close to despair. Clif had not come yet, or had come and gone before she arrived, or wasn't coming at all. Still she watched the entrance arch like a hawk.

Jody was midsentence when she saw Clif arrive. "Excuse me," she murmured in haste, leaving a friend of her mother's agape behind her.

"Happy New Year, Clif," she said, conscious of a nervous tremor in her smile.

"Happy New Year, Jody," he responded, his tone so noncommittal that he could have been addressing a toll booth collector.

She'd have felt hurt, except that his eyes told a different tale, eagerly scanning her face and coming to rest on the pendant. He touched it lightly, then pulled his hand back quickly and jammed it into his jacket pocket. His expression was once again distant. "Glad you liked my little gift. I ordered them a couple of weeks ago. Well, guess I'd better circulate since I'm not staying long."

He walked swiftly away and Jody was left open-mouthed. Why had he said "them" when he mentioned his gift? Had he meant both the pendant and the chain? This was no time to ponder his meaning, nor was she about to let him just walk away from her like that! Determined to carry out her plan, she followed him to the bar and tapped him on the back.

"Clif, could we go somewhere and talk?"

"Talk? What do we... Look, I know I left rather abruptly the other night.... I can't explain, so why don't we just..."

"Clif, please?"

"If you insist." He gestured in the direction of another archway. "Seems to me there's a solarium or something through there. We can give that a try."

There was and it was empty. The jungle of ferns and the tropical greenery that twined around every available surface provided the privacy and intimacy needed for their talk.

"So, what did you have to say?" Clif rested against a long table, his gaze fixed on an idly circling foot.

Jody hesitated, not knowing how to begin. He was making it so hard. She had expected a smile, at least. Of course, as far as he knew she was still the same person who had burbled along about the Boundary Waters and strummed a poignant guitar—the person he wanted nothing to do with. She had to get on with it, let him know she'd changed.

"I...well...do you like my dress?" she blurted, realizing immediately what a stupid thing it was to say.

His eyes drifted over her, mouth set in a grim line. "It's fantastic—perfect for you. Any man would love it. You wanted to talk about clothes?" He resumed his downward stare.

"No. I . . . ah . . . this is so hard for me. I'm sorry to be stammering around, but . . ."

"Yes?" His foot ceased its motion. He raised his eyes to meet hers, puzzled and concerned.

"It has to do with my morals . . . I mean, my integrity . . . oh, damn! Will you please make love to me?"

Joyous astonishment flickered across his face, followed by a look of doubt and then by what Jody took to be a suggestion of amusement.

"If you laugh at me, Clif McClelland, I'll heave a plant pot right at your head!" She glanced down and picked up a promising specimen, each thick leaf ending in a wicked thorn.

"I would never, ever, laugh at you, Jody."

Surprised at the seriousness in his voice, she said nothing, merely set the pot down and waited.

Clif briefly studied the toe of his shoe, marshaling his thoughts she supposed. Though why he didn't simply say yes and get on with it was puzzling. Finally he spoke.

"Have you been thinking that this is the reason I said goodbye? The reason I needed some thinking space?"

"Well, yes . . . isn't it?"

"In a way it is, but not because I'm tired of waiting for you." He paused again before he went on. "Jody, making love is part of a total commitment for you. I respect that—value it even. I was afraid that if I were with you anymore I might forget the promise I made to you, that I would push you into saying no or yes. And I was afraid that if you said yes in the heat of the moment you'd be sorry afterward. I'd wind up hurting you and it's the last thing in the world I want to do."

"Clif, I know how you feel about permanent arrangements. I mean, much as I appreciate your not wanting to hurt me, we wouldn't even be having this conversation if I hadn't cleared that up with myself."

He shook his head. "You *think* you have. You think you've cleared it up. I think you're kidding yourself, and I'm saying no because I refuse to hurt you."

Jody stared at him in bewilderment. His refusal was the last thing she'd expected; she hadn't even considered the possibility. How, after assuring him that she understood herself perfectly, could he still be saying no? She'd just offered herself boldly and blatantly only to be turned down. Forget all his fancy reasons and concerns about hurting her, the bottom line was that he'd rejected her. Didn't he think the humiliation hurt? She lashed out at him in anger.

"My goodness, you're almost too thoughtful to stand being around. And how fortunate for me that you're more privy to my own thoughts and feelings than I am. Otherwise, I might be hurt. Heaven forbid! Well, *Saint* Clifton, at least you can get a laugh out of the afternoon—one more idiot female ready to fall into your bed means one more notch for your bedpost, or wherever it is you keep score."

Clif flinched at the sarcasm and rage in her voice as if she'd struck him. It was precisely what she would have liked to do, but she needed all her strength to hold back the tears. Her overriding wish was to get home, home to the sanctuary of the Point and her bedroom. She turned and left.

Conscious that he was following her, Jody chose to ignore him, racing along a hall to a side door and fresh air. Blessedly, the door opened out near the parking area. Seeing their car, she sprinted toward it. She heard Clif call her name as he ran to catch up with her. Then suddenly a door slammed and Carl's voice boomed across the lot.

"McClelland," he commanded.

She whirled to see her brother running for Clif, grabbing his shirtfront and saying something. His fisted hand went back—

"Carl!" she screamed. "No!"

But Carl wasn't swinging, just shaking his fist and whipping some angry words at Clif before he ran to Jody's side. He guided his obviously distressed sister between vehicles to the shelter of their own. "Honey, what happened? Was he trying to come on to you?"

Hysterical laughter tripped out over the strangled sobs. "No, no, not that. Not that at all. I can't tell you. Just take me home, please. I'll be fine, as soon as I'm alone for a while."

"I'll get your coat," Carl offered.

"Please, just get me home. I'll get the coat later."

ALONE BEHIND THE CLOSED DOOR of her own room, Jody slipped on an old robe and warm slippers. She tucked herself into the familiar window seat, knees hugging her chest, thinking that she was surely going to wear the cushion right out worrying over that obnoxious Clifton McClelland. Only he wasn't obnoxious at all; he was wonderful and she loved him. All those horrible things she'd said weren't true at all. He *was* thoughtful, he *was* protecting her; and, maybe, just maybe, he knew better than she what her reaction would be after loving him.

So where did she go from here? She was getting sick and tired of regrouping, but there was little else she could do. At least she knew he still wanted her—some consolation when he refused to act on it. Perhaps he was relieved to be rid of her, thinking she was not the casual type, and might refuse to let go when the time came. Wouldn't that be embarrassing. Jody tried to picture the suave Clifton McClelland with a panting, adoring, lovelorn puppy scampering along after him every place he went. Such a bother. The annoying embarrassment of it all.

Her fury returned at gale force. Jumping to her feet, she hurled the cushion across the room and then let fly with a handy book. It crashed quite satisfactorily against the door. She tugged on ski pants, sweater and jacket to take her nieces and nephew for a therapeutic battle. A couple of hours building elaborate forts and bombarding each other with snowballs ought to clear her head.

Her call to arms resulted in a clamor of confusion, with children tearing about in search of mittens and earmuffs. In the middle of the racket, Jody had a sudden memory; Clif in the solarium, loosening his tie, and on that tie a gold tie tack gleamed. A cuckoo, twin to her own. His use of "them" to describe what he'd ordered was no longer a mystery, but why buy one for himself? Did he think he was cuckoo, too? Probably yes, because he'd been idiot enough to have wasted so much time on her. Her train of thought was abruptly halted by imperious shouts and pleas to "come on." Damn the man, she thought, and then put on a big smile for the youngsters so eagerly awaiting her.

THE NEXT WEEKS limped by, not helped in the least by the quiet, empty house after Carl and his family had returned to Seattle. Inventory at the store had alleviated things somewhat. Dull as it had been, a chore really, it at least kept her busy. And how much easier it would be next year, with the computers to help. Mentally she'd thanked Clif a dozen times during the task, and then forgotten to say so when he'd brought his father into the store to meet Jack right after the holidays. Seeing him that day had been the highlight of the month so far. Those brief moments had kept a good three days alive for her. Clif's ''matchmaking'' had been a great success—the two men had even gone over to the Athletic Club for a game of chess after spending an hour in Alferic's.

But all that was over, and Jody found herself, late on a Friday afternoon, sitting at her desk idly pushing papers from one spot to another and accomplishing exactly zero. The weekend loomed gloomy and hollow.

''January's a dumb, boring month,'' she announced, and then sat back with a rueful laugh. January had nothing to do with it. Clif was the reason she was feeling this way. Any month of the year would be the most glorious, exciting month on the calendar if Clif were with her.

Chin resting in the palm of a hand, Jody beat a tattoo with her pencil as she thought. *Just when do you plan to forget that man and get on with your life? You could start this very evening, if you wanted to. You could pick up the phone, call Tommy and see if he's free tonight.*

But she didn't want to be with Tommy. Even though he was nice, presentable, reasonably intelligent and courteous, he was still a bore. The only man she wanted to be with was Clif. They were meant to be together. If she were patient he might discover it for himself. If not, she would have to think of some way to bring him around.

CHAPTER NINE

A PERSISTENTLY RINGING telephone woke her the next morning, shattering a lovely, lazy Saturday-off dream. Now she would never know why Clif was beckoning her up a mountain or what was in the brown bag he was carrying, or why he had a Ping-Pong net draped around his shoulders. Even her dreams about him refused a neat category!

The call was from her closest neighbor at Lake of the Isles, telling her she'd best come by and check her house. The thermometer had plunged to a bone-chilling twelve below during the night and pipes had cracked in many of the homes in the area. Her neighbor's house was in such a mess that he and his wife had only had time to dash through the upper floors of Jody's place, but not the basement. Everyone had calls in to the overworked plumbers, and he suggested that if Jody needed repairs done they could share the first plumber who arrived on the scene.

Well, she reasoned, as she scrambled into her car, you buy an old home and you buy lots of problems. Not that new pipes didn't break, too. It was just indicative of the sort of things that had been happening since she'd moved in. Fuses blew, wires sizzled, faucets rumbled, grumbled and finally shot out geysers of rusty water, and drains fussed and bubbled. She had an arm-long list on a kitchen counter of "things to be fixed.'' It made no difference. She loved the house, and she loved the area.

As Jody drove along, she wished it were spring, when the two islands in the lake became a resting place for ducks and geese on their journey north. In the morning the water was still and clear, with tendrils of mist hovering above the surface. Canoes replaced ice boats, and joggers trotted the lake's three-mile perimeter on their lunch hours.

Lake of the Isles was really an urban park area, with a neighborhood of single-family dwellings. Its proximity to downtown was one of the reasons Jody had wanted to live there. But the main justification for spending all her graduation money and inheritance on the down payment for a run-down old house had been to raise a family there. She intended to make this house, on a lake dredged from swampland, into the same beloved sanctuary for her husband and children that the Point had been for her.

The basement was Jody's first stop when she arrived, and she found that she was in trouble, along with everyone else. A fine mist was spraying from a crack in a short connecting pipe from her washing machine. Fortunately, the only damage was to a box of detergent sitting underneath; it had been reduced to a sodden, frothy glob. All she knew about plumbing was that when one turned on a faucet, water appeared, arriving at its destination through some system of pipes. The crack was getting larger as she scowled at it, and it was obvious she was going to have to come up with some instant plumbing expertise or have a flooded basement to greet the plumber.

"Ingenuity," she decided. "A little old-fashioned ingenuity is what's needed here. The water is escaping from that crack, ergo, plug the crack. Simple!"

She dashed upstairs for some florist's clay since it, by definition, must stick when in water, and so it did—sort of. At the widest point in the break, the pressure kept nudging it out. Tape then. Scotch tape was all she had and was, of course, useless. Then she remembered a box of odds and ends on the back porch left by an electrician. That black tape he used might work, providing she wound it round a dry area of pipe.

"Jody, you are one smart lady," she congratulated herself, at the same time giving the tape and clay firm instructions to stay put until the real expert arrived.

By this time it was nearly eleven and she'd had neither food nor coffee. She couldn't remember what she'd left in the cupboards when she'd moved home to help her mother, but she was sure there was a can of coffee in the freezer. A little foraging turned up a lone tin of beans and a can of Crisco. She decided to get both brew and beans started before running next door to tell them she had joined the line awaiting a plumber. The doorbell rang just as she plopped the beans into a pan, and she opened the door, not to the neighbor she expected, but to Clif. He was carrying a large, brown grocery bag.

"Hi," he said, and then his eyes twinkled. "Jody, what have you been up to? You're a mess."

"I've been up to plumbing. Come on in, you and your brown bag both. What's in it this time?" Jody's lighthearted banter belied the euphoria she was feeling inside.

"Lunch is in it. Someplace I can set this down?"

"Right this way." As she led him to the kitchen her feet seemed to barely touch the floor. "It's the one room in the house that's livable," she explained.

Clif looked around the large room in admiration. "This is great, absolutely great. Reminds me of the kitchen at your mother's house, which is no coincidence, I bet."

"You're right, no coincidence. For me, a kitchen has to be the heart of the house, so—" she swept an arm around the room "—fire, couch, big old table, big gas stove... Sit down, Clif, I've got some coffee made. How did you know I was here?"

"Your mother. She also told me you'd disconnected your phone here, otherwise I'd have called. Do you mind my coming?"

"As long as you brought food, no," she teased. "I'm famished. I rushed over here without any breakfast to check on the water pipes, so I'm ready to gobble up an elephant."

"In lieu of elephant, how do Reuben sandwiches and potato salad sound?"

"Heavenly. But, first, I've got to run next door and tell them that if a plumber ever shows up, I need him, too."

"Madam, you insult me! The plumber is already here, and you're looking at him."

"You know about plumbing?" Surprise was more than evident in her tone.

"Sure. Read all about it in a book once. Nothing to it, so your problems are over."

As Jody led Clif to the basement she thought to herself that reading about plumbing in a book hardly made him an expert, and it was quite likely that her problems were just beginning.

Clif took in her knobby repair job, and while he grinned at her efforts, he also complimented her. "Not bad, not bad at all. Quite innovative, in fact. No problem fixing this, just replace that short section. Good thing it happened where it did. This your only casualty?"

She nodded.

"Suppose I get started while you're rustling up the sandwiches. Where's the water turn-off, and I'll need a pipe wrench."

"Water turn-off? I don't know where it is; I never looked for it. The people I bought the house from said that all that stuff, the controls or whatever, are in the back, by the basement door."

"The controls?" Clif smothered a laugh. "Yes, well, that's one way of putting it. Never mind, I'll find it. How about the wrench?"

"Won't pliers work? They get pretty wide if you jiggle them around a bit."

This time a huge laugh greeted her words. "No, pliers wouldn't work, even after jiggling. Let's see your toolbox."

Clif pursed his lips in fresh amusement as he lifted the lid and saw three lone occupants. "You're trying to renovate a house with a hammer, screwdriver and pliers?"

"Well, it's been enough so far. I've mostly just painted and wallpapered, and I plan to hire professionals to do the rest. I don't know much about building and rewiring and all that."

"Is that so? I'd never have guessed."

"Are you making fun of me, Clifton Mc-Clelland?"

The amusement in his eyes softened to tenderness, and he answered by taking her in his arms, a finger beneath her chin to raise her face to his. "Yes, but only because I ... I think you're so cute in that big old shirt and jeans with your hair all piled up helter-skelter, a smudge on your nose..."

And then he was kissing her, gently and lovingly, while Jody's thoughts and feelings tumbled in confusion and joy. Everything in her world seemed right when she was in his arms. He must love her as she loved him. Otherwise, how could he kiss her with such sweetness? How could he release her with such obvious reluctance?

"You're probably wondering why I'm here," he said. "I came because I owe you an apology, Jody. Several in fact." He tried a careless laugh, but it didn't come off very well. "My behavior decorating your tree, and on New Year's Day...well...I don't seem to be very consistent, do I?"

"No, you don't," she admitted, disappointed that he hadn't come back because he'd made a decision about them. He was still in a quandary. But mindful of her decision not to push him into anything, and noting his discomfort at the topic he himself had brought up, she smiled and went on, "Why worry about it? It's enough that you came here to apologize. Let's let it go at that. You also came bearing gifts and I'm still famished, so come on upstairs and keep me company while I heat up some lunch."

His look of relief at her words was almost comical. "Sounds great. Except that, instead of keeping you company, I'm going to tell your neighbors you're doing fine and then run to the hardware store for a wrench and some pipe. Any chance for a quick tour before I leave? Your patch job should hold for a while.''

''With pleasure! This house may not look like much right now, but when I'm done, it will be gorgeous. I'm absolutely in love with the place.''

Jody's amazement grew apace as Clif enthused his way along the three upper stories. It was the last sort of house she would have expected him to like, but like it he did.

He poked and tapped at walls and woodwork, let out a chortle of delight at the turret room ringed with velvet window seats and mumbled something about hide-and-seek and Easter eggs as he peered into sundry small rooms and cupboards, the original uses for which were a mystery to him. Presented with the third-floor ballroom, he let out a deep sigh of satisfaction and rested his back against a wall.

''What a fabulous house,'' he said.

''With some great stories. Would you like to hear one about this ballroom that one of the elderly neighbors told me?''

''By all means. Fire away.''

''It seems that during bootleg days, the people who owned the house had vats and vats of whiskey and gin around, and threw the wildest parties imaginable. The lady who told me was a little girl at the time and remembers the gramophone blasting away with ragtime, madcap Charleston dancing, the black bottom, too, all of which she watched in her nightgown from her bedroom window next door. But the most exciting night of all was when a party guest pulled out a revolver and shot down all the chandeliers, everyone cheering him on and scrambling for cover at the same time.''

Clif laughed uproariously. "No doubt flooding the street with indignant neighbors. What fun those people must have been and what fun this house will be."

"Clif, you surprise me. This house isn't the least bit efficient, or any of the qualities you value."

"Jody, it just may be that you don't know all of the qualities I value. What you have here represents the best of yesterday, in my opinion. A home is to live in, not function in. Home should be easy and comfortable, not a place you race through efficiently. Like my grandparents' home...it was my favorite place in the world when I was little, especially on rainy days, when we'd go up in the attic and empty old trunks full of Civil War uniforms and dresses with ten pounds of beading. Sometimes we'd run across old tintypes of grim-faced ancestors or letters. Once I even found one of my father's report cards from college, with enough C's for blackmail purposes, if I'd chosen to use it. Anyway, in the unlikely event that I ever have a home and family, I do not want modern efficiency any place in the house, except the bathrooms and furnace. Well, enough said. That pipe won't hold forever." He pushed himself away from the wall and headed downstairs to be off for the hardware store.

Jody gave Clif directions to the store and reminded him to check in with the neighbors. Then she started emptying the grocery bag. She was glad he'd left, otherwise he'd be hearing her chuckles. Instead of Swiss cheese, he'd bought mozzarella; instead of rye or pumpernickel, he'd bought a dark, sourdough French bread. He had enough corned beef for a dozen sandwiches and enough sauerkraut for a regiment. Unfortunately, he'd forgotten butter, or assumed she had some. She'd have to use the Crisco for browning.

Since there was a definite frigid draft around the big table, she added warped storm windows to her "fix it" list, and she set up the coffee table in front of the fireplace. By the time Clif came through the back door in a swirl of cold, stomping snow from his feet, Jody had everything ready, including cushions pulled from the couch onto the floor to serve as chairs.

"Smells terrific." He sat down cross-legged and picked up his sandwich. "Isn't it odd that the Germans put this on a French bread?"

"Yes, isn't it."

He took a bite and said, "I got the wrong bread, didn't I? Damn!"

And as the stringy mozzarella stretched from his mouth back to the sandwich, they both burst into laughter.

"Struck out here, too. Pizza cheese. This *is* corned beef, isn't it? I must have gotten something right."

"You got two things right. The sauerkraut's the real thing, too."

"Batting five hundred, at least. Does it taste okay to you?"

"Fabulous... hits the spot... oops..." She had to stop and break off a strand of cheese that was as elastic as a rubber band. In fact, it was winding all over her chin.

"What a mess. I put way too much cheese in these. My face is going to be covered in it before I get done."

She finished the first half of her sandwich, conscious of Clif's steady scrutiny, and wondered if he was remembering and feeling what she was. The drippy cheese had brought instant recollection of the croissants and jam on the couch in her office, and had conjured up all the same sensations. With great care she began on her second half, determined to avoid any dangling bits of cheese. Part way through, she realized that Clif had stopped eating. A quick look at his face showed her why. He was concentrating on her mouth. Her heart gave a jump, and she lost her own concentration. There she was, breathless, with mozzarella-bedecked lips and chin.

Clif slid around beside her, quickly pushing another cushion behind her. "Let me, Jody. Once more, let me," he said, bringing his mouth to hers.

This time she made not the slightest effort to damp down her responses. She encouraged every new caress, opened herself to his urgent exploring and as she heard his words of wanting, she was sure that nothing could stop their perfect fulfillment. Nothing, that is, except cushions that persisted in zipping out from under them.

"This is a helluva poor arrangement," he protested, and stood up. "I'm going to get us more comfortable. The couch—it makes into a bed?"

She nodded as she folded the bed down and brought the comforter from the top of the cedar chest. "It's where I sleep when I'm here." And then, to her distress, he frowned.

"Jody, are you sure?" he said.

In reply, she went into his arms, drawing his lips to hers. "Absolutely sure," she whispered.

"I hope so. God, I hope so. If you're just succumbing to the...the...well, magic will do. If you're just succumbing to the magic..."

Wishing he'd never had any time to think, she said, "What could be wrong with succumbing to magic?"

"That it's gone after the succumbing."

"It won't be. It could never be gone."

His answer was a rumble low in his throat, and then she was lying in his arms, lost in the wonder of his loving. This is how it should be, she thought. She and Clif loving each other completely. Here is where she belonged. Here was the man she'd been waiting for, was born for. She could lose herself to him...trust him, cherish him. But wait. He didn't love her, he wouldn't cherish her....

Abruptly, everything seemed wrong, and she knew Clif had been right in his reasons for refusal. She knew that no matter how deeply she might love him, without his love and dedication flowing toward her, she would not be complete.

Later, holding her close against him, Clif tipped her chin up so their eyes met. "You're not happy, Jody. What is it?"

Jody knew that Clif had felt her absence of fulfillment, and his concern seemed genuine. "It's not your fault, and I'm not unhappy." It was true. The sensations that had shivered through her told her that fulfillment was but sleeping within her, waiting to be awakened. Apparently it would take a man as devoted to her as she was to him to prod it from its slumber.

"Maybe you're not unhappy, but you're certainly not happy, either. Don't pretend with me; it won't work you know. Covering feelings never works for you. Come on, out with it."

She turned onto her back and pulled the sheet up. "For openers, we're doing far too much talking and worrying. How can anything be free and happy when we're stewing about pros and cons? This is my doing and my problem, and now let's drop it."

"I think...Jody, look at me. I think the real opener is that loving will never be free and happy for you without the promise of permanency. I was right on New Year's Day."

"You were right," she answered.

A hand on either side of her face, Clif kissed her lightly. A look akin to relief was in his eyes. "You're as true and clear as a perfect diamond, Jody Jenson, and I can't say that I'm disappointed." With that enigmatic remark, he stood to get dressed.

One arm into a shirt-sleeve, he halted his progress. "Fidelity," he exclaimed as though he'd just experienced a revelation. His next words were pensive and deliberate. "There's the promise of fidelity in that integrity of yours. Why haven't I thought of that before?"

Jody got up and put on an old robe, shaking her head over his apparently astonishing disclosure. Had he thought she wasn't a loyal, faithful person? "Clif McClelland," she mumbled to herself. "Sometimes you are just plain stupid!"

She started tidying the kitchen as Clif finished dressing, then went to the basement to replace the pipe. He'd gone down whistling confidently, but the cheeriness didn't last long. A string of oaths soon flew up the stairs, stopping her dishcloth in midswipe. *I was right, too,* Jody thought. *The problems are just beginning.*

"Jody?" he yelled up. "Don't you have a bucket in this damn place?"

She went to the head of the stairs. "In the laundry sink. There's a mop right next to it," she added as an afterthought that he probably didn't appreciate. All she could hear was some distracted muttering about water still in the pipe even after he's shut it off. She tiptoed to her sink.

A crash was followed by a series of clankety-clanks as metal rolled across the cement floor. Jody cringed. The pipe had clearly taken on a life of its own. A new and definitely blue volley of epithets proved her surmise to be correct.

Whack! Whack! Whack! It was the sound of a tool being banged furiously against an undisciplined pipe, Jody guessed. And then there was silence. She was just breathing a sigh of relief when she heard the bucket fall over. "Where's that blasted mop!" Clif's roar from below was embellished by a few sloshing sounds.

Jody started to laugh. Unable to stop, she rocked on the edge of the bed, one hand clamped to her mouth to smother the sound, the other pressed against her aching stomach. She heard the bucket clatter into the sink, the mop thump into its corner and then the forceful stamp of feet on the stairs. Trying frantically to smooth her face into appropriately serious lines, she got to her feet.

"It's fixed," Clif announced grimly as he tromped to the sink to wash his hands. "Damn pipe wrench must have been a second—ought to give that hardware store a piece of my mind." He snatched the towel off its hook and nearly impaled it when he put it back.

Jody tightened her lips against a persistent smile. "I've heard that the easiest reading makes for the hardest doing."

A snort of disgust was his only reply. Scowling at her, Clif noticed her barely suppressed merriment and his lips began to twitch in response. A few chuckles escaped, grew in volume, and then they were both collapsing in hilarity.

When they'd calmed down, Clif said, "Good thing I don't have to make my living plumbing. Or, sawing. Meet Mr. Klutz in the do-it-yourself department."

"Well, Mr. Klutz, you saved the day for me. Look out the window. Half the men in the neighborhood are out scanning the street for a truck that says 'Night and Day Plumbing' and I'm home free."

"Well—" he cleared his throat "—it might be best if you had a real-life plumber take a look . . . I mean, it'll hold all right, but just to be on the safe side."

"Good idea. It always pays to be on the safe side," she agreed with a straight face.

"Yes . . . well . . . enough on the plumbing. Before I leave, Jody, there's something I want to talk to you about."

"Fine by me. Come sit down at the table, I'll get some coffee. What is it you want to talk about?"

"One of my nephews. Jody, I need to be sure that you understand my reluctance toward marriage, understand why I'm so adamant on the subject. I think meeting Mike would help."

"I'd love to meet him. When and where?"

"The when I'm not sure of. The where is on the ski slopes."

Jody rolled her eyes in dismay. "Dear heaven, what have I gotten myself in for?"

"Some fun, I hope."

"But I don't know how to ski. I don't even know how to put the silly things on."

"I know, but neither does Mike. Lesson time for both of you—and they're not silly things," he corrected her.

"You haven't seen them on me, yet. But never mind, I do want to go, since that's the only way I'll meet Mike. How about a little background on him?"

"Gladly—might make it easier when you meet him. He's a bit difficult to communicate with...seldom gives anything of himself. Anyway, he's eight years old, sensitive, talented, bright, and I...Jody, I love him very much. In fact, he's the one I was talking about shepherding along. I've sort of been a surrogate father to him."

"His own father? He doesn't..."

Clif gestured dismissively. "My honorable older brother hasn't got time, and my former sister-in-law works all day. Thinks she's some hotshot career woman. They don't need her income. If she had to work to make ends meet I could understand it. But how she can leave Mike every day when he's obviously so unhappy is beyond my comprehension. If one of my children ever looked like that..." He stopped, jaw clenched and a near murderous look in his eye.

Jody's heart had already gone out to young Mike. She knew and loved a boy that age and also knew what they should be like. Ivar was eight. His face was as merry and blooming as any parent could wish; he was as loved and cared for as any child could ever be.

"Mike's the same age as Ivar," she said.

"I know. The contrast nearly broke my heart, and watching Alf and Britta with him, and with Kirstie—there's so much love in that house. While Mike...well, you'll meet him and see for yourself, *if* I can persuade his mother. She hasn't much use for me, I'm afraid. Says I'm meddling. Anyway, the kid's a born athlete and I'm trying to get something started that doesn't involve teams and practice schedules. No one would take him to them, but the skiing bit I can do myself on weekends."

Jody got up and went around the table to give him a kiss.

"What was that for?" he asked. "Not that I'm complaining, mind you, just curious."

"Because I like you, Clif McClelland."

He stood up and took her in his arms. "And I like you, Jody Jenson. I like you very, very much."

Before his kiss could deepen, he stepped away. "Time for me to be heading out."

She handed Clif his coat and started for the door. "I'll be waiting to hear from you, though not for the skiing lesson, I'm afraid. Just for the pleasure of meeting Mike."

"Don't knock the skiing too hard yet. It's one of my favorite pastimes and it will be one of yours, too. You'll see. By the way, Clark mentioned that Renard is due back in town on Monday."

"That's right. I think it's a waste of time to meet, but Warren thinks we should. I'm sure not looking forward to it."

"No. I don't suppose you are. Be alert, Jody. Don't let the guy fool you . . . trap you in some scheme."

"Don't worry—my intuition will be on red alert."

He smiled and pinched the tip of her nose playfully. "Okay, I won't worry. Clark can tell me how you fared, and I'll call you as soon as I get something worked out for Mike."

The door closed behind him and Jody sat down on the bed with a weary plump. "If one more person tells me to be cautious . . ." she mumbled. She sighed and got up to begin dressing, continuing to muse as she did so.

It was interesting how anxious Clif was for her to meet Mike. She wondered if it was his own determination that needed bolstering. Maybe more than showing *her* why marriage was out, he needed to show himself again. Of all the reasons he'd given her, she was willing to bet that Mike was going to be the most impelling. Could he be worried that she'd neglect her family for Alferic's? She knew she would never do that, but Clif didn't. She could only hope she'd get a chance to straighten that one out.

If it wasn't one thing it was another. Jody shook her head in dismay as she slipped on her coat. It was time to get back to the Point. And there was nothing to look forward to except another meeting with Mr. Renard. What a dreary, disgusting prospect! At least Monday was just a day away, and then it would be over and done with.

CHAPTER TEN

JODY HAD FIRMLY INTENDED to avoid a second settlement conference, positive that it would be a waste of everyone's time. However, after listening to Warren's insistent and persuasive voice extol the virtues of sitting down together and talking, she'd reversed her decision and consented. But she did have one condition—the conference must be held at Warren's office. She was not about to chance an unexpected meeting with Clif and have the added complication of pretending to be casual, especially after Saturday's encounter. Disguising her feelings at any time would be hard enough; to play nonchalant when her wits had to be sharp would be impossible.

As she and Warren walked down the hall to the meeting, he filled Jody in on a few last-minute details. "By the way," he concluded as they reached the conference room, "Clark's had to go to Chicago after all, so Clif's sitting in today."

Jody halted in midstride as she gaped in dismay. The news that Clif would be there shattered her composure.

Thinking to reassure her, Warren took her by the elbow and said, "Nothing to worry about; Clif's one of the best and Clark will be back in a couple of days."

Jody had no choice but to accept Warren's guiding hand and carry on—it was too late to deputize Alf to replace her. Mustering her courage, Jody entered the room.

She smiled at Clif and walked toward him, hand extended for a shake. No more than a simple greeting to a friend. His reaction was equally pleasant and noncommittal, and she was relieved at the ease of it all. Jody turned to acknowledge Mr. Renard briefly. To her surprise, instead of the old roué she'd previously met, she found herself being introduced to Renard Junior, who had come in his father's stead. Urgent business in New York was the reason given.

"Miss Jenson—" he took her hand "—I'm pleased to meet you." His handshake was followed by one of the most captivating smiles she had ever seen.

He's a gentleman, she said to herself while making the appropriate responses. Not like his father at all. That's worth a point or two in his favor right at the beginning.

Though approximately the same height as Clif, Alexander Renard's slender frame made him appear slightly taller. He was a pleasant-looking man, but his coloring was rather nondescript—a thatch of sandy hair, a brush of sandy mustache, eyes of light brown. Seated beside his acting attorney, he seemed pale, cast in shadow by the intensity of Clif's cobalt eyes, ebony hair and tanned skin.

The contrast also marked their speech and mannerisms, but to a lesser degree than the visible differences. Where Clif's words were clipped and emphatic, Alex's were precise and firm. This suggested to Jody that Alex was not an indecisive man, but rather a cautious one. His gestures did not have the power of Clif's, but they were strong. Jody's overall impression was of a good man who deliberated before taking action, a man who lacked the excitement of Clif's bold energy.

Jody shook her head impatiently. In her eyes, any other man would be eclipsed by Clif. Her feelings would make it difficult to judge Alex fairly, but she was honor bound to make the effort.

Clif, at the moment, was giving a quick précis of the previous conference to make sure both parties understood each other. He then went on to say, "Alex has a compromise offer to present on behalf of his father for your consideration. Alex, the floor's yours."

Jody shifted her eyes reluctantly from Clif's face to that of her adversary's and prepared to listen.

"Thanks, Clif," Alex said, his eyes focusing on Jody's. "I believe in being direct, Miss Jenson, so I'll present our plan to you in a nutshell. My father is going to give the bookstore to me. You would remain the manager, and the name Alferic's would be kept. In this way, your uncles' business could be saved, while leaving you in charge of the store. Now, you may be wondering why my father has suddenly turned altruistic—saving you, as well as Eric and Nils. The truth is, he's doing it for me. You see—" he sent Jody that smile she'd found so delightful "—my biggest interest in life is rare books and my dream is to own an antiquarian bookstore. We'd have no trouble getting along at Alferic's."

Jody hoped her eyes weren't popping as he finished his speech. Who would ever have thought of an offer like this? This was no mere sop thrown in her direction if she'd sell. Mr. Renard's compromise meant saving her uncles *and* Alferic's. The only loss would be outright ownership of the building and that would be in the hands of an antiquarian book lover.

"Mr. Renard, you've certainly caught me by surprise... I hardly know what to say. Though one question comes to mind immediately. Why wouldn't you want to manage your own store? Why abdicate in favor of me?"

"Because I want to learn appraising, travel in search of treasure—the British Isles, Europe, the Orient—and I'd be glad to have you doing the day-to-day business... making the decisions required. You do it exceedingly well, you know."

A little icing on the cake, Jody thought in amusement, though she didn't let it show. A simple nod was all the response she gave.

"In fact," he continued, "the only trouble you'd have from me would be making shelf space for the booty I sent you."

Jody joined in the general laughter at Alex's assessment of his trouble-making capacities, at the same time thinking that everything was surely falling into place. It was all as neat and tidy as... as a preconceived plan! The words thudded in her brain. "To plan his next move," Clif had said in December. "What happened to getting this wound up today?" Warren had asked. Could Renard Senior have returned to New York and worked all this out with his son? *Plan* was an odd word to use for an offer. There could be something underhanded going on. Alex may have come because, as a book lover, he could better persuade her. But why would they be that determined to get the Jenson Building and Alferic's? Why not simply turn a Renard outlet over to him for his kind of bookstore?

Jody silenced her troubling thoughts to listen to Warren and realized that he was asking a question that should have occurred to her. She admitted to herself that lawyers were sometimes a definite asset.

"Mr. Renard, who would own the building?"

"Your concern is understandable, Warren. You don't want me renting from a third party. The building will be mine."

Warren pondered for a moment. "Well, you seem to have covered most of the bases. I'm not prepared to ask my client for any sort of decision right now, of course. We'll talk it over and get back to you. How long will you be in Minneapolis?"

"For as long as it takes. Whatever time Jody needs to make her decision is hers. I'll wait."

Tactical error, she thought. I haven't given you permission to use my first name, nor I'll bet, did Warren. "Mr. Renard, there's something about this that I don't like."

"What would that be, Miss Jenson?"

"It's far too perfect for me to trust. Doubting perfection may seem absurd to you, but that *is* how I feel—doubtful."

Glancing at Clif, Jody noted the astonished expression on his face and her heart turned heavy. *Does he think that I should be shouting for joy and grabbing the nearest pen? Might as well forget having him in there pulling for me.*

Alex leaned forward in Jody's direction. "Miss Jenson, conference tables make forbidding barriers. At least, I think so. Perhaps if we got better acquainted, you'd have an easier time considering our offer. Would you do me the honor of letting me buy lunch for you?"

Jody nearly responded with an instant no. It seemed an inappropriate invitation to her, and she didn't want to accept at all. However, if there truly was a plan, this could be part of it. She would never find out if she didn't spend a little time with the man. She glanced at Warren and he nodded his approval. Her decision was made.

"All right, Mr. Renard. You are quite correct in saying that I want to give thought to your compromise. Having lunch with you seems as good a place as any to begin."

Warren asked for a few moments with her before they left, at which time he cautioned her to make no promises, to go slowly and merely get to know Alex a bit. Though the new offer seemed too conveniently all encompassing, Alex appeared to be a decent man, not at all like his boorish father, and Warren could see no harm in listening to him.

When she joined Alex down at the taxi rank, he confessed to a tourist's inclinations, and asked if she would mind eating at St. Anthony Main. He'd read about it in the hotel guide and thought it sounded fascinating. Jody said she wouldn't mind at all.

The cabbie beamed at their decision and promptly launched into a full description of the wonders to be found at this renovated factory. There were some sixty specialty shops and five major restaurants, a small park that overlooked the River and Nicollet Island Inn, and even a restored livery stable with hansom cabs for hire. Their informant's enthusiasm became understandable when he said that his first job had been right there, although it had been the Salisbury Mattress Factory in those days.

Jody and Alex strolled through the arcades, admiring the shops and old brickwork, while Alex decided

upon a restaurant. His choice was one that special-
ized in crepes.

They sat opposite each other beneath a red-and-
black striped awning. One of Lautrec's blowsy can-
can dancers flipped her skirts at them from a poster
over the table. Glasses of wine in front of them, Jody
felt the time had come to get on with the business at
hand.

"May I call you Alex?" she asked to start things off.

"By all means . . . Jody." He lifted his wineglass in
salute.

"And now, let's get to the reason for our being here.
Why doesn't your father simply buy you a store, any
old store that you could turn into an antiquarian
bookshop, at far less money than he's offered for Alferic's and the building? Or transfer an existing Renard outlet to you? All this seems absurdly complicated
if the purpose is just to give you a chance at your
dream."

"I'm not surprised at that question. The answer is
that he can please both himself and me with the
building. The rental income for Pop, the store for me.
There's an additional bonus for me—an established
name in books, plus a capable, built-in manager. I get
to do all the fun stuff."

"Such as mail off enormous cartons from faraway
places, all brim full of treasure," she said with a smile
to answer his. "Your reasons make sense, though there
are surely other buildings in other cities that would
serve your purpose, and you could hire a manager.
Why Minneapolis?"

"This is terrific book country and Pop thinks I'll
have a better chance of success out here in the hinter-

lands. Shall we order?'' He hailed a waiter before Jody could reply.

Hinterlands! she thought. Tactical error number two. And he sure zipped by the success angle in a hurry.

When the orders had been given, she resumed the conversation. ''This is terrific book country, Alex. You'd be surprised at the caliber and number of requests for books. But even though your answers are making sense, it seems to me your father is going through a lot of hassle just to get our building—flying between Minneapolis and New York, conferences, a legal tangle, all of them disrupting your lives and schedules. It seems a bit much.''

Alex surprised her by laughing. ''If you must know, I think Pop has got his back up over you. Being beaten out of what he wants by *anyone* just makes him plant his feet deeper. And to be defeated by a 'feisty, stubborn, articulate, intelligent female' was more than he could stand.''

''He said all that?''

''He sure did. Stomping around his office like a mad bull. He was nearly beside himself.''

''Well, at least you two know that my feet are pretty firmly planted, too.'' She sat back as their food arrived.

''Not bad,'' commented Alex after his first bite. ''Not bad at all.''

''You weren't expecting good food in the 'hinterlands'?''

Alex sent her a sharp glance. ''Why do I get the feeling you didn't appreciate that choice of word?''

''Probably because I didn't,'' she said without elaborating.

"Sorry. It's just that I've never heard much about Minnesota, except in history texts, usually dealing with Indians or iron or corn. I didn't mean to be derogatory."

"That's good, because I'm more than proud of my state. Why does your father think your chance of success is better here than elsewhere?"

His eyebrows lifted. "You're not much on mincing words, are you?"

Jody looked at him, a glint of shrewdness in her eyes. "Does it bother you?"

"Nope," he answered, but she detected a flicker of unease. "However, I can see that I'm going to have to watch my tongue, since you pick up on everything. But to answer your latest question, the truth is, Pop doesn't think my chances of success in antiquarian books are good anyplace in the country. He has no use for them; why would anyone else? He looks down on the whole field of literature, unless there's money in it. For that matter, he dismisses most of the arts. He thinks music begins and ends with Sousa, barroom type pictures are the state of the art in painting, and as for books, Zane Grey said it all. My tastes parallel my mother's . . . you'd like my mother, Jody."

And by implication, he was saying she'd like him, too. Aware of this, she let his comment pass with a slight smile. "You obviously want a full-service store, probably an atmosphere conducive to browsing. How can you bear to be associated with Renard Books?"

Alex was clearly puzzled. "Bear it? Pop expects it of me. I'm the only son. Naturally I have to follow him into the business. Anyway, our sort of operation means megabucks, lots of extra cash for treasure."

She merely nodded in acquiescence, though she was disturbed by all his references to his father. The man seemed to be the dominant factor in his son's life. An unpleasant indicator of future influence if Alex owned the store. However, she didn't pursue it right then, saying instead, "I should be heading back to the store pretty soon. Why don't you get the waiter's attention for some coffee and we can be on our way."

"Already?" he objected. "Jody, we've barely begun to get acquainted. I was hoping you'd consent to a tour of the Twin Cities this afternoon. How about it? I'm positive you'd make the best tour guide I could have."

Jody's first inclination was to say no. She didn't trust this man. But on the other hand, if his plan was legitimate, it would bail out Uncle Eric and Uncle Nils. She owed it to them to give Alex a chance before saying "no, see you in court." And the longer she dilly-dallied over her decision on the offer, the longer Alex would hang around. Maybe she could get the niceties over within one day and give herself some room to think.

"You have no time limits to your stay here?" she asked.

"None. In fact you can take weeks to decide if you want. Time with you is time well spent as far as I'm concerned." And out came that devastating smile to punctuate his words.

Terrific, Jody thought. Now he was going to start flirting with her. Still, she had to persevere.

"There's nothing pressing that I know of at the store," she said, "so I'll play tour guide for you. Let me call just to make sure, while you get our coats and think about what you want to see."

She got a go ahead from Alferic's, and they hailed a taxi to take them to the parking garage where she'd left her car. On the way, Jody tried to pin Alex down on his preferences for sightseeing.

"I don't really know," he admitted. "You plan the itinerary. It'll all be new to me, so I'm not particular."

"In that case, I'll give you a choice of two tours. The first is a chamber of commerce sort, highlighting things such as our mills, the university, art galleries and museums."

"Sounds good! What's the alternate tour?"

"The alternate choice is a historical tour. That means waterways around here, because our history is all wound up in the rivers and lakes. We'd begin up north at St. Anthony Falls and drive south to Pig's Eye—the original site of St. Paul—wind up at Lake Pepin, and I'd bombard you with native legends and folklore along the way. Our final stop would be Minnehaha Falls and you'd have to sit through a recitation of my favorite poem, 'Hiawatha.' Now, which do you choose?"

"History," Alex answered promptly. "I'm not about to miss the story of 'Hiawatha'! Didn't he marry Minnehaha? Or is my memory faulty?"

"Your memory's not faulty, and I promise not to try recalling the whole thing. I'm really pleased that you want the history tour. It's one of my favorite subjects. In fact, there's a good chance that you'll be bored to death."

The tour had quite the opposite effect on Alex. He had not been bored. Instead he had been most enthusiastic, eager for every bit of information Jody had given him. By the time they had pulled up in front of his hotel and her accompanying lecture had ended, she felt comfortable with him, her distrust all but laid to rest. How could a lover of antiquarian books and history be other than honest and good?

Since her father had died, she had not met anyone who shared her love of history the way Alex apparently did. But it had become increasingly plain on their tour that he was interested in more than just her words and knowledge. This development left her less than comfortable.

"Now, where shall I take you for dinner?" Alex asked the instant Jody turned off the ignition.

She restarted the car, stating rather tersely, "I'm going home, Alex. No more shared meals for us, I'm afraid."

He sent her a mournful glance. "You sound altogether too definite. To think you'd abandon a visitor from New York to a lonely dinner in a sterile hotel— most inhospitable. Sure I can't change your mind?"

Jody laughed at the hangdog expression he had pasted on. "I'm sure."

"Well, can't blame a guy for trying. Thanks for the afternoon, Jody. It was very special for me." He hopped out of the car and vanished into the hotel.

Driving home, she felt the teeniest bit guilty, thinking of him eating by himself, spending the evening alone in a strange city. But it was hardly her responsibility, and he must have been prepared for that when he flew out. She shifted her focus from Alex, and concentrated instead on the long, hot bath and quiet evening by the fire that awaited her.

AFTER CHECKING that her mother was comfortably asleep, Jody indulged in her well-deserved bath. Then,

wrapped in a cozy robe, she went in search of something good to read. She remembered her grandfather's journal, still in the attaché case she carried to
and from the store. Between the holidays and the legal wrangle, she'd completely forgotten about Clif's
find. It would be a perfect companion in front of the
cheerful fire she'd built earlier in the kitchen.

Snuggled up on the couch, Jody read about her
grandparents' first home and the beginnings of Jenson & Sons Milling. Alternately chuckling and shed-
ding a few nostalgic tears, she laughed aloud over a
paragraph concerning her grandmother and the outrageous fashions she wore. She was still dashing the
dampness from her cheeks when the next entry caused
her to sit bolt upright:

My dream, the one I told Joanna about when we
were courting, is to be realized. We are going to
build our bookshop. It's a dream that has its seeds
in my youth, planted shortly after I came here
from Sweden. In order to learn English as rapidly as possible, I all but lived at the public library. It was my first insight into the power of
books.

But how much more satisfactory to own one's
own volumes, to have them at one's fingertips in
a home library, to read and reread, discuss with
family and friends at leisure. I vowed I would
someday make the volumes available for purchase in my own bookshop. My dear wife and I
both feel that the poorest man in the world is the
man who doesn't read, because he is doomed to
remain within his *own* small sphere of experience. There is wealth to be mined in books, and

it is our intention to make this wealth available to the fine people of our city.

Jody flipped a few pages ahead and found more references to Alferic's:

I bought a lot on Nicollet Avenue today. We have decided to construct a four-story building, with office space above the bookshop for rental income. It will be the Jenson Building, its most valued tenant, Alferic's, on the ground floor. Joanna chose the name, deriving it from mine— Alfred Eric. I admit to being pleased. Next week I will have my will rewritten to ensure the passage of both bookshop and building to my heirs and their issue. It is my fervent wish that Alferic's never leave this family! That it be a tradition, from generation through generation, for the name Jenson to mean fine books for the people of this great state. Minnesota has brought me wealth; I intend to return, albeit in a different coinage, as great a measure as I am able.

Jody's throat was tight with pride in her grandparents, her thoughts filled with determination that their dream would not die. She, too, would disseminate the wealth of the written word "in as great a measure as she was able." Dramatic as it might sound, it was a noble dream.

Closing the journal for the night, she ruffled the remaining pages and the word *scandal* caught her eye. Her grandfather involved in a scandal? No one had ever told her about that.

My business acumen was asleep when I invested in that fool Beacon Tower. The perpetrators of the project are nothing but scoundrels, selling stock only to manipulate it into money for themselves. Along with a few others, I intend to expose this deceitful scheme!

Jody could find no further references to the scheme, nor any mention of the ''scoundrels''' names. The whole thing must have just blown over and been forgotten. Interesting, though. She would have to ask her mother about it.

Meantime, Jody was glad she had put off calling Alf and Warren until tomorrow. These words of her grandfather's would surely constitute a heavy weight on her side of the scale. In fact, if it weren't for the seriousness of the situation with her uncles and the mills, she would ignore Alex's offer altogether.

As she set the journal aside, Jody had a thought that brought fresh amusement. Clif had been the one to find the very evidence that might swing the case firmly in her direction. How ironic! She doubted that his senior partner would thank him for his discovery, but she most certainly did.

CHAPTER ELEVEN

As JODY HAD EXPECTED, Warren had been delighted over the evidence in the journal. It would cement the "intent" angle in no uncertain terms. However, given Jody's expressed wish to help her uncles if it were not at the expense of Alferic's, he still thought she should get to know Alex better. Alf had agreed. The character of any future owner would be paramount to reaching her decision. So when Alex had called to ask if he could spend the morning in the store, she'd said yes.

Since his hotel was just down the street, it seemed that he was in her office at almost the same instant she'd hung up the phone.

"Got here as quick as I could." He grinned.

"Any quicker and I'd have expected wings. Come on, I'll get back into the tour business for a few minutes and then leave you on your own."

"You mean I'm being left alone again?"

Jody laughed and started downstairs. "Hardly, Alex. Between customers and staff, you'll have plenty of company."

She showed him around the store, pointing out various features as they moved along. "Be sure to check out the stockroom before you're done, right through that door under the stairs. We're preparing to go modern in there—computers for all the ordering, deliveries, inventory and so on. Should have done it ages ago. And the staff knows your name, so simply introduce yourself as you go along. There, I guess that's it.''

"Okay if I come up to your office when I'm through?''

Jody said it was, then went back upstairs and left him to his solitary inspection.

The top priority on her agenda was one she thoroughly enjoyed—placing an order from a publisher's new list for the season. The representative of this particular publishing house had been in the previous day and "talked through" the list while Jody made notes in the margins of the catalog for later study. It was now decision time. The things she had jotted down as the rep talked enabled her to order with intelligence and precision, and Jody wondered, as she had in the past, why any bookseller would prefer to order "cold" from these catalogs, bypassing the support and advice of the publisher's own representative. Jody believed that any bookseller who did not utilize such valuable aid was certainly less than astute.

The majority of the list took very little time since she had pretty well made her choices during the rep's visit, but there was one title that required some pondering. The question was not whether or not to buy it, but rather how many. Jody was still tapping a pencil against her teeth in thought when Alex walked in. He came around the desk and glanced at the catalog she was studying.

''Now, there's the sort of new season list I like,'' he commented. ''Not one title mediocre enough for Renard's!''

"The perfect compliment. I'll pass it along to the rep, tell her she's got a winner."

"Not financially, she doesn't. Hey, is that coffee I smell?"

"Right over there. Help yourself."

He did and also refilled her cup. "Why don't I run out and get us something to go along with this? The Danish pastries in these parts ought to be fabulous— more Danes around here than in Denmark, I'll bet."

Instantly an image of Clif flashed before Jody's eyes. Clif holding her, touching her, on the couch right there. Clif taking the last bit of croissant from her lips with his own and then . . .

"No!" she almost shouted. "That is, I'm not hungry, but thank you anyway. There's a place in the Crystal Court, if you want some."

"Not really . . . we'll have lunch instead. Did I say something wrong? Danish pastries upset you?"

"No, of course not. I'm just being silly. Come on, pull up a chair and let me run an idea past you, if you don't mind? It has to do with the store."

"Mind? I'd love it." Sitting forward in the chair next to her desk, Alex was clearly interested and attentive. "Shoot."

"There's a book on this list that I'm thinking of doing a promotion on. The title sounds about as stimulating as a classroom text—*Transport On The Waterways of Minnesota*—but just listen for a minute before you decide I'm crazy."

Jody's idea was to have a topographical mock-up constructed for Alferic's large center window. The display would show the Great Lakes and St. Lawrence system and also the Mississippi River from its source in Lake Itasca all the way to the Gulf, complete with scale-model ore boats, barges rafting lumber, all the commercial carriers and maybe even some old riverboats, side-wheelers and stern-wheelers.

"A 'Minnesota, provider to the nation' sort of thing," she concluded. "So what do you think?"

"Terrific! Absolutely terrific!" Alex's eyes danced in anticipation. "I had a thought while you were talking. Why don't we have the little boats move? You know, a tracklike affair with the machinery underneath the mock-up? An ore boat leaving Duluth and docking in Chicago, or Gary, or Pittsburgh, or wherever it is they go."

"What a great idea. The paddle-wheelers could paddle. And maybe we could put little people on the decks—like a gambler all in black with a sleek mustache and looking the sly villain. Anyway, there would be copies of the book in the window and I'd have a breakfast to honor the author, invite him to autograph the books that people buy...lots of possibilities."

"Jody, we're going to have the most marvelous time with this, working together, being close...I can hardly wait to get started. How much time do we have?"

Too late Jody regretted her enthusiasm. She'd all but said that there would be a partnership. At least, Alex could certainly interpret her words that way. There was a more pleasing aspect, however—the two of them seemed to be quite comfortable working together.

"Plenty of time," she replied. "The exhibition isn't until May. Meanwhile, I'll order a galley proof of the book and see if I think it measures up. I may choose—"

A knock interrupted her sentence. "Come in," Jody called, and the door was opened by Ed, a longtime employee.

"Excuse me, Jody, there's a gentleman downstairs insisting upon a copy of *The Black Forest: Its Clocks and Birds*, which, as far as I can tell, has never been published. He told me to check with the boss since Alferic's is famed for its service, including the search for rarities."

"What does the gentleman look like?"

"Tall, black hair, intense blue eyes. Fine-looking chap, but rather insistent."

"I think I know who he is." Jody felt like leaping up and running down to him, but managed a sedate rise from her chair. "I'll talk to him myself."

Alex was quickly at her side. "I'm coming with you. The fellow may get nasty. Why doesn't he just settle for a book on Bavaria?"

"I suggested that, Mr. Renard." Ed stood aside to let Alex precede him through the door. "He claims that won't do at all. A very particular fellow."

"Ha! Hard to please sounds more like it."

"Alex, please." Jody turned back on the bottom step. "I'm almost positive it's Clif."

"Clif? What would he...by God, you're right! Here he comes."

At the sight of Clif's expression, the first word that popped into Jody's mind was *jolted*. His eyes flicked between her and Alex briefly, and then he smiled as if everything were exactly as it should be.

"Well, Renard, I certainly didn't expect to see you here. In need of some reading matter to wile away the hours at the hotel?"

"No, just getting acquainted with my future." One arm swept an arc to encompass the floor. The other made a slight, but noticeable motion in Jody's direction.

Clif's eyebrows rose. "Progress along a broad front, I see."

Jody had stepped farther away from Alex at his gesture and sent him an annoyed glance. "Not really. We're still very much in the talking stages of any sale. Alex, you can go back upstairs if you like. I'll see what I can do to help Clif and be up in a few minutes."

"Sure thing. I'll keep busy perfecting *our* ideas on the window project." His emphasis on the word carried the ring of someone staking a claim, and Jody was more than annoyed—she was indignant.

"Well, well," Clif commented, his gaze fixed on Alex's retreating back. "How things have changed since the contretemps over the conference table."

"They have, and they haven't. I can't imagine what possessed him to talk that way. We're involved in business—period."

"As far as you're concerned, maybe, but be on your toes. Alex has definitely widened his field of conquest."

She dismissed his caveat with a flick of a hand. "I doubt it, but thanks anyway. Now let's see what we can find out about the Black Forest."

Clif stayed her arm as she turned to walk toward the reference shelf. "That was just for laughs, Jody. Figured you'd know who it was down here, though the good Ed insisted upon exhausting all the possibilities before bothering you. He's a topnotch employee, by the way. The real reason I came by was to see if you'd

go skiing with Mike and me this Saturday afternoon.''

Jody's eyes lit up in delight. ''His mother said yes—
how wonderful! I'd love to. That is, if you don't think
Mike will mind?''

''He said he wouldn't. He's so happy to be going
that I don't think he'd object to an entire regiment
tagging along. I'll pick you up about eleven-
thirty... here? Or your house?''

Jody thought for a moment. ''Neither. Alf and
Britta's would be better—I can borrow Britta's skis.''

''Fine with me. And get her poles, too. They should
be the right size. We'll rent the boots. By the way, I
met your uncles yesterday. They were on their way to
lunch with Clark, and they asked me to join them.
Fine men. Both of them.''

''Of course they are! What else could a Jenson be?''
Her answer was flippant, yet she was concerned that
Clif would consider her not only foolish, but also un-
caring in her desire not to sell. He liked her uncles and
she was blocking their only chance to salvage their
business.

''Right! A Jenson could only be the best of everything,'' he agreed with a smile. ''And about my
uneasiness over Alex's interest in you—that guy can be
a smooth operator when he chooses. Be alert.''

''I will be. It's good advice.''

With a reminder of Saturday's time and place, Clif
left and Jody went upstairs. She found Alex standing
at her office window.

''Did you see anything interesting?'' she inquired,
knowing full well he'd been unabashedly observing her
and Clif.

"Matter of fact, I did. What happened to the search for the book?"

"That wasn't what he really wanted—just a joke between us. So, tell me, have you come up with dozens of new ideas for *my* mock-up?"

Alex grinned at her pointed reminder of his own choice of words. "Sorry if I made you angry. Clif was obviously none too happy at the sight of me standing next to you, and I couldn't resist trying to crack that cool facade."

"It's not a facade. Now, if you don't mind, I'd like to get back to work...."

"Hey, you promised to have lunch with me, remember? In lieu of Danish, you said yes to lunch."

Jody sighed. "Alex, I did not say anything of the sort and you know it."

"Well, you didn't say no, so I took it as assent."

"You shouldn't have. Remember, I also said no more meals." She tried not to sound irritated.

"No law against changing your mind, is there?"

Of course he was right about that, and maybe she should change her mind. It would provide an opportunity to probe into his past a bit, to get a handle on the degree of influence his father had on him.... She had to know that before coming to any conclusion.

"All right, I'll go. It's early, but let's leave now. We'll be sure to get a table that way."

Mitterhauser La Cuisine was practically next door, and Jody thought their lace tablecloths and flowered wallpaper would provide the relaxing atmosphere she needed right now. Fortunately, Alex enjoyed Hungarian food so he accepted her suggestion readily. Jody chose a light dish, but Alex went the route, with Chicken Paprikash and all the trimmings.

"Jody," he began, once the orders were given, "I don't mean to be pushy, to be forcing myself on you...it's just that I need you to get to know me—fast."

She nodded. "I see that, but it's awfully hard to build trust in a hurry, and that's what a business association needs—any association, for that matter. Can I trust you?"

Her direct query seemed to bother him. He was clearly uneasy and no answer was forthcoming.

Jody spurred him on a bit. "Renard does mean 'fox' you know. It's a bit of a misnomer, I hope?"

To her surprise, he didn't laugh, didn't even smile, at her jest. "I'll let you come to your own conclusions."

"Then I think a little exploration of your life is in order, but only what you want to tell me. No prying intended, just what you might tell any prospective business partner."

He said nothing, his eyes resting on her as a series of emotions drifted over his face. Fear? Hope? Indecision? Jody wasn't sure, but she thought she saw all three.

"Actually, I think I'm going to do a bit of soul baring for you."

"Please don't tell me anything you'll regret later. There's absolutely no necessity for such revelations."

"I know. That is, the need is all on my side." His gaze was intent as his words.

"In that case, carry on."

"My life begins with my father," he said, "and it begins with fear of him. My mother, my sisters, myself—we're all afraid of him. He..."

"Alex, no!" Jody protested. "This is all too personal! Please..."

"I want to. You're the first person I've trusted enough to tell this to. I feel like talking about it and I want you to understand me. Unless it will make you too uncomfortable?"

She propped her chin in her hand and stared at the flowered wall. Was this part of some plan, too? His trust in her was suspiciously sudden. But suppose he did need someone to talk to? Perhaps by listening she could determine his true motive.

Jody directed her gaze across the table. "No, not too uncomfortable. What worries me is that you'll be very sorry you've said anything. Please understand that I'm not going to allow personal matters to influence a business decision. I can't do that."

"I wouldn't want you to. And you can trust me there!"

"Okay, so back to your father, then."

"Obedience is the key word in our household, and always has been. Obedience to Pater from day one. You probably think it's weird for a man nearly thirty to be talking about minding his father, but childhood patterns are a lifelong prison. Does that make sense to you?"

"Yes," she replied. "We're all shaped by childhood experiences."

"Well, the lessons dinned into our young ears went something like this—first, last and always, father knows best. Then, forget the eye for an eye bit, it's two eyes for an eye in Pop's lexicon. And last, win at any price, losers are no better than worms."

Too appalled to speak right away, Jody simply sat there. She finally managed to say, "A charming man, your father." A less than adequate remark, but all she could think of.

Alex grinned. "Oh, he does have his good points."

"You could have fooled me! What possible good points could a tyrant have?"

He did not appreciate her terminology one bit. "Jody, I love and respect my father. He raised us the best way he knew. His own childhood was a nightmare. He really can't help what he is. It's just that he's made it a little hard for me to become my own man."

The understatement of the decade, she thought. "That's to be expected, I suppose, and I didn't mean to be rude. However, I'm not going to retract my description."

The arrival of their food came as a welcome distraction, and Jody hoped it would permanently derail the topic of Alex's home life. No such luck.

"In case you're thinking I never make a move on my own, let me tell you about my years at Harvard. Pop was in Europe all during my freshman year, with the happy result that I was free. Better yet, since he was there for a rest cure for some heart problems, mother had instructed me not to bother him with anything controversial. So there I was, away from Pop. It was safe to be just plain old me and, presto-chango, obedient Alex metamorphosed into a tiger. Instantly! I proceeded to change everything Pop had planned. Hey, you look like the Cheshire cat. Why so pleased?"

"For tigers there's hope. Sheep don't have much future," she said, instantly ashamed of this additional discourteous remark. What was the matter with her? Why had she suddenly developed thorns? It wasn't like her at all.

"You sure don't pussyfoot around, do you?" Alex questioned angrily. "I'm not a sheep."

Immediately her hand went to rest on his arm. "I'm sorry, I've been rude again, and it was unfair besides. I had no right saying such a thing after this short conversation. But you've made it sound as though you'd follow whatever your father wanted done. And, if we were in business together, it's possible that *he* could run Alferic's through you."

"No way!" The emphatic denial was tinged with real fear. "He wouldn't even be here in Minneapolis. Anyway, we'll have a contract, so how could he?"

"A good point. However, that's all in the future and I'm really interested in what changes you went through at Harvard."

He relaxed and gave her a wide smile. "Actually, I can't imagine why I got upset. One of the reasons I trust you is that you come right out with what you think and feel. A great trait and one I've seldom, if ever, run across."

"You ought to spend more time in the hinterlands," she said, adding a smile to soften her rather sharp reminder.

A huge laugh greeted her comment. "Nothing but good honest folk around the haystacks, is that it? Well, you might have a good point this time. At any rate, it's a statement I can validate for myself, since I plan to be spending more time around here. A lot more, if I have my way. Still want to hear about Harvard?"

"I do, and I'd also like some coffee."

Alex flagged a busboy, waited while he filled their cups and then continued his tale.

"First, I switched my major from business to the classics. Then I switched my roommate. You see, Pop had crossed a few palms with silver and gotten me bunked with a student from a socially impressive family. He turned out to be a good friend later, but I don't think that would have happened if I'd been shoved on him that first semester. Instead I teamed up with a fellow classics major, and we stayed together the entire four years. We're still good friends today. But all I wrote to Pop was that I was getting along with my roommate and pulling A's in all my courses. If he'd even remotely suspected that by courses I meant medieval history and literature, Greek and Hebrew, St. Thomas Aquinas, art and the church, he'd have slammed me into the military and found another heir. By the time he got back to visit...but, that comes later. Meantime, I did a third thing, and this one would have brought on a massive coronary—I went out for hockey."

"Hockey? *Ice* hockey?" Jody could hardly believe it, but he was nodding his assent. Carl had mentioned that Clif played for the 'U' and that seemed somehow fitting and appropriate—all that aggressiveness and competitive energy needed the outlet of a body-crunching sport—but, Alex? Book-loving, slenderly built Alex?

"I know it sounds incredible," he admitted. "I hardly seem the type—a mite small for all that crashing around. Actually, I never have figured out why I decided to try hockey. Something about proving my independence after all Pop's directives, I suppose. Whatever the reason, it turned out that my speed on the old blades made up for my lack of brawn, and then

I learned some other ways to compensate. Matter of fact, I became something of a star.''

"Good for you," she said. "Tell me, why would your father have had a coronary over you and hockey?"

"Pop doesn't believe in team sports. He claims they make you dependent on others for success, which is an underscored no-no with him. In our family, you win or lose on your own merits, and you'd best win if you don't want the back of his hand!''

Jody just shook her head in disbelief. She really didn't want to hear any more about this unhealthy relationship, and she suggested to Alex that they finish their coffee and go.

Jody firmly but politely turned aside his request for the chamber of commerce tour, stating her intention to put in a full afternoon of work. Leaving Alex to explore the city on his own, Jody returned to Alferic's. But she found herself accomplishing close to nothing, despite her good intentions. Images of Alex's face kept rising in front of her. Or, to be more precise, faces. The conversation had left her feeling there were two people under one skin—the gentle scholar and the young man rigidly controlled by his father. Both seemed real, but in truth, she didn't want to deal with Alex at all, one face or a dozen.

However, it wasn't that simple. Her commitments to Alferic's and her family demanded she explore the possibility of a partnership. As she always did when things got in a muddle, Jody picked up the telephone and dialed home.

"Mom? How are you feeling?"

Mrs. Jenson didn't give her a direct answer. "Jody, your voice tells me you need something. For that, I'm always feeling just fine."

"I love you, Mom, even if you are becoming a mind reader. I'll be right home."

FORTY-FIVE MINUTES LATER, she was seated beside her mother's bed, happy to be sharing her dilemma. Mrs. Jenson listened carefully to Jody's recap of her time with Alex, her impressions of his character and of his problems. Jody concluded by saying, "I wish you'd agree to meet him, Mom."

Her mother patted her hand in understanding. "I know you're worried because it's my money. Don't. Your father and I have had our day with Alferic's. It's your store now. I only want to save it for you. Why ever should I meet Alex? I said at the outset that your own judgment is sound, and I still feel that way. But that doesn't mean I won't talk it over with you."

"That glint in your eye tells me that in fact you're dying to, right?" Jody said, chuckling.

"Of course! You know how I love to talk, but first off, I have some news for you...both bad and sad. I heard from your Aunt Kirsten and Aunt Hulda this morning. Eric and Nils didn't get the extension on the loan that they asked for. It's being called in a week from Monday."

Jody slumped back in her chair. "Great! Just great! No chance in the world for a court date before then."

"Well, I wouldn't know about that, but Hulda did say they could get an extension on the basis of a signed contract for the sale of Alferic's."

"How very convenient!" An expletive burst from Jody as she got up to pace the floor. "Sorry about that. It just slipped out."

"No apologies necessary. It was warranted."

"Something fishy is going on . . . everything is playing into the Renards' hands. And darn it, with Alex here instead of old Mr. Renard, Clif isn't even on my side . . . not that he ever really was, I suppose."

Mrs. Jenson leaned forward from her pillows. "Why would that make a difference to Clif?"

"He didn't like Renard Senior at all. Called him a 'goon' and warned me not to be alone with him. He cautioned me about Alex, too, but basically thinks he's okay."

"Hmm . . . interesting. How about Alf? How does he feel?"

Jody shrugged. "He hasn't said anything except to get to know Alex better. Now that the extension on the loan has been turned down, he has to be torn in two over the whole thing. His mother must be upset."

"I agree. Except Kirsten didn't seem too upset. It was Hulda who was in tears. But then, she's always been a bit volatile. Kirsten's as stable as a mountain."

"Any suggestions?" Jody resumed her seat.

"Yes, though these are ideas I had before you told me about Clif's appraisal of Mr. Renard. Honey, the son may not be all that different from the father. Just better camouflaged. Anyway, here's what I was thinking this morning. We are firmly situated between the famous rock and a hard place. Two cornerstones of our lives are being threatened—the family and Alferic's. Which do we value most?"

"The family, naturally. But they got themselves into this mess. They made the mistake . . ."

"Jody, we *all* make mistakes and we all expect help from our loved ones. Now, while I'm fully as angry as you over their lack of foresight, I had pretty well decided that the happiest solution would be to trust in the Renards and hope both cornerstones would be saved. Though I wasn't going to say so unless you asked."

"Which I have. But are you saying that you don't feel that way anymore?"

Mrs. Jenson nodded her head emphatically. "I am indeed. If Clif is right, if *either* of the Renards is a goon, then it seems perfectly natural to suspect the validity of their dealings with Eric and Nils. Goons are not noted for being on the straight and narrow!"

Jody hopped to her feet. "You're right! If a person's that way at all, he'll be that way with anyone. My hesitation may actually help Eric and Nils in the end. So, now what? Some serious investigating, I should think."

"Exactly. You'll have to see more of Alex, I'm afraid."

Jody pulled an unhappy face. "Yuck! But you're right again. We can't let the note be called in just on the basis of some vague suspicions. What if we haven't got anything concrete by then?"

"We'll worry about that when it happens. Meanwhile, get started on finding some proof."

"What time is it?"

Her mother looked understandably bewildered at the abrupt topic change. "Three-thirty, why?"

"I'm going to call Clif right now." Jody rose to leave. "Mom? Why the big grin? Don't you think I should?"

"I think he is precisely who you should call. He's the one with the distrust of Renard Senior and the doubts about Alex, which makes him the logical choice. I'm just amused at your instinctive desire to talk things over with Clif. A very good instinct to follow, by the way. So let me know what he says. I'll just rest a bit while you call."

Jody gave her mother a kiss on the cheek and went to her own room down the hall to make the call in private. Unfortunately, Clif was with a client, but his secretary said he would return her call—it would just be a few minutes. For Jody, it was time spent having second thoughts about bothering him at all. He might think she was invading his requested thinking space. Maybe she should cancel the call and get hold of Warren instead. But, if something underhanded were indeed going on, he would want to know. His loyalties would then be solidly lodged in her camp.

The phone jangled.

"Jody, what is it? Can't you go skiing?" Clif's voice held more than enough anxiety to drive all thoughts of concern from Jody's head.

"No such luck, mister," she answered. "You're still going to be stuck with two novices on Saturday."

"Well, that's a relief! I mean, it's fun we're after, so the more the merrier," he hastily amended. "What can I do for you?"

"I'm not sure you can do anything, but I wanted to tell you about something that happened today and see if it raises any doubts in your mind about the Renards. My uncles had asked for an extension on their loan and it was turned down. They fully expected to get it, and there's no reason for a refusal. We've been in business here for over half a century."

"No defaults in the past?"

"Not that any of us, including my uncles, knows about. But, the thing that really makes me wonder, that makes me think it's all just too pat, is that the bank *will* extend the loan on the basis of a signed contract for the sale of Alferic's."

Clif pondered the situation for a few moments. "That is a bit too pat, I must admit. What bank is it?"

She told him and Clif jotted the name down. "I'll see what I can find out. I don't bank there, but I know someone who does. Better not get your hopes up, though. I realize that some wrongdoing would simplify your decision, but... I can't imagine Alex involved in dirty pool. He's a smoothie, but compared to his father he seems quite harmless. Tell me, what do you think of him as a person?"

Jody was silent, then finally answered, "I don't."

They both had a good laugh over her cryptic answer, and Clif prompted, "Do you mean that you don't think about him as a person at all or that you don't know what to think?"

"That I don't know what to think. He defies a neat file folder, as far as I can figure out."

"You mean he can't be categorized?"

"Not exactly. I mean, he loves history, books—old ones, rare ones, the antiquarian sort—and that should mean that he's gentle and ... well, comfortable to be with. Instead, he's uncomfortable somehow. For me, that is."

"Well, he still sounds harmless and certainly not much like his old man. Anyway, I'll get right on this, and I'll come by the store tomorrow... late afternoon, after my appointments are finished. Meantime, just relax. I'll take care of everything."

He rang off, leaving Jody in a glow of warmth, worries banished by his confident assurance. If only something would turn up. Then Clif would be at her side, and the two of them would rescue her uncles, and Alferic's would be saved. The world would be a most beautiful place, and they'd all live happily ever after. She laughed at herself as she returned to her mother's room to tell her the news.

CHAPTER TWELVE

THE BUZZER on Jody's desk sounded at four in the afternoon to announce Clif's arrival. Her request to send him right up elicited first a "will do" response and then a "wait a minute...Jody, I've lost him!"

"Never mind, I'll find him," she said, thinking that he might have gone into the stockroom to see how many of his suggestions had been implemented. But he wasn't there, so she went back out and scanned the selling floor. Clif was not among the customers, either. Perplexed by his vanishing act, she was just about ready to go back to her office when she decided to try the Rare Books room. And there he was, nose pressed to the grillwork of a case.

She could have hugged him on the spot, but she squashed the impulse and greeted him with a warm laugh.

He turned to her with a grin. "Came in for a sniff test and guess what? You were right. A very interesting smell—a bit musty, but interesting. Is that a de-humidifier I hear humming?"

"That's what it is. We really have to be careful of the temperature and humidity in here...like in a wine cellar, I suppose. Anything you'd like to see? I've got the keys if there is."

"No, I don't think so. Why the lock-up arrangement? Can't imagine anyone stealing a book, of all things." His expression added the unspoken phrase, unless he was an idiot.

"Surprise, Mr. McClelland, some people find them valuable enough to take the risk. We haven't had much trouble since Dad put the grilles and locks on. I've only had to handle one shoplifter."

"*After* the locks? How could anyone?"

"By being an old customer we never suspected. A man we'd known and sold to for years, a dear man really, who'd outfitted himself with a topcoat lined in huge pockets. We'd been obligingly opening the cases for him, and he'd been walking right out the door with a 'thank you for the delightful browse.' Poor man." She shook her head sadly at the memory.

"Poor man! He was a thief. What happened to him?"

She smiled and shrugged. "We didn't press charges. His daughter had leukemia, and he'd been selling the books to pay doctors and hospitals. He wasn't really a thief, just a desperate father."

Clif put an arm around her shoulder and dropped a kiss on the top of her head. "Soft heart you've got inside that beautiful package. I like that. So—" he stepped away "—I've got some news for you. Where shall we talk?"

The room was empty except for them, and there was a pleasant nook with a table and chairs. "Why not right here?" she suggested. "It's hardly the busiest part of the store, and I like it." She got them some coffee and then sat down to listen to his news.

"You were right on target in thinking things were far too pat. The loan officer who turned your uncles down came here three months ago from a branch facility just outside New York. And guess what? Our files show that Renard banks with that bank, albeit at the main operation downtown, but he just happens to live in the community where the branch in question is located.''

''Good Lord, that can't be a coincidence!''

''I'm more than a little inclined to agree. It's just too damn neat. Renard must have staged all this, although Alex may not know about it . . . about his father's part in it.''

''Remember my wondering how Renard knew about my uncles' financial straits?''

''Yes, I do. Right after that first conference . . . and Alex knew, too. Although that doesn't indicate that he also knew what his father meant to do about the loan. And of course, we don't have any proof of anything, period.''

''The bank officer didn't know anyone named Renard?''

''I didn't ask my friend to find out. I think we have to be careful, at this point anyway, not to tip our hand. I think you're just going to have to spend more time with Alex, and hope he drops some clues we can follow up.''

She smiled inwardly and allowed a faint curve to settle on her lips. All those lovely plural pronouns! ''You've been saying 'we' and 'our.' Does that mean *you* think I shouldn't sell?''

''Not necessarily, Miss Jenson.'' He winked at her. ''Don't go leaping to conclusions. Although I'm certainly not about to say 'sell,' either. I'm in the neutral camp, I guess you could say—suspicious, but no conclusive proof.''

Jody sat back, a dejected look on her face. ''I don't want to see more of Alex, but I agree with you. It's the only thing to do. Did you say anything to Clark about this?''

''Not specifically. But, I did ask him if he had any ideas on why Renard wants your particular store and building so badly. His answer was, 'Because he can't stand being thwarted and the man's as twisted as a corkscrew. Bordering on the insane, if you ask me. Though Alex seems rational and quite sane.' ''

''Looks like I'm the only one worried about Alex.'' A light bang of her fist on the table showed her frustration.

''Listen to me, Jody.'' He bent forward and took her hand in his. ''Your own instincts are perfectly sound. Go with them. If when the time comes, you want to say 'no sale,' don't listen to anyone else. It's your store, your career, your decision, and you have to live with it. Understand?''

''I understand and thank you . . . very much.''

He squeezed her hand and then released it. ''Good. One more thing. Since something about Alex is making you uncomfortable—and me, to some degree—and there's a good chance Renard is unstable, I'm not happy thinking about you alone with either of them. Would you please be sure other people are around when you're with Alex? Not even ride in a car with him alone? At least, not with him at the wheel. Can you manage that?''

''I *will* manage that,'' she answered, hugging his concern to herself as one more indicator of how much he cared. One of these days he would surely admit it to himself.

As they were leaving the room, Clif looked around and slowed his steps. ''There wouldn't happen to be anything by Dickens in here, would there?''

"I'll check," Jody said quickly, praying that she'd find something really special to pique his interest. A look through the record book hanging by the door revealed she had a true treasure in stock. "We sure do, a terrific one." She unlocked a case and handed him a copy of *A Christmas Carol*.

"Nice binding," Clif commented, slowly turning the pages. "Interesting printing.... And I'll be damned. The paper *does* feel good." He turned back to the title page. "'Published 1843.' Jody! What's this?"

"What does it look like?" She joined him to read the inscription on the frontispiece. "To my very dear friend, Annette." It was signed, "Charles."

"Are you trying to tell me Charles Dickens wrote this?" Clif obviously thought it was a forgery of some sort.

"It's been authenticated," she told him, trying not to laugh at his expression.

Clif didn't say anything for a while, just held the slender volume, smoothing the leather cover with a finger. "Charles Dickens handled this very book himself... wrote in it ... gave it to someone he cared about. My father would love having this."

"It is for sale, you know. Do you want to buy it?"

"I most certainly do." He handed it to her and began pacing alongside the wall of cases, staring in through the grilles, seeing it all with new eyes. Then he walked to the door and his gaze swept the main floor.

"I've never been much of a reader for pleasure," he admitted when he returned to her side. "Facts, learning, yes. But not for pleasure. I think I've been missing out on something." His eyes roamed the room once more.

Jody slipped her arm through his. "One of the great things about reading is that it's never too late to start. There's a whole new world out there for you to discover."

"I'll count on you to introduce me." He smiled down at her. "Later, though. Right now I've got to get to a dinner meeting."

Before they left the Rare Books room, Clif took a last, ostentatious sniff. "Nice, but I prefer your lilacs any day of the week."

Jody laughed. "Well, I certainly hope so. I'd hate to lose out to a room, no matter what department."

They walked to the door, his arm across her shoulders. "Therein lies my problem. I've almost come to the conclusion that you wouldn't lose out to a single person or thing in the universe in any department at all!"

"Why, you poor man. Imagine having to deal with a mind-boggling problem like that. I do feel sorry for you."

"Hush, woman, I'm simply trying to proceed slowly for once in my life. I'm having a hard enough time as it is without the sparkling mischief in your eyes throwing me off stride."

Jody closed her eyes as she opened the door for him. "Is that better?"

"No," he grumbled. "You're still throwing me off stride."

"Well, don't stumble and fall on your way out."

He chuckled and brushed a kiss on her forehead. "I probably already have. See you Saturday. Be careful, and let me know if you get any glimmers of what's going on."

It wasn't until she'd gotten back to her desk that she remembered she hadn't thanked him again for finding her grandfather's journal or told him about all the reinforcement for their case, and that odd reference to a scandal of some sort. Oh well, Saturday would come soon enough.

She glanced at her phone. Stuck on it was a message to call Alex. She picked up the receiver and dialed his hotel.

He had three requests of her. The first was dinner that night, which she turned down. The other two seemed reasonable so she said fine to them. Yes, he could come into the store the following afternoon, and yes she would go to a hockey game at the university afterward. Plenty of people would be around, and she was quite sure she could persuade Britta and Alf to go to the game, too. Better yet, Alex could meet her at her cousin's and she need never be alone with him.

Next she called Britta, who brushed aside Jody's apologies for using their home as some sort of way station in her social life. She also said that they would love to see a hockey game. A quick call back to Alex resulted in his reluctant consent to a foursome, and Jody hung up the phone feeling confident that she had arranged the evening in a way that satisfied her—and would please Clif.

ALEX'S BEHAVIOR the following afternoon reinforced Jody's impression that Alferic's would be safe under his ownership. Assuming, of course, that Mr. Renard stayed away. But his father wasn't anywhere near the store on this day, so Alex could most definitely be his own man. He did so by remaining in the Rare Books room for most of the time, talking to the appraisal expert Jody used. That gentleman was highly complimentary of Alex's scholarly background and his quickness to learn. Thus reassured, Jody relaxed and prepared to enjoy the hockey game.

The four of them were part of a very large crowd as they approached the field house that evening. Both Britta and Jody expressed amazement at the numbers interested in a college hockey game.

"I understand it's *the* game of the regular season," Alex explained. "Seems the University of Denver knocked you out of the divisional play-offs last year, so your Gophers are primed to wipe the ice with them tonight."

"A real battle in the offing," said Alf. "As in, war games on ice."

"Right you are and believe me, these guys will have forgotten all the rules of sportsmanlike conduct, if they'd ever heard of them. Should be a slam-bang game."

Their seats were excellent, had cost a fortune according to Alex, but were well worth the money and wrangling it had taken to get them. Alf looked around at the varsity-jacketed people they were surrounded by and commented that they seemed to be in the alumni section. No wonder the tickets had been costly. They were some of the best seats in the house.

Jody hardly listened to her companions' conversation because, directly below them, in the row behind the Gopher bench, she had spotted a letterman's jacket on a familiar back—Clif's. Her instant elation at the sight of him was just as rapidly banished by another sight. Next to him sat a woman, black-haired and wearing a sweater that did nothing to hide her voluptuousness. *Good heavens*, she thought, *if that's what he likes, I might as well forget it. A more opposite appearance from mine I can't imagine.*

A raw wound began opening inside her. Somehow she'd thought—hoped—that he wasn't dating others. It had clearly been a vain hope and probably foolish, given his life-style, a life-style that obviously hadn't changed. The wound spread and throbbed, even as she forced herself to focus on the game.

Happily the speed, excitement and razzle-dazzle of the action soon pushed the hurt from her immediate consciousness. Jody's familiarity with hockey consisted chiefly of cursory glances at the television when her father and Carl had been watching a game. The brilliant skating going on before her eyes came as a surprise, as did the actual sight of the goalies.

How the men could even move was beyond her comprehension. With chest, back, arms and legs encased in thick padding, gloves the size of slabs of bacon and a full mask, they each reminded her of herself as a toddler, bundled up by her mother to brave below freezing temperatures. She'd been immobilized by the sheer bulk of her clothing.

"Oh, no!" she groaned as Denver scored.

"Damn," muttered Alex. "Idiot defenseman screened his own goalie."

As the teams faced off again, Jody tried to imagine either Clif or Alex down there thumping into the boards, careering off to crash into an opponent, then whizzing down the ice after the puck, viciously bumping everyone out of the way. It wasn't at all difficult to superimpose Clif on a player down there—he was always stomping over the opposition—but Alex of the rare books? He wasn't feisty, didn't behave like a commanding general leading a charge.

Her thinking came to an abrupt halt as Denver scored again, just as the buzzer sounded to end the first period.

They stood to let some people past, including Alf and Britta who wanted Cokes. Jody could hear Alex grumbling.

"Good Lord, what a sorry show your old Gophers are putting on. I expected a real fight, not a pushover."

"Maybe this is their game plan. There *are* two more periods, aren't there?"

Alex hooted with laughter. "Some game plan! Nope, that's not it. The coach must be a real loser, nothing's happening along the boards or in the corners."

"Nothing's happening? Where have your eyes been for the last half hour? On the crowd? Alex, it's a wonder the players haven't all been piled into ambulances by this time."

He chuckled and touched her cheek lightly. "What I meant was that, with a little moxie, there are ways to slow up your enemies, even put them out of business for a while. Remember I mentioned yesterday there were other ways to compensate for lack of size? Well, that's what I meant. All you have to do is make sure the ref doesn't see you."

Clif had stood up to stretch and scan the arena. When he met Jody's eyes, she could almost see the answering light in his. He was over his seatmate's knees and by Jody's side in seconds.

Alex was obviously annoyed and he made no effort to hide it. "McClelland, you keep turning up like the well known bad penny. What are you doing? Tailing us?"

Clif laughed, not in the least put out by the insolent questions. "No, but maybe I should be, if it bothers you so much. I'm just here to cheer my alma mater on to victory. What about you?"

"This was my game back at Harvard and I brought Jody thinking we'd see a real contest here, but it looks completely hopeless. Your alma mater's fielded a bunch of wimps."

Jody laid a restraining hand on his arm. "Alex, please. Clif played for the 'U.' They're not wimps, and there is still time left in the game."

With a visible effort to quell his anger, Alex produced a smile. "Right. That remark was premature. Maybe they'll pull it out of the fire yet. Why don't you amble down and give them some pointers, Clif?"

"They don't need any advice from me. The coach is more than capable. By the way, if you want anything to eat or drink, you'd best get going. I'll stay and talk to Jody. No point in her going with you and getting splashed with catsup and pushed around in the crowd."

It was easy to see that Alex wanted to protest the arrangement, but he could hardly do so without appearing to want Jody elbowed and bespeckled with hot dog makings. He marched off in a grump.

"Pleasant fellow," Clif observed. "And if I needed any proof of his intention to widen his field of conquest, I just got it. Come on, let's go find a wall to lean against."

"Anything suspicious turn up?" he asked, once they'd found a bit of privacy.

"Not a thing, except his irritability just now. Something positive, though, has come out of the day." She told him about Alex's time in the store. "So I'm sure I'm right to think we could work together with no trouble."

"Hmm...could be our worries are groundless, I suppose. We'll see." He glanced down toward his seat and gave a grimace of annoyance. "In a few minutes I'm going to have to go back and endure that silly female my so-called buddy scraped up for me. Didn't even ask me, the bum. Just brought her along."

A surge of happiness rushed through Jody. "You didn't ask her?"

Clif stared at her, an expression close to astonishment on his face. "Good God, no. Is that what you've been thinking? I would never ask anyone...for weeks and weeks...no one..."

He was clearly distressed, and Jody knew that not only had he not dated anyone else since he'd met her, he also wanted to be very sure that she knew it.

"Clif, I'm so glad..."

A tremendous roar reverberated through the stands as the Gophers took to the ice for the second period. Alex appeared, handing her a Coke she really didn't want. He sent a curt nod in Clif's direction and guided Jody firmly to her seat. Sliding in along the row, she glanced over her shoulder to see Clif watching her progress. He smiled and saluted her with a small wave, then went down to his own seat.

Alex clicked their paper cups in a toast. "Here's to a more successful second period for your 'U.'"

"It will be," she replied confidently. "How about telling me what you think should be going on along the boards and in the corners?"

"Sure." He began to drape an arm over the back of her seat, caught the warning look in her eyes and rested an elbow on his own seat instead.

"The thing to do," he confided, "is to get them where they're not padded, right here in the solar plexus. Ram the butt of your stick into the guy. It'll double him up. No need to look so horrified; everyone does it. Sure, it's illegal, that's why you've got to hide it from the ref. Another good one is cross-checking. Say a guy's skating close to the boards—you come up on him, stick held parallel to the ice and slam into him so the stick catches him across the shoulder blades. Mashes him right into the boards. Harder to get away with, but very effective."

Jody was genuinely shocked. A queasy sensation rose in her stomach. "Your coach taught you that? He wanted you to play that way? Alex, that's sick!"

"No, it's all part of the war. Winning's all that matters in a war. From the look on your face, I'd best not elaborate on the action in the corners."

"It's not a war, it's a game and winning is not all that matters. You sound as bad as your father."

"No, I'm not. Don't ever say that, or even think it. That was just my attitude on the ice, and I wasn't the only one out there who did those things by any stretch."

"Well, I don't like them, either," she snapped at him.

"You're not much of a realist, I'm afraid."

"That depends on the reality you perceive. Let's concentrate on the game. Is it my imagination, or is Minnesota looking better down there?"

"It's not your imagination. Something's sure lit a fire under them. They're out-skating Denver and . . . a breakaway!"

The stands erupted in yells, everyone scrambling to his feet to urge the Gophers' flying right winger down the ice. Denver had a lone defenseman to stop him, and he might as well have been with his teammates at the opposite end of the arena for all the good he did. The Minnesotan slipped past him, lured the goalie out of position with a brilliant feint, then scooped the puck over his sprawled form into an upper corner of the net.

"He scored!" Alex grabbed her in a bear hug and lifted her off her feet. "By God, they'll do it yet."

He was right. Another goal was scored in the second period an instant before the buzzer, and a thriller of a third period resulted in two more goals. Minnesota handed the Denver champions their worst defeat of the season.

Pandemonium had Jody covering her ears. As she joined in the cheering exuberance around her, she was unable to hear a word Alex was saying. Clif was nowhere to be seen. He and his friends must have already been headed for a victory party. Caught like a twig in a current by the raucous mob heading for the exits, she accepted the security of Alex's arm holding her tightly against him. She let herself be carried along, bellowing the University of Minnesota's fight song along with everyone else. By the time they reached the car, her voice was hoarse, but she was still carrying the tune in a hum as she climbed into the back seat.

"College songs are fun," Britta exclaimed, "and so are college sports. Thanks, Alex, for including us in your plans."

"My pleasure," he answered, though he sent a rueful sidelong glance at Jody.

Coming out of the parking lot, Alex peered out the window to study the downtown Minneapolis skyline.

"That star sure isn't much of a beacon anymore, is it?"

"What star?" asked Alf. "Oh, you mean the Beacon Tower? The star on top?"

"Yes, that's the one. Damn near eclipsed now by all the other lights and taller buildings. Too bad."

It was on the tip of Jody's tongue to tell Alf about their grandfather's reference to the tower and a scandal, but something held her back. She kept quiet, realizing it was an odd reference for Alex to make. Why would he care about the old Beacon Tower with its bright North Star on top? How had he even heard of it, for that matter? The guidebooks pretty well ignored it in favor of more impressive sights that warranted mention. She hadn't thought of it herself for years, and here, in the space of one week, it had come up twice. What, if any, significance this might have escaped her, but she remained silent just the same.

Jody said good-night when they reached Alf's, her excuse being that tomorrow was a working day. Alex walked her to her car and then leaned against her door as if prepared to chat.

"I'm going back to New York tomorrow," he informed her.

"Oh?" Jody didn't know whether to be happy over this turn of events or distressed. She might be forced to come to a decision based solely on the skimpy evidence she had now, none of which could be proven.

"For how long?" she asked.

"Until next Friday, a week from tomorrow."

The last working day before the note fell due. How interesting, and how clever! Another push to get her to make a decision with insufficient information, Jody decided. They certainly knew the pull of family on her.

Alex had the grace to look somewhat embarrassed. "I know. This wasn't my idea. Pop's recalling me, as it were. Left on my own, I'd stay right here because I want you to be comfortable with whichever way you chose to go. I know you have to feel easy about my owning the store before you can make up your mind, and you can't very well do that long distance. But there it is."

"Yes, there it is. However, it isn't really you I'm hesitating over so much, it's your father, and the speed of all this."

Alex flashed a smile. "Thanks for the trust. I assure you it's well placed. You can have Alferic's and save your uncles at the same time, believe me. I'll make it happen."

Strange phraseology, she thought. Why would he have to "make" anything happen after an agreement?

As if on cue, Alex said, "I've had Clark draw up a contract for Warren to look over. It should be in his office tomorrow. Maybe it will be helpful to have our offer in black and white, even if you don't sign it. Anyway, you can study it, see what you think."

"Sounds fine to me. I'll probably hear from Warren tomorrow." She stamped her feet to warm them up and stretched out a gloved hand. "Thanks for a fun evening and have a good flight home."

Alex took her hand and held it. "I'd much rather be staying...much rather. Seeing Pop right now is something less than appealing, especially when there's so much appeal right here. I'll be calling you from New York, and I'll see you on Friday."

She withdrew her hand but smiled and said that a phone call would be fine, then got in her car and left with no mention of Friday. Driving away, she felt troubled. He'd seemed so sad, clearly unhappy over having to go back, uneasy over facing his father. If there was any underhanded plan afoot, she didn't think Alex was very enthusiastic about it. And then there was that odd "make it happen" phrase he'd used. As far as she was concerned, every time she thought about Alex he came up a large question mark...almost a nonperson. Except for one definite trait—he was his father's errand boy, as thoroughly conditioned as one of Pavlov's dogs.

Well, tomorrow she could see the offer in writing. Maybe having a document to study would help clear her mind. Meanwhile, she'd cease brooding over him and focus on what she wanted in the contract to protect Alferic's. She'd best get them written down for Warren.

THE EXPECTED CALL from her lawyer came the next morning, and Jody went over to his office at noon to hear his thoughts.

"The contract looks quite acceptable to me," Warren assured her, glancing over her list of items to be included. "Most of these I've already covered. Here's a copy of the clauses I've added. One of them gives you the right of first refusal should Renard decide to sell, another makes sure that the name Alferic's remains with you. The other conditions you can read for yourself. Hmm. You want a proviso to guarantee Jenson management in the future should you decide to step down. That's a tough stipulation to uphold in court. Competency would be a factor, for one thing. However, I'll think of something and include it."

Warren took off his glasses, thumb and forefinger rubbing the bridge of his nose. "Jody, I'm here to see that you get what you want. As concisely as possible, would you please tell me exactly what that is?"

"To save Alferic's and to save Uncle Eric and Uncle Nils," she proclaimed.

Warren laughed at her single sentence. "Not only concise, but succinct, and precisely as I surmised. All right, the contract would seem to be the answer, if—and it's a very big if—if we can trust the Renards."

"Why would that be so very important? I mean, wouldn't the contract protect me? I thought that's what it was for."

"It is, and it will. My concern hasn't to do with your rights under the law if they break the contract. What bothers me is that no matter how many legal fences we construct, we're faced with another hassle should they decide to jump them. I'd hate for that to happen to you. You've been through quite enough this past year. Tell me, do you find Alex a trustworthy man?"

Jody hesitated, unsure of just how to answer. "I've only known him for four days. All I can really say is that I don't have any concrete reason to distrust him. And now he's back in New York."

Warren's fist hit his desk in anger. "Jody, that is insupportable! Completely unacceptable. Why?"

Jody shrugged. "Renard Senior 'recalled' him, to use Alex's word. Warren, could something fishy be going on?"

"My dear young lady, something fishy can always be going on. What did you have in mind?"

She told him what she and Clif had learned about the bank refusal, also about Clif's general unease and her own discomfort with Alex.

Warren sat up straight, glasses decisively replaced. "That does it! You're not signing a thing. Having Alex absent himself so conveniently, thus preventing you from having a fair chance at getting to know him, is bad enough. Now the loan. I've known your family for years, and I admit to being astounded when I learned about the bank's refusal to grant Eric and Nils an extension. I assumed there was something in the past that I didn't know—default history or some such thing. Now it all seems highly questionable to me. Therefore, all I'm going to do is get our version of the contract completed and give you a copy. Maybe I'll call Clark and see if we can get young Renard back here before Friday. Meantime, I want you to do nothing this week. We'll just let it ride. Does that meet with your approval?"

Jody said it most certainly did, and she walked back to the store on light feet. No worrisome thoughts for a week, hallelujah! There were times when lawyers could be the very best people of all to have around. And tomorrow she'd be seeing her favorite one. The thought brought several more hallelujahs and even lighter feet to breeze her through Alferic's door in a near dance step.

CHAPTER THIRTEEN

"AUNT JODY, Mr. 'Clelland's here." Kirstie banged the front door open. "You have to ski now. Mr. 'Clelland's here." Having blasted her announcement at triple forte, she tore back to the driveway to join Ivar, who was shaking hands with Clif and being introduced to Mike. Like some diminutive snowbird, Kirstie darted around herding them to the porch, where Jody, Britta and Alf waited.

Jody's heart began tugging at its moorings the second she saw young Michael. He was so like Clif in physical appearance, but lacked his life and energy entirely. His eyes, the same heavenly blue of Clif's, were grave and weary. His fine mouth seemed pinched, and his demeanor was one of rigid endurance. Standing before her was the oldest, saddest, eight-year-old she'd ever seen. But one look at his jawline told her he'd make it with a half a chance.

"Hello, Mike," Jody said, extending her hand in matching gravity. "I see that you have your uncle's determined chin. Great success in your future, young man." She winked at him.

Her reward came instantly with an answering bit of light in Mike's eyes, a brief twitch of his tight lips.

"Are you a fortune-teller, Miss Jenson?"

"Only when I'm positive about something," she answered.

"Oh," was his only response, and then he turned his attention to Ivar and Kirstie, both of whom had set up a clamor, begging to be taken along on the outing.

"Not today." Britta shushed them with hugs. "As soon as Aunt Jody becomes the champion of the slopes, I'm sure she'll take you along."

"Britta, they'll be ancient if they wait for that unlikely day," Jody protested with a laugh. "Don't worry, kids, I'll take you as soon as I can stand up for five minutes running. That ought to be this year sometime."

"Promise?"

"Word of honor."

They began exhorting Mr. McClelland to teach her fast, and instructing Jody to pay attention and learn it all today. Then they were shushed once more, this time by their father. "Enough already! You can check out Aunt Jody's progress in a few hours. Your mother has asked them to have supper with us when they're done, so just hold your horses and settle down."

During this exchange Clif had been quietly observing Michael, who, in turn, was observing the children, his expression that of pure bewilderment. He hadn't said a word, but now that they were leaving he was forced to respond as Ivar spoke.

"I'll show you my fort when you come back, Mike," he said.

"Okay," Michael mumbled, a careless lifting of his shoulders adding that he couldn't care less.

Clif put a hand on his nephew's shoulder and offered the other hand to Ivar for a shake. "Thank you. We'll count on that, although if we don't get going, we won't make it back until bedtime."

They drove off to a chorus of well-wishing and farewells from the whole Jenson family.

"Whew." Jody turned to look at Michael in the back seat. "Was all that a bit much for you? I'm afraid we're a noisy group, everybody talking at once, and all the time."

Another shrug from Michael. "I didn't mind," he mumbled and then fell silent.

"Good," she replied, as if that was all the response she expected, and then she turned back to chat with Clif.

"How about some pointers before I have to tackle an honest-to-goodness hill?"

"Stay loose." Clif grinned at her. "I mean it. Relax—knees flexed..." He went on about where to keep her body weight and how to lean just a bit on the downhill ski to change direction. From time to time he commented over his shoulder to Michael. No responses were forthcoming from the back seat.

They began the afternoon in the ski shop, getting Jody equipped with boots and Michael completely outfitted. While Mike was busy trying things on with the help of a clerk, Clif drew Jody aside.

"Any luck during the rest of the evening with Alex?"

"No, unless more doubts than ever count. I'm really coming to the conclusion that he jumps when Papa whistles, regardless of his own wishes. Makes me wonder how much I could count on Alex in the store."

"You should wonder. It's got to be no go if Renard is in the picture. You didn't sign that contract Clark drew up, did you?"

"Heavens no! Warren and I went over it, added some clauses, but we still have a week. And, guess what? Alex is back in New York until Friday, summoned by you know who."

Clif made a face of disgust. "Another maneuver to pressure you. Damn them!"

"I feel the same way. There's another thing, too, something that won't quit wandering through my mind." She recounted the mention in her grandfather's journal of a scandal during the building of the Beacon Tower, then Alex's surprising interest in the very same building. "There's no reason in the world to connect the two things. Maybe I'm just getting overeager about finding incriminating evidence."

"A little woman's intuition at work?" He smoothed an affectionate hand along her cheek. "Pays to follow up on those hunches. What year was the tower built? Did your grandfather say?"

"No, the journal rambles along as if he just wrote down the things that he wanted to, or thought were important."

"Well, here comes Mike, so we'll have to get going, but first thing next week I'll do some checking in the newspaper archives and see what I come up with."

"Clif," Jody protested, "you're doing all the legwork on this—"

"While you've been stuck with Alex. That's work enough. I'll tackle the newspaper. And now, you two, time for some intensive instruction."

They headed for the bunny hill, where Clif immediately left a wobbly Jody and a still silent Michael to talk to the instructor about his new pupils. Gamely trying to stay upright and get a feel for the skis, she nearly fell over when she heard Mike's voice beside her.

"We aren't allowed to make noise at my house. It makes my mother's boyfriend mad. And I've never been a success at anything, so that was a dumb fortune that you told."

Jody stopped her floundering efforts and stared down at the defiant young face at her side. "Well—" she groped for words "—I will say one thing, Mike. When you do say something, it's sure worth hearing!"

Defiance changed to surprise and then to a tentative smile. "You're not mad at me for saying all that? Calling your fortune dumb?"

"No, of course I'm not. You're entitled to your own opinion, even if it's wrong. And it is. That was a true prophecy, you'll see."

"Crap!" He spat the word, followed it with a contrite, "sorry" and then looked over his shoulder at his uncle to see if he'd overheard.

"He's still busy with the teacher. He can't hear a word we say. Why wouldn't you have wanted him to know what you said?"

"I don't know." Mike cast his eyes downward and began busily sliding his skis forward and back in embarrassment.

"Because he'd be mad at you?"

"No, he's never mad at me. But...maybe he wouldn't like me anymore." His skis were sliding furiously now.

"Your Uncle Clif loves you. He told me so."

"He does? He said that?" Mike smiled as brightly as the snow they stood on.

"He does. He did, and here he comes. I'm not looking forward to this lesson."

His astonishment was huge. "You're not scared, are you? Uncle Clif won't let anything happen to you."

A spray of white fluff and the savior was at hand. "Darn right I won't, son. Nothing but fun today—no fears. The class starts in five minutes. Let's do a little practicing while we wait."

Jody was so upset by Michael's words that she could barely pay attention to Clif's patient instructions. Here was a truly tragic reason for denying marriage. Marriage would mean children to Clif, and he would never chance a union that might put his youngsters in Mike's shoes, would never permit one of his own to be in the position of coping with pain he was too young to bear and knowledge he was too young to understand.

But a more important concern for her at the moment was, what she could do to help this little boy in his anguish. All she could think of was giving him a quick hug as the instructor lined them up. She promptly fell down, bringing chuckles from the group, a resigned sigh from the teacher and solicitous help from Michael. He certainly wasn't having any trouble with these cumbersome boards!

"Mike," she grumbled, "it's not fair for you to look as if you'd been born on skis when I look like Calamity Jane."

"You'll do better in a while," he assured her in all seriousness, but when he saw her smile he actually laughed.

For what seemed like hours, Jody tried hard to get the hang of a sport that she was becoming increasingly convinced was the most difficult in the world. Trying to snowplow, she kept falling forward. Herringbone climbs had her tumbling every which way.

Downhill runs had her closing her eyes in prayer, and the rope tow had her swearing words she wasn't aware she knew. Michael, on the other hand, was by far the best in the class. Every feature on his face glowed in enjoyment, and for Jody, the sight more than made up for her own dismal progress.

Clif had gone off to make a few good runs of his own but was right there when the class ended. "Well, son, I could see that you were the star of the group—a real natural."

"I was the best." Mike drew himself up proudly. "Will you take me on a real hill now?"

"I sure will. Where's Miss Jenson?"

Michael pointed to the top of the bunny incline. "She's that yellow blob up there that just fell down. Uncle Clif, I don't think she's a natural."

"Just wait here a minute. I'll go get her."

Jody saw him coming as she tried to rise from her latest sprawl. The effort only made more sitzmarks in the snow, so she gave it up and sat there.

"You all right?" He had her on her feet in an instant.

"Yes and no. Yes, because Mike's so happy and because I'm in one piece. No, because every muscle aches, I'm sopping wet and I'm the worst skier this little bump of a hill has ever seen."

"Yes...well...it all takes a while...lots of patience..." Clif looked concerned as he gestured at her damp jacket and pants. "Does this mean you'd like to leave?"

"Not on your life. Do you think I'd let the likes of this slope defeat me?"

Clif laughed and exclaimed, "Good for you. I'd hate to take Mike away right now. Haven't seen such joy on his face in years. Come on, I'll coach you down.''

Jody shook her head. "Thanks, but no thanks. You and Mike just go on your merry way. I'll manage by myself. Shouldn't take me more than three hours to conquer this thing and heaven knows, I've got enough instructions clogging my brain."

"You sure?"

"Positive."

He seemed on the point of giving her a kiss, but apparently thought better of it. "In that case, I'll pick up the champ down there and see how he does on a tougher run."

"Give him a great big hug from me."

"Will do, and thanks for hangin' in there."

"You're welcome. I think."

He left with a chuckle and they waved to her from the bottom of the slope before skiing over to a chair lift on one of the steeper hills. The hill they were about to ride up made Jody shudder just looking at it.

To her surprise, maneuvering her skis seemed much easier without the rest of the class around, without an instructor calling out commands and without being concerned about holding everyone else up. Her first attempt got her to the bottom without a spill. Of course, she'd traversed about five times instead of going straight down, but who cared? She'd made it. The rope tow behaved itself, and she made yet another successful run. On the third try she decided to attempt a straight line and forget all this zigging and zagging. She reached the bottom in an upright position. Why, this might be an enjoyable sport after all, Jody thought enthusiastically. One more identical run and her hopes were soaring.

Clif and Michael chose this moment to do a little reconnaissance of her progress. Filled with newfound confidence, she imitated their skating motions to reach the tow and decided that it was a simple maneuver. She grabbed the rope like an old pro and after it towed her to the top of the hill, she came down in one smooth motion with a nice crouch and sideslipped to a stop. Their cheers were the first she knew of their presence.

"Hey, how about that, guys?" she crowed.

"That was great, Miss Jenson." Michael came up and executed a neat hockey-type stop.

"But I'll never match that move, I'm afraid. You look terrific!"

"Thanks. You'll match it, just keep practicing." Michael was clearly reveling in his status as an expert in Jody's eyes.

"He's right, Jody, you're doing great. Come on with us now. It's time you tried an intermediate run." Clif pointed at the very hill she'd shuddered at.

"Clif, no. I'm not ready for that. Anyway, it's sure to have modules on it and I don't know—" Mike and Clif suddenly burst into laughter, interrupting her statement. "What's so funny?" she demanded.

"Jody," Clif coughed out, "it's *moguls*, not modules. Modules . . . dear Lord."

"Clifton McClelland, stop laughing this minute." The indignation in her voice was feigned, and Clif simply went on laughing, but Michael took it seriously. His amusement ceased instantly and he looked frightened.

Jody winked at him again and, as had happened earlier, a bit of light rose in his eyes and a smile twitched his lips. She returned her attention to Clif, whose laughter had finally subdued to a wide grin.

"Really," she scolded playfully. "It is quite too much to expect me to do computers and skiing all in the same few weeks. All in the same year, even."

"Yes, ma'am, no more laughter at your expense. That's a promise. Now, shall we be on our way?"

"I really don't think I'm ready. I've only just gotten comfortable with this."

"Listen, I'll be right beside you every minute, with Mike on the other side. Just give it one try. You'll never know what skiing really feels like on this little bump, as you called it. That's a long run over there, but a very gentle one."

"We'll protect you," Mike added confidently.

"Okay," she said reluctantly. "One try and one try only. But, be prepared! I'm going to traverse the entire thing because it only looks long to me. Forget gentle."

The chair proved much easier to get on than the rope; all she had to do was sit down when Clif gave her the word. Getting off was another matter altogether. She did everything Clif told her to and—splat! Falling wasn't too bad really. If she'd learned nothing else all afternoon, she'd most assuredly learned how to get up.

Clif positioned the three of them at the top, Jody in the center, and all of them pointed toward a line of trees on the other side of the run. She arrived at that destination with no problem at all. In turning around to face the direction from which they'd come, she only got her skis crossed once, and Clif caught her before she fell.

After several successful runs, she decided to try a steeper angle. Halfway across she heard a shout from above them, turned her head to see what was going on and gasped in horror. A giant of a man was hurtling toward them, poles windmilling wildly, plainly out of control. Clif gave Jody a shove, snatched Michael's hand, and sent them both flying toward the trees. Then he took off after the terrified skier, shouting at him to drop his lethal poles. Jody had a brief glimpse of him reaching the man's side and starting to help him, before she felt herself falling.

She did a sort of sideslip on her rump and lost her poles. But miraculously she wound up with both skis still on and parallel, her behind firmly perched about eight inches from the backs, in a picture-perfect crouch position. And then she began sliding slowly downhill, her speed increasing gradually until it reached an alarming rate. Jody closed her eyes, realized her folly instantly, and reopened them.

Oh no! she thought. *People all over the hill, me headed straight for them, and it's miles to the bottom.*

"Look out below," she yelled, seeing nothing but a blur of startled faces as she shot between skiers. Jody began to smile as the bottom of the hill came encouragingly close. The smile never reached her lips. She was headed straight for a stand of trees!

"Oh Lord...goodbye, Clif...I love you...." She hugged her knees, forehead pressed between them, eyes squinched shut—and drilled a perfect line between two pines.

Minus skis at last, she landed in a heap at the feet of a portly gentleman onlooker, his eyes starting from their sockets and a hot dog halfway into his mouth.

"Your mustard's dripping," she quipped, and then laughter began bubbling helplessly, uncontrollably building on itself, until Clif's frantic voice finally brought her to her senses.

"Jody! Jody, my God, are you all right?"

"Fine. I don't know why, but I'm fine. Did I hurt anyone?"

"No, not a soul." He helped her up.

"I didn't protect you," a sad-faced Michael said.

"There's no way on earth you could have, so don't even think about it. You wanted to and that's what counts. You're a gallant young man, Michael McClelland."

The overweight gentleman was still standing there, though he'd managed to swallow the hot dog. "This place is too dangerous," he announced, then stalked off, shaking his head and swiping at the mustard on his coat.

Clif retrieved her skis from the copse she'd hurtled through and came back looking both cross and worried. "I don't know how you ever made it! Why in God's name didn't you just sit down when you started moving?"

"Sit down? That's precisely what I've been trying not to do all afternoon. Of all the ridiculous... anyway, I never thought of it." Her admission brought on another bout of hilarity.

"Well—" Clif hugged her hard "—next time, think of it. If anything ever happened to you..."

"It won't, for the simple reason that there isn't going to be a next time. I'm exhausted and dripping wet, so I'm off to the ski shop to trade in these boots for some smashing après-ski clothes. Much more my speed—a fire, a gorgeous outfit and maybe I can rustle up a backgammon devotee."

"Are you sure you won't give it another try?"

"I am very sure. I got the feel of skiing and I pass. It's all yours and Mike's with my blessing, so get a move on. I'll wait in the lodge."

A feeling of deliverance accompanied Jody as she left, though there was a measure of sadness mingled with it. Clif had wanted her to enjoy the sport he loved, and she didn't. Even if she made a further effort to learn, it simply held no interest for her. Maybe he liked to dance, she thought. Jody could dance straight through into next year and keep on going. She'd have to hope for other activities they could share, and forget about the skiing.

Her rather desultory look through the après-ski clothes resulted in the purchase of a lovely, coral-colored velour warm-up that she could wear any number of places besides a ski lodge. Jody changed into it and stuffed her soaked garments into the bag her purchase had been wrapped in. By the time Clif and Michael came looking for her, she felt one hundred percent more comfortable.

Clif let out a slow whistle of approval. "Smashing. What do you say, Mike?"

"I like it," he mumbled, abashed at the question.

"Now I know I made the right choice." Jody gave his shoulders a quick squeeze. "There's one more purchase I want to make. Come over this way."

She led them to a shelf that held stuffed animals in a variety of skiing postures and pointed to a series of smallish bears.

"Now this I figure is me." She took down a woebegone bear, his posterior planted ingloriously in the snow, skis spraddled toward the heavens and scarf trailing behind him.

"And this," she continued, "this I think is Mike." Now she had a fierce, determined bear, obviously roaring downhill, knees properly bent, poles correctly angled and scarf as stiff as a pennant in the wind. "A winner," she explained. "Now you pick out your Uncle Clif."

Mike looked disbelievingly at the toy she'd handed to him. "Are you going to buy this for me?"

"As soon as you find your uncle up there."

"Why?"

"Because I like you very much and because I want us all to have a reminder of this afternoon."

Michael held tight to the little bear, a smile playing at the corners of his mouth, and then he began examining the choices. He took a long time about it, studying each one carefully.

"I must be a real problem," quipped Clif.

"No, I just like looking at them and thinking, but I've decided now—this one."

He gave Clif a triumphant bear, with a touch of arrogance about him, standing straight up and displaying a medal on his chest.

"Because Uncle Clif always wins everything," Michael explained.

With eyes suspiciously bright, Clif accepted his nephew's choice. "Mike, I don't always win, though now that I have this to live up to, I'll have to see that I do. Thank you, Son."

When it came to putting his toy into the bag, Michael resisted the clerk's efforts.

"Never mind a bag," Jody said. "We'll each carry our own souvenir. So, I guess that's it. Shall we get back to Alf and Britta's? I'm hungry as a . . ."

"Bear," supplied Mike, swishing his gift through the air in a spectacular run as they walked to the car. "I skied pretty hard and I'm starving."

Clif slid the skis into the car rack. "You skied *very* hard and very well. We're going to make a regular thing out of this, Mike, and you're going to end up a real pro."

"Hey, do you think I could go to the Olympics some day?"

"Never can tell. If that's what you want and you work hard enough for it, you'll make it for sure. You've got the ability; I can see that."

As Michael helped with the skis, he checked to make sure that Jody was in the car and then said to his uncle, sotto voce, "She's a nice lady, Uncle Clif."

"Yes, she is. A very nice lady."

"I feel like talking when I'm around her."

"I know what you mean. Okay, hop in. Time we took up Mrs. Jenson's supper offer."

Mike was a different child on the trip to town than he had been on the way out. If he wasn't talking to his bear, he was chattering to Jody and Clif, and he kept bouncing around exactly the way an excited, happy eight-year-old should.

"Are you looking forward to seeing Ivar's fort?" Jody asked him.

"Sort of." The lightheartedness ceased.

Jody could have bitten her tongue in regret. *What did I have to go and bring that up for? Some unfortunate memory...* Mike's voice interrupted her thoughts.

"My dad started to build me one once, but he hit his thumb with the hammer and quit."

Jody heard Clif mutter something about his brother always being a quitter, and then she reached back and put a hand on Michael's knee. "I'm sorry, Mike. I'm sure that disappointed you a lot."

Mike's young shoulders lifted in yet another shrug. Jody thought that an eight-year-old master of shrugs bordered on the unhealthy. She tried to change the subject.

Michael, however, seemed anxious to pursue it. "He even went away from my mother and me. Guess he doesn't like fights."

Clif's only response was a rasp of disgust, so Jody faced the back seat once again. "Mike, I don't imagine anyone likes fights but they do happen. That's the easy part. The hard part is finding the reason for the fight and clearing it up. Would you believe that I have a terrible temper? Your uncle called it a 'pepper pot' temper. My brother always called it 'Jody's buzz saw.'"

An instant smile came from Mike at this news. "I have a temper, too. Some things make me real mad. Like when a guy stole my best baseball card. Boy, was I mad!"

"I should hope so," said Clif. "Can't go around like someone's lapdog. Did you get it back?"

"Yep. 'Course it was in three pieces after I grabbed it from him, but that was better than him still having it. Then he punched me one and we had a fight. But that was okay. He got a big, old black eye and all I got was a little tear in my shirt."

"Good for you, son. I'm sorry you got into a fight, but I'm glad you were able to defend yourself."

"Really?"

"Really."

Jody glanced back at Michael, and instead of the happy smile she'd expected to see, she surprised a deeply thoughtful expression crinkling his brow.

"Miss Jenson didn't quit. Every time she fell down she got up, until she was all wet and tired. She never lost her temper. I guess she's a different kind of fighter."

"Out of the mouths of babes," murmured Clif.

"Mike, thank you! You make me sound downright heroic."

"Well, I just thought it up," he answered her smile. "Maybe Ivar could come along next time," he suggested abruptly, effectively dismissing the previous topic.

"Great idea." Clif sent his approval via the rear-view mirror. "We'll ask him. Jody, how about you? Game for another try?"

"No thanks, I've had my whirl with skiing, I think."

He took her hand in his before continuing. "Have you ever considered cross-country?"

Visions rose before Jody's eyes of flat terrain, the occasional gentle—truly gentle—incline, a leisurely pace, peace and quiet. Her expression was one of pleasant surprise. "I think that could be terrific fun. It doesn't seem quite your style, though—not exactly exciting, you know."

"It is a mite slow and easy," he admitted, "but I've always thought I'd try it someday, so we will. Together."

As they pulled into Alf's driveway Jody was thinking that there just might be a way for them to share this sport after all.

The idea of cross-country had elicited no response from Mike, and he tugged at his uncle's hand as soon as they got out of the car. "You'll still want to ski on hills, won't you?"

"You're darn right! I'm not about to give up all that fun. Not to worry for a second, Mike."

His reassurance earned a loud "whew" of relief as they got to the door.

While Alf and Clif had a drink in the living room, Jody lent a hand in the kitchen. To her delight, Britta treated Michael as one of her own, sitting him down by one twin's high chair, and Ivar by the other, equipping them both with spoons and bowls of food.

"Better sit back farther. She'll spit it in your face if you're not careful," Ivar cautioned Mike.

"Why? Aren't they hungry?"

"They're always hungry. Babies just like to spit and throw stuff around. Don't ever get one at your house. Nothing but trouble. And noise."

"Maybe they'll get better, like we did."

"Mike, they're girls! It's hopeless."

"Yeah, I forgot about that. Too bad."

When they sat down to supper, Michael's initial attitude was one of reticence; not shy exactly, just observant. Then he got off a one-liner that had the table erupting in merriment, and from then on he was so much a part of the group that one would think he'd sat there for years of meals. Jody thought Clif might burst with pride before they were through.

The children were excused early, so the adults could have coffee in peace. They scrambled from their chairs the very second Alf gave them permission. First stop would be the fort for a quick look, then next would come two activities that had Mike's chin dropping in amazement—roller skating in the basement and painting pictures on the basement walls. Except for the furnace room, Ivar explained, the basement belonged to Kirstie and him and they could do almost anything they wanted down there.

Mike looked wide-eyed at his uncle. "Boy, I never saw a family like this," he exclaimed, then, face shining, he raced off after his friend.

With coffee and dishes done, Clif wondered if perhaps he should get Mike and leave. Britta went to the basement door and swung it open. Shouts and laughter floated up the stairs, along with cries of "watch me" and "I can do that." She shut the door. "He's having a wonderful time. Don't take him away yet."

"I didn't really want to. I just didn't want us upsetting your routine any more than we have already. How about a walk, Jody?"

"Great," she agreed. "Might even work off a pound or two. I must have gained at least three tonight."

"You're not alone." Clif chuckled and gave Britta a hug. "You're too good a cook, madam, but I'll come back anytime!"

It was a night that seemed made for walking . . . and for lovers, Jody thought. Flakes of soft snow drifted down to powder their heads and mist the streetlights, and it wasn't cold enough to be uncomfortable. A romantic gift from nature, this still and tranquil slice of time. She took Clif's hand as they strolled along.

"I like holding your hand," he said.

She tightened her hold in response and waited for him to break the silence.

"That's how a home should be." His voice was firm with conviction.

"I agree."

"How does she do it when she's working?"

"Britta doesn't work," Jody answered in surprise. Then she remembered the wrapping desk and understood his question. "Except at Christmas, in the store. She only does that because both grandmothers vie for a chance to take the children shopping, do Christmas baking, things like that. If they weren't lovingly taken care of, she'd never do even that much."

Clif looked down at her, the lines between his brows telling her that he was troubled over something.

"Neither would I," she offered.

"At Christmas, you mean?"

"I mean if I had a young family, I wouldn't work outside my home...period. Unless I had to for financial reasons."

"But, Jody! Alferic's...you're not saying you'd give that up? It's too important to you. You're dedicated to it."

Grateful that the subject had arisen so naturally, Jody proceeded to try and remove it as a stumbling block for him. "I *am* dedicated to Alferic's, you're absolutely right. But I am *not* dedicated to being in charge forever. All that matters to me is that it remains what it is—a quality bookstore. *That's* what I'm dedicated to. Choosing the right management would accomplish that end."

Clif halted and faced her. "Suppose you had a family and a lousy manager?"

Jody had to forcibly quell a flicker of annoyance at the question. Patience, she admonished herself. "You must have paid some attention to the reason for the stew I'm in right now—namely, family versus store. And these are only my uncles, for heaven's sake. Not even immediate family. No way would I take over from a lousy manager on a full-time basis. I'd fire him, fill in while I found another...part-time would probably be enough...take the children with me...leave them with Mom or Britta...I don't know, but I am certainly capable of juggling more than one ball at a time, and I would never do anything to hurt my children. Family always comes first.''

''Sorry.'' He resumed walking, his hand still clasping hers. ''I'm pretty hung up on this idea of women with careers and children left home with baby-sitters. They don't mix, in my book. Look at Mike. As fine a son as...''

Jody's annoyance boiled over. She stopped and forced him to look at her. ''Clif, you blame your sisters-in-law for everything and that's not fair! Yes, I know we went over this before, but you only gave token consent to the idea that your brothers might have a fault or two. Just keep quiet and listen to me for a minute. Plenty of women work full-time and raise fine, happy children, including perhaps, Mike's mother if she hadn't had to cope with your immat...irresponsible brother. Maybe she even *has* to work. Maybe he isn't paying the child support. Who knows? Do you?''

''No, can't say that I do.'' He looked rather nonplussed at her angry attack.

''Then check into it before making judgments! Heaven knows I'm not about to start castigating people I've never even met, nor am I about to take your word for it. And while you're delving into the situation, you should keep in mind that I am not your sisters-in-law. I'm me! So, don't go dumping me into some convenient little category you've cooked up to rationalize your own shortsightedness. I won't fit.''

Furious at the way the lovely evening had turned out, Jody whirled and headed back to Alf's at a brisk clip. So before he'd consider a commitment, he wanted her out of the store... probably even before she had any children, Jody brooded. Well, she was not willing to do it, even for Clif. But she really couldn't be angry with him. He felt strongly about this and she understood why, even though she thought he was mistaken. Yet, feelings seldom responded to logic. Her feelings about Alferic's were a perfect example. No amount of logic in the world was going to change how she felt.

''Jody! Wait!'' Clif caught up and slowed her down with an arm around her shoulders. ''I admit... ah... well, I'll do some rethinking... some objective looking into... damn it! You keep knocking down all the barriers.''

He was so cross with himself that Jody nearly laughed. ''Is that so bad?'' she asked.

''I'm not accustomed to throwing out cornerstones of my life.''

''A rather nice man I know once said that life is about change.''

Clif tossed his head back in hearty laughter. ''Okay. Serves me right, but what do you mean *rather* nice?''

Slowly Clif pulled Jody close to him. He lifted her face to his and his mouth claimed hers, not roughly, but so strongly and passionately that he might as well have said, *I love you*. But he didn't. He didn't say anything. He just walked her up the door, opened it and they went in.

The anger she'd thought had melted arose once more to niggle the edges of her mind. If he couldn't manage an *I love you* after such a day, when would he ever be able to? What was the matter with him? How could he, a man who handled all the business of life on a straight shot of road, be stumbling about in an emotional maze, bumping into dead ends? Could he ever find the way out? Maybe not. Maybe she'd been right on the afternoon they'd made love—he'd never change. And while these thoughts hurt, they also made her angry.

Clif was sending her looks of concern; he knew something was wrong. But Mike was there, and they were saying good-night. Jody settled for giving all the children a hug and linking her arm through Britta's to walk to her car. She got in and drove off with a smile and a carefree wave in the general direction of the entire group, nothing special for Clif.

She was still angry and hurt late the next morning when he called, clearly worried about her state of mind.

"Jody, what happened? Something I did?"

"No, nothing you did."

"Then why the furious expression last night?"

"Because I was mad." *Because you're so stupidly slow to see the obvious, if you ever do!*

"Well, something's the matter." He sounded suddenly impatient.

"Guess you'll just have to figure it out for yourself." *And don't get impatient with me, Clif McClelland. You're the stubborn slowpoke around here, not me.*

After a few more inconclusive remarks Clif's temper snapped. "I'll call you tomorrow." His sentence was punctuated by the slam of the receiver.

Good, thought Jody as she gently placed her receiver in its cradle. Be mad. Maybe a hefty dose of banging and crashing around would bring him to his senses. If it did, she'd be here waiting. If, that is, he didn't take forever about it.

CHAPTER FOURTEEN

LAUGHING SOFTLY to herself, Jody started for the kitchen to fix her mother's lunch tray. What a foolish statement she'd just made. As if she wouldn't wait for Clif until all those foot-dragging cows came home. She'd wait, all right; patience was a long suit of hers when it came to something she truly wanted. And she'd never wanted anything more in her life than to love Clif openly and freely, knowing that he loved her in return. So, yes, she'd wait...but it was getting darn hard!

Why didn't he hurry up and get on with it? Of all the times for *him* to practice patience...she had to laugh aloud this time. Here she was, going through life grumbling and complaining because everybody and everything had to travel Federal Express these days, while she was back in the dust with the Pony Express. Then, when Clif opted for dropping back along the trail and hopping into the saddle for a gentle canter, she got upset. She just had to relax and let him lope along. He'd get there—he had to!

She'd no sooner gotten the tray settled on Mrs. Jenson's lap than the telephone shrilled once more. This time it was Alex.

"I've missed you, Jody," he said.

A little taken aback at his words and the sincere tone of his voice, she stammered over her response. "You have? I mean . . . we didn't see all that much of each other . . . that is, I'm surprised."

Alex sounded amused. "We saw each other enough for me to miss you and think that Friday is aeons away. What have you been doing?"

She told him about the skiing, without mentioning Clif's name, and they went on to have an easy, comfortable talk. Jody wasn't quite sure what to make of his continually flirtatious attitude. Did he really mean it, or was he just trying another tactic? Not that it mattered much at long-distance range; she'd be able to evaluate his motive when he got back to Minneapolis. At this point, she was only very careful not to encourage him, merely agreeing that he could call her during the week and that she'd see him on Friday.

Funny, she thought after hanging up, she'd shared dozens of interests with Rich and Alex and yet neither of them appealed to her as men. Zingless relationships is what she called them. The only one who brought her alive was a man as different from her as one could get.

CLIF DROPPED BY the store the next morning with the information he'd found in his search through the newspaper archives.

"Jody, your intuition has paid off in spades. The primary mover behind both the building and investment of the Beacon Tower was one Alexander Renard. Alex's grandfather, I presume."

Her expression could only be described as gleeful. "Something concrete at last . . . I mean, there must be a tie-in. Otherwise, why didn't Alex say something that night after the game to explain his interest in the old Tower? I tell you, if he's knowingly mixed up in anything shady, I'm going to bonk him over the head with a baseball bat.''

Clif smiled at her threat, but then pointed a stern finger at her. "You let me take care of any bat swinging that's needed, hear?"

"I hear and I'll think about it. But forget Alex, what about the scandal?"

"Well, it was some scandal, all right. Renard had concocted a stock-selling scheme to raise the money and was later accused of manipulating the stock. He wasn't the only one involved—no other names I recognized though—but they were all exposed. Some of the men served jail terms, but Renard apparently did not. Can't imagine why, but he wasn't mentioned in that write-up."

"Was Grandpa's name in the paper?"

"No, it wasn't. I imagine he was one of the investors who got taken in."

Jody agreed. "His sleepy business acumen. Well, it's all very interesting and I just know it figures into all this somehow, but . . . how does it help us?"

"Beats me." Clif got up to refill their coffee cups and then resumed his seat. "It does mean that underhanded dealing is not unknown in the Renard family, and that Minneapolis has more significance for them than they led us to believe. I'm more and more uneasy over this whole thing."

"I am, too. Alex called yesterday."

"Oh? Trying to talk you into signing?"

"He didn't even bring it up." She bit her lip, hesitating over her next sentence. "He seemed a bit . . . well, flirty."

Clif snapped to attention. "Flirty? How?"

"Nothing offensive. Innuendos, mostly. He missed me . . . things like that."

"Terrific!" he fumed. "Just what I need going into trial. Alex chasing after you."

"You're going into trial? Then you shouldn't be concerning yourself with anything else at all. Just drop the whole Renard business. Alex is probably trying out some new ploy and, anyway, how much chasing can he do from New York?"

"Enough to make me madder than hell. And I'm already stewing over why you were miffed on Saturday." He glared at her as if she'd committed a crime.

"Don't. Don't stew over anything. Listen, I have a friend who's married to a lawyer, and I know what happens when her husband is in trial. He sees nothing else, hears nothing else and speaks to her in monosyllables—if he says anything at all. Mostly he paces around muttering to himself and grabbing law books off the shelf. Total focus on the matter at hand."

Clif grinned and then turned quizzical. "Would that bother you? If you were in her shoes?"

Jody stifled a grin of her own. "I don't see that it would be much of a problem. Or should I say, trial?"

With a laugh, he drew her to her feet. "Trial will do admirably. And, to pile pun on pun, I'm finding it a trial to think of being away from you for the next few days. Still miffed?"

"No, not miffed at all."

He kissed her lightly, then rested her head against his shoulder, just holding her close. "I hope to have my case wound up on Friday. I'll call you then...maybe before, I don't know. I have an idea for Saturday." He raised her head for another light kiss before he let her go. "I'm going to be officiating at a snowmobile race out at White Bear, a fund-raiser for Winter Carnival. If you could come out with Alex, I'll make an opportunity to ask a few pertinent questions...see if we can hook the Tower into the move for Alferic's.''

"That should be easy. He's already said he wants to see me. I'll just say we're going to the race and that's that.''

"Good," Clif agreed, but he didn't look too happy over the idea. "I don't want you trying to find out anything from Alex yourself. From what I've been hearing about the Renards, having him suspect that you're on to something scares me. God only knows what he might do. And no riding with him at the wheel, remember. Promise me.''

"I promise, though I really think Alex has my best interests at heart now. He doesn't worry me the way his father would.''

"I don't agree with that. I think they're both worth worrying about. So even if you're right, let's just play it on the safe side. One more thing...'' He paused, clearly uncomfortable with what he was about to say. "I've been wrong about the value of Alferic's. It belongs where it is, as it is, with you in charge, and owning it. Forget the dollar signs, and never mind whether or not something shady is going on. No one but you should own the store. Don't sell, unless *you* want to.''

And there it was. He was irrevocably on her side. "Thank you. Thank you for saying that. I've been hoping you'd feel this way for so long.''

He smiled down into her shining eyes. "And now I do. No more neutral camps for me. Stick to your guns. I'll be right there backing you up.''

Another brief kiss, and an assurance that he'd call her Friday, and Jody was left gazing at an empty doorway. Honestly, she said to herself, Clif was umpteen times more amorous when he first knew her than he was now. He never touched her at all anymore. It bothered her, especially today after hearing the glorious news that he was on her side at last. But somehow she knew it would all come together. She just knew it....

FROM THAT NOON HOUR ON, the week had been a steady downhill slide. On Tuesday, Alf had greeted her by saying that Aunt Hulda was driving his mother nuts by coming over constantly, bawling and carrying on over the "coming catastrophe." Then in the middle of the same afternoon, Anna had called to say that Mrs. Jenson was in terrible pain, and the doctor couldn't understand Anna's broken English. Jody had called the doctor herself and had left immediately for home. When the doctor had arrived, there was little he could do except increase the dosage of his patient's medication, rendering Mrs. Jenson too dopey to even communicate. At Jody's objection to so much of the drug, he had replied that it would only be for a day or two, and there was no other course to take.

By Wednesday morning Alf was in her office again, this time much more annoyed than before over Hulda's behavior. "Do you know what the 'coming catastrophe' really is?" he asked, sitting down with an angry plop.

Jody sat back in surprise as she realized that she didn't actually know. "The end of Jenson & Sons is what I've assumed, but I never even asked. Why? Isn't that it?"

"It is not. To think it's taken this long for me to get around to asking for specifics . . . Anyway, the big disaster is that the North Dakota operation would have to be closed down. And of course we both know why that won't do."

Jody smiled and nodded. "Of course we do; it's Nils Junior's baby. Still, I'd be sorry to see it happen to him."

"Well, sure, so would I. N.J.'s an okay guy and deserves his chance—it's just that we've been thinking it's much worse than it is. Dad thought we knew the situation—by osmosis presumably—so he never bothered to elaborate. Pays to ask questions, that's obvious."

Jody didn't comment. She was busy trying to recollect what she'd heard about N.J.'s project. "Alf, didn't I hear some talk about how grateful the farmers were when we built there? That we created enough jobs to employ some of the wives? Mortgages were being met again? Things like that?"

"Yes you did. I remember that, too. And I see what you're getting at...the ripple effect. Good Lord, here I'd hoped to ease your mind a bit and I've made it worse for you."

Jody dismissed his final sentence with an impatient gesture. "No, you did the right thing in telling me. I need to know everything I possibly can. If I'd refused to sign and then found out about all those people being laid off, I'd have been heartsick. This way I can be heartsick starting this very minute."

Alf's eyes widened. "You've decided not to sign?"

"No, I haven't decided anything yet. It's just that the thought of bringing misery to people who have nothing to do with the problem, people who count on the Jensons, doesn't make for happy thoughts.''

''That's for sure! Well, kiddo, now that I've brightened up your day so admirably, I'll just be moseying back to my domain. I'll drop by later on.''

''Sans news, I hope.'' Jody scowled at him.

''Sans news. I promise,'' he answered solemnly, then grinned at her and left with a wave.

Before she had time to even begin mulling over this fresh complication, Anna was on the phone again. Mrs. Jenson flatly refused to take any more of her medication. Jody headed for home, feeling as though she'd tumbled into a whirlpool. Her mother was in agony, the remedy for which was worse than the hurt. Store business was stacking up on her desk, she had no time at all to think about the contract, and Clif was too deeply involved in his case to be distracted. Jody spent the afternoon reading to her mother, and going through her own agony at the sight of her white, tightly controlled face.

She'd all but forgotten Alex until he called that evening, full of anticipation at seeing her in a day and a half. As before, he didn't mention the contract at all, putting all his efforts into upcoming plans for the two of them. Jody mentioned the snowmobile race, and Alex was delighted.

''Say, since it's a fund-raiser, any chance I could rent one of them and get us into the race?''

She had never been on a snowmobile and had no real desire to ride one, but it just might be a perfect way to gain some insight into Alex's character, his competitive nature. ''I'll find out and tell you Friday,'' she answered.

"Great," he said. "And Jody...I've seldom looked forward to anything more than seeing you again."

She frowned at the receiver as she hung it up, not at all sure that this was going to be a pleasant situation to handle. And she most assuredly could not work up any enthusiasm for snowmobiling!

On Thursday, she decided that the prospects for the weekend loomed emphatically unpleasant. An early edition, beautifully bound, of "Hiawatha" was delivered to her at the store. From Alex, of course. As enchanted as she was with the gift, it took her no time at all to decide that she would refuse it. It was far too special for her to keep, under the circumstances. The delivery did serve to remind her that she must stop by Warren's office on her way home and pick up a copy of the contract. He'd added the provisos they wanted, and she planned to study it once her mother had gone to sleep.

Mrs. Jenson's pain had happily lessened somewhat, but it was still a melancholy evening for Jody. Her blues stemmed from having no one to talk over the contract with. Her mother might be better, but she certainly didn't need to be bothered with this. Carl hardly knew what was going on and had never met Alex or Mr. Renard. And today Alf had confessed that Hulda had finally succeeded in upsetting his mother. Kirsten now claimed that if *her* son were involved in any shutdown, she'd probably sacrifice the bookstore, too. Jody felt that she couldn't very well call Alf, who now knew where he stood now.

Actually, she didn't want to talk to any of them anyway; she wanted to talk to Clif. Even though the decision was hers, and hers alone, she wanted to work it out with him, see him, be with him. But he hadn't called, nor stopped by, so the trial was obviously consuming all his time and thoughts.

So, where was she now? She had some hints of wrongdoing that were completely inconclusive—a scandal that involved grandparents and some possible hanky-panky at the bank. Clif's and her instinctive feel that something was being covered up was hardly enough to go on. And definitely not enough to warrant closing a plant and laying off dozens of people. The only thing she had going for her was time. She had until Sunday night to come to a decision. Alex was coming tomorrow, and perhaps his words or actions might point the way. But best of all, she would see Clif on Saturday. His very presence would be a help.

Jody opened the refrigerator to see what was available for her solitary supper. She had a choice of cold meatballs or salad. "Some choice," she mumbled. "I don't want either. I want Clif and chocolate mousse with a ton of whipped cream!"

She felt most virtuous, fixing a green salad with oh-so-healthy sprouts and sunflower seeds. Eating it, she felt as if she were munching her way through an alfalfa field. She knew that slenderness was a full-time job, one she was used to and didn't really mind. The bothersome thing on this particular evening was that she also knew the bowl of greenery would taste every bit as luscious as chocolate mousse, if Clif were sitting across from her.

ALEX WALKED through her office door on Friday bearing a large bouquet of creamy yellow roses. Genuine delight lit Jody's face at the sight of the flowers— here was a gift she could accept in good conscience, and maybe it would soften her refusal of the book.

"These are lovely. And the scent. I won't want to leave my office all day," she exclaimed.

"That won't do at all—doesn't fit in with my plans for a minute. Here, I'll pin one to your blouse, and then you can enjoy the fragrance wherever you go."

There was a corsage pin in the florist's box—a bit too handy, Jody thought—and he had the flower securely attached in no time at all. He took the opportunity to hold her by the shoulders and search her eyes. "It's so good to be with you again." He touched the rosebud gently and stepped back.

His words were not enough to make a fuss over, but they troubled her. "Alex, the flowers are a marvelous gift and I love them. But the book . . . I love it too, but it's much too special for me to accept."

An angry expression flitted across his face. "I see. You think I'm trying to bribe you into signing the contract?"

Jody's jaw dropped in astonishment. "The thought never even crossed my mind. I suppose it should have, but it didn't."

He was all smiles now. "Good, and in that case, please keep it. Call it a gift from one book lover to another."

"No, I'm really not comfortable . . ."

"Please? For the weekend at least?"

"For the weekend," she agreed. "I'm sorry I won't be able to join in the plans you've made, but I simply must get this desk cleared off today. The week's been so hectic that I'm days behind."

"If you must, you must. But I insist upon dinner, in the most elegant spot in town."

"Done," she said with a smile.

They decided on a restaurant, and Jody said she'd meet him there. That qualification didn't please him at all, but she wasn't about to get caught in the intimacy of a late night ride back home to The Point.

THE DINNER with Alex could not have been more enjoyable, nor more compatible. The two of them laughed and talked their way through a multitude of subjects, sharing opinions about the theater, the arts, education and politics...everything but Alferic's. Alex was proving to be a fascinating companion, but the omission of any discussion regarding the store became more and more glaring as the meal progressed. Finally Jody brought it up.

"Are you reluctant to talk about the contract?" she asked.

"No, I just don't want to be pushy. Time is pushing you enough. As I said last week, it's necessary that you get to know me—fast. Has that happened?"

"I think so," she said tentatively. "I assume you saw Clark today and read the changes Warren put in?"

"I did, and they're fine. I want you and the future of Alferic's protected in every way possible." This was stated so firmly that Jody wondered if he thought protection necessary.

"Will your father agree?"

"He will. Not that it matters much. I have his power of attorney, so we can wrap it up any time you're ready."

"*If* that time comes," she said as they rose to leave.

Alex made no particular effort to prolong their good-nights when they got to her car. He simply looked at her with gentle affection and then waved as he watched her drive away.

Jody arrived home having pretty well decided she would sign. Nothing had been said or done that evening to increase her suspicions. Indeed, everything had served to all but banish her concern over selling. Renard Senior might be a shyster, but Alex was not. Alferic's would be safe in his hands. Maybe she would tell Alex as much at tomorrow's outing—after she'd seen him in action on the racecourse....

CHAPTER FIFTEEN

THE CROWD milling about the starting line for the White Bear snowmobile fund-raiser was raucous and boisterous, an indication that this contest was purely for fun. The contenders jockeyed for position, gleefully bumping friends aside, shouting playful insults, and generally causing the officials to give up on any efforts toward a smooth start.

Seated at the timekeeper's table, Clif spotted Alex and Jody the moment they arrived. Jody was aware of Clif's presence, but Alex had not seen him. Just as well, thought Jody. Alex needn't know at this juncture that Clif was here.

An announcement that the starting gun was about to go off brought renewed clamor and increased bumping, with Alex doing a bit more than his share of elbowing and pushing. At the signal, he had them securely in a front slot.

For the first leg of the course, he seemed content to stay with the pack. Jody could tell, though, from her position behind him on the snowmobile seat, that annoyance was gradually replacing his contentment. She thought it was probably because everyone kept cutting in front of one another, just for laughs, and she tightened her arms around his waist. He patted the clasped hands at his midriff and apparently leashed the rising impatience she'd sensed. But it didn't last.

A few more cut-ins and his emotions slipped all restraints.

"No need to win this crappy little race the fair way," he yelled back at her. "I'm going to get some speed out of this baby." He hit the throttle and sent them shooting off the course.

"Alex, the markers! The course goes between the markers!" Thoroughly alarmed, Jody's arms nearly cramped from the effort to hold on. "We're trespassing," she shouted. "This is someone's field!"

But Alex had cranked the speed up so high that the wind tore the words away from his ears. Not that he would have paid any attention. As he turned his head to check on the other racers, she got a look at his face and felt a surge of panic. Alex was scarcely recognizable. His features were twisted in the grip of some maniacal drive, and he revved the speed still higher until they were rocketing across the snow, icy particles stinging her cheeks, the wind screaming past. Jody grabbed his arm, but he tossed her hand away, intent on the distant flags marking the finish line. He was going to be first, disqualified or not. She gave up any attempts to slow him down and concentrated on hanging on. Another quick glimpse of his face and she shuddered. Now his lips were drawn back in a malicious grin, his eyes glittering in some consuming madness. She prayed they would get to the end of the race in one piece.

"Alex!" she screamed, pointing frantically at the line of fence posts dead ahead. Buried in the snow, only the tops were visible. Too late, he spotted them, tried to swerve and couldn't. One of the runners caught on a top wire, slewed the snowmobile violently, then flipped it wildly, somersaulting them both into the air.

Jody landed on her back, spread-eagled as though she were making a snow angel. Vaguely disoriented, but not in pain, the first sounds she heard were Alex's frantic shouts as he plowed toward her, arms windmilling to maintain balance in the deep powder.

"Are you hurt? Jody, answer me!"

She turned her head as he fell in a swirl of snow at her side. "I'm fine," she answered, but cried out as she felt a stab of pain in her wrist when she tried to get up.

"Oh God, what is it? Where does it hurt?"

"Just my wrist...nothing serious...help me stand up...I'll be okay in a minute...."

He put one arm behind her back and carefully lifted her to her feet, babbling all the while. "Goddamn fence...should have stuck a flag on it...couldn't see it at all. If you're hurt, I'll kill that goddamn farmer...too lazy to..."

"Alex, be quiet!" she snapped at him. "Stop blaming the poor farmer for your reckless idiocy!"

Jody moved her wrist experimentally, and even though she was biting her lip in agony she was sure it was just a sprain. "Nothing to worry about," she said through clenched teeth.

"Thank God! But you're whiter than this snow. I'll carry you to the lodge."

"Don't be silly, I can walk, for heaven's sake. Nothing's wrong with my legs."

They both looked up at the sound of approaching snowmobiles. Thank heaven, she thought, someone saw the accident. Now we can ride back. The driver of the first vehicle was half standing, black hair tossing in the stream of wind, broad shoulders hunched in an effort to move his machine even faster. Jody didn't need to see the man's eyes to know that they were the blaze of blue she loved. In seconds, she was gazing into Clif's face, filled now with tender concern.

"Do your neck or back hurt?"

She shook her head and he scooped her into his arms, telling the other driver to take "that ass." It was the first and only acknowledgment he made of Alex's existence.

His repeated insistence all the way back to the lodge that they go to an emergency room for X rays nearly brought Jody to tears.

"Please, Clif, can't I just put an ice pack on it? Look . . . full mobility. It has to be a sprain, not a break. I'll elevate it on a cushion in front of the fire. I'm so cold, and upset . . . please?"

"Sure," he relented. "I don't suppose there's any great rush, and there are bound to be some doctors in this crowd. Unless . . . Jody, are you very sure nothing else hurts, or is even uncomfortable? Head, neck, back? Inside your chest or abdomen?"

"Not even a twinge."

Clif swept her into his arms and carried her up the steps of the lodge. Held firmly against his chest, her forehead brushing his chin, and her arms around his neck, Jody did begin having sensations in her chest and abdomen. Far from uncomfortable, however, these were sensual and exciting. She was tempted to act upon them, but it was too late. Clif was already depositing her in a chair by the fireplace. Then he set off to find a doctor.

He came back with three physicians in tow, one of them an orthopedic surgeon. They all examined the now plump wrist, held a brief consultation and agreed that the swelling was due to a sprain. The recommended treatment was elevation, ice packs, aspirin, and as many rum toddies as she could handle. They suggested she see her own physician the next day. He would order the X ray.

Alex, who had been hovering about in the background, left with alacrity to fetch the rum anesthetic. When he returned, he delivered the mug to the tune of renewed apologies.

"Dear God, I'll never forgive myself for this. Every time I get into a competition, it's as if the old man is sitting on my shoulder yelling at me to win, never mind how, just win. That was a lunatic stunt . . . racing off across the field."

"Damn right it was, Renard." Clif secured an ice pack to Jody's wrist with gentle fingers. "You could have killed her."

Alex downed his Scotch in one gulp and signaled for another before answering. "But not to worry, the cavalry always comes galloping over the hill. What is it with you, McClelland? Haven't you got anything better to do than sneak around after us?"

Clif leaned an elbow on the mantel, glanced at Jody's anxious expression and shrugged. "We do seem to wind up in the same places. Just coincidence," he replied, reining in his temper for Jody's sake.

Alex snorted his disgust and downed half of his fresh drink. "Not surprising, I guess. I thought Minneapolis and St. Paul were cities, not villages between the corn stalks. Jody, I'm going to take you to New York, show you a place with some real action, where you can go three years running without seeing the same people—and where there's some class," he added as he scanned the lodge derisively.

Jody hastened to forestall any comments from a now tight-lipped Clif. "I told you on the way out here that this lodge was a converted barn. It's *meant* to look like a barn, and it's a fine example of rustic charm—and sophistication. But if you can't see that then I can't imagine why you want to live here."

"Just kidding. Anything to stir up the omnipresent counselor, here. And by the way, McClelland, I have ways of dealing with guys who horn in on my territory. The scene when you rescued Jody back there was interesting to observe. I'd suggest you be somewhere else by the time I get back here." He grabbed Jody's still half-full mug and headed for the bar.

Clif slipped another pillow under her wrist. "I will not offend your ears with the response I'd like to give that animal."

"He didn't mean what he said. It's just one side of him...."

"That's no excuse, and if you're right, he's too damn unpredictable to be around. One thing for sure, I'm driving you home, even if I have to drop him headfirst into a snowdrift."

"Clif." Jody tried to sound chiding, but couldn't help a giggle.

"Here you go, just what the doctor ordered." Alex swooped her toddy through the air, handed it to her with a flourish and then glared at Clif.

"Good Lord, McClelland, you still hanging around? What's wrong with your hearing? I told you to get lost, so get moving. Jody and I have plans to make."

"Such as?" Clif sat down on the hearth and arranged a pillow behind his back, underscoring his intention to stay put.

Alex bit back whatever words he'd intended to spit out and twisted his mouth in a smile. "Such as a trip to New York for the two of us."

Jody made an impatient motion. "Alex, I do not want to go to New York. I saw enough when I was at Wellesley to last for a long time. Anyway, I'm perfectly happy right here."

"So, McClelland." Alex stretched lazily in his chair, choosing to ignore Jody's rebuff. "What do you do for excitement when you're not traipsing around after us? I imagine you find the Midwest pretty dull fare. Provincial, I'd say. Don't you agree?"

Feeling Clif's anger, Jody closed her eyes and waited for a cutting reply. But when he spoke, his voice was surprisingly mild. "Depends on what you mean by provincial."

"Well, let's see." Alex sipped his drink in leisurely fashion, apparently reflecting on a difficult subject. "Certain words come to mind—insular, unsophisticated, unrefined..."

Jody's laughter rippled across his words. "Good heavens, you sound like King George the Third dismissing the colonists as a bunch of yokels, to his eternal regret, as you'll recall. I think I'd like to go home now, if you don't..."

"Bartender!" Alex shouted, "another round over here." Then he turned to Jody. "One more drink. Three doctors' prescriptions call for three drinks. Not that you seem to be finishing any of them, but it'll give us a chance to hear from *the law* here on the subject of provinciality."

Clif studied Alex's face for a moment or two, reflecting on his response. Into the silence fell a harsh laugh from Alex.

"Come, come, counselor," he said, "a lawyer's supposed to be quick on the uptake. Or isn't the quick wits department your forte?"

Clif chuckled and shook his head. "Just debating over whether to give you the lecture you deserve or a concise answer."

"Well, could be I was a bit hasty there. After all, Jody comes from the Midwest and she's all that's good and—"

Jody cut his words off. "Please, Alex . . ."

"I didn't mean to embarrass you." He laid a hand on her arm and she promptly shook it off. "The Midwest's fine, I was . . ."

Clif stepped in smoothly. "Glad to hear you say that, Alex. I should hope you'd feel that way. Didn't some of your family come from Minneapolis?"

Alex did a double-take. "What? No, they did not! What makes you ask that?"

"I was doing a little research in the newspaper archives the other day and ran across some articles on the building of the Beacon Tower."

Alex's face tightened like a vise, but he made no comment.

Clif went on. "Seems the Tower plans were put in motion by one Alexander Renard. That wouldn't be your grandfather, by chance?"

A telltale deep breath preceded his answer. "Seems to me I did hear something about that. I guess my grandparents must have lived here for a while. But that was long ago and of no interest now." He yelled for yet another drink.

Jody stood up. "Time I got home," she announced.

Alex jumped to his feet. "Good. Also time we found a more congenial spot."

Clif set his pillow aside. "I'm taking Jody home, Renard. You've had too much to drink, and one accident a day is one too many."

Alex cocked an ear with a finger, a parody of listening. "Do I hear the distant beat of cavalry?"

"I don't want to go home with you, Alex, and that's that!" Jody didn't have to say she was furious with him, the tone of her voice told him in no uncertain terms.

"The contract?" he said.

"I'll call you later, after I decide." And then she hit her forehead with the heel of her hand. "Clif, *I* drove out here. I totally forgot. Alex came with me."

"Good—" he smiled at her "—because you're the one who was going to get the lecture, for not keeping your promise. No problem—I'll take you home in your car. You can't drive with that wrist anyway."

Clif arranged for a friend of his to follow them to The Point and then bring him back for his own car. Alex said he'd call a cab.

"Well, this has been an eye-opener," Clif said as they left the lodge behind. "Are you persuaded not to sign?"

"Yes, I suppose I am. For one thing, the mills aren't in as much trouble as we thought." She told him what Alf had passed on to her. "So the only one to really suffer, in the family that is, would be Nils Junior— N.J. as we call him. The North Dakota thing was all his idea and he begged for the chance. He did a good job, but the market's been off—something like that—

anyway, it was a bad time. I don't know, Clif, let's not talk about it right now. I want to hear about your trial and about Mike."

He said Mike was fine, spending the weekend with his McClelland grandparents and, wonder of wonders, his father was planning to take him to the zoo on Sunday. For the moment, all was well there. About the trial, he was pleased, and proud as could be—Jody ought to have been there when he'd wound things up with his final summation to the jury.

"I wish I had been. Okay if I come next time?"

"You'll get an engraved invitation." He smiled and took her hand. "Jody...why did you add, 'in the family' when you mentioned N.J.?"

She laughed, but it was a small, sad sound. "Nothing's ever simple, is it? Opening that plant has been a real boost for the farm communities in the area. So many farmers are in financial trouble and we've employed a lot of the wives. They're helping bring in enough to at least pay the interest on their debts, give the families hope, restore some pride. If the plant closes, all those people will be hurt by the shutdown."

Clif raised her hand to his lips. "Always the ramifications to contend with. But you can't save the world. Alferic's is important in a lot of lives, too."

"I know." She stared out the window for a minute. "If I sign and it doesn't work out, I *can* relocate. The meaning of the store is what matters, not the location so much, and not at the expense of people's lives. The only thing is, what if the Renards aren't on the up and up? What if we *all* get hurt in some way or another?"

"Precisely why I'm saying don't sign. Let the court decide. Something is very wrong. I can smell it. And the family Renard doesn't even begin to pass any sniff test! Well, here we are," he said as they pulled into her mother's driveway. "And good buddy Brad's right behind, so no time for us alone."

"Well, win some, lose some, as a rather nice man I know is fond of saying," she quipped.

Brad declined Jody's offer of coffee or a drink, saying that he'd just wait in the car and see her again some other time. He hoped her wrist would heal rapidly. Once inside, Clif got the household organized— a clucking Anna headed for the kitchen and an ice pack, Jody's mother phoned their doctor as Clif had suggested. And then he said goodbye . . . a very tantalizing goodbye. "Sleep well, darling," he said, taking her gently in his arms. "I'll call around noon tomorrow and I'd like you to plan on spending the rest of the day with me. I hope to have a gift for you—I say hope, because I'm not sure I can get it on a weekend. At any rate, tomorrow is decision day for you and if you're willing, we can make that decision together."

"I'm willing, more than willing . . . not even a hint about the gift?"

"Not even a hint," he whispered as his lips met hers in a very thorough kiss. Reluctantly he pulled away and headed to Brad's car.

Between that kiss and his calling her darling, Jody felt justified in thinking that his gift would be well worth the wait. And then the telephone jangled, ending her euphoria abruptly.

Aunt Kirsten's voice was pleasant; her words were not. She began by apologizing for interfering in Jody's affairs, but then claimed that Eric and Nils badly needed her cooperation, to say nothing of Nils Junior. The North Dakota expansion held great promise, would benefit the whole of Jenson & Sons, and N.J. was doing a magnificent job. He shouldn't be made to suffer for the sake of a bookstore. The Renard proposal sounded eminently reasonable. Taking the matter to court could lead to years of wrangling, therefore would Jody please reconsider?

Close on Kirsten's heels, so close that Jody couldn't help but think conspiracy, came a call from Aunt Hulda—nearly hysterical Aunt Hulda. Just what did Jody think she was doing? Was she out to ruin her cousin? The family? Jenson & Sons? Did she enjoy having everyone in an uproar? Spending sleepless nights? And all this because young Jody wanted a bookstore to amuse herself with until something better came along. Hulda wound up her tirade in tears, labeling her niece an irresponsible adolescent and a spoiled little girl.

Jody hung up shaking her head in amazement over her aunt's outburst. However, Hulda aside, Kirsten was right about any courtroom confrontations being lengthy, and any victory for herself would be but a Pyrrhic victory at best. There was N.J. to consider, as well as all the employees dependent upon the Jensons, and Jody knew that she couldn't live with the specter of letting them all down without solid proof of foul play on the Renards' part. Her mind was made up. She decided to sign.

A call to Alex telling him of her decision had him all ready to hop into his car and come to The Point. Jody said no to that. The lobby of his hotel would do perfectly well and yes, she was able to drive. The ice packs, aspirin and bandage had rendered her wrist all but painless.

In the end, her choice of meeting place didn't work out. Alex said he was waiting for a phone call, and he asked Jody to come up to his rooms. Less then pleased, she complied just to get it over with.

He welcomed her with a wide smile, took her coat and ushered her into the suite's sitting room. A romantic setting, Jody realized in dismay, taking in the champagne on ice, the soft lighting, the flowers and the hors d'oeuvres.

"What a relief to hear that your wrist is better. Sit here on the couch. I've got a great champagne for us, caviar and all the trimmings."

She avoided the couch and sat in a wing chair, annoyed at him for assuming she'd come to his suite. "I can't say I feel much like celebrating, Alex. One glass of champagne and then I'm leaving."

"Maybe I can manage to change your mind, but first things first, have you got the contract?"

Jody pulled it out of her purse and, before she could have any second thoughts, wrote her name on the designated line.

Alex scrawled his and then let out a whoop of pleasure. "All wrapped up at last. Pop's going to be one hell of a happy man!"

They toasted their future association, Alex grinning from ear to ear, Jody grim of face.

"So, partner," he said. "And does that sound wonderful—partner. Anyway, partner, I want to apologize again for this afternoon. Bad show on my part, but teamed up with you now, I'm going to get over that sort of thing. Time I quit jumping at Pop's every appearance in my life."

"I'd certainly agree with that and I'm glad to hear it. Now I really want to get back home. What with one thing and another, it's been a wild day, and I'm tired. Sorry about all the trouble you've gone to." She gestured at the full coffee table.

"Jody, come on, just a few minutes? We have things to talk over . . . about Alferic's . . ."

She stood up. "Next week will be ample . . ."

The telephone's shrill demand interrupted her sentence, and she nodded an impatient yes to his plea that she wait while he took it. But she got her coat from the closet, buttoned it securely and pulled on her gloves. The minute he was done, she was going out the door!

Meanwhile she wandered around the sitting room, her eyes drawn to a stack of books on the desk. She picked one up to look it over.

"What an odd title," she murmured. "*Allison's Secret*—never heard of it."

A brief perusal of a page came as a jolt. She was reading pornography! What on earth was Alex— Quickly she flipped to the title page, wondering who published such trash.

Fox Enterprises Incorporated, she read. Never heard of them, either, and why did this New York address ring bells? A second jolt hit her, this one triple-barreled. Renard meant fox, and the street was the same one as Renard Books. Quickly Jody snatched the contract from the table to check the street number. Two digits different. They were right next door to each other!

When Alex entered the room Jody was methodically ripping the signed document to shreds.

"Oh God," he gasped. "You heard me! I can explain . . ."

"I didn't hear anything. I saw something—this." She held up her evidence, then started for the door.

"Oh God," he cried again, darting ahead of her to grab her by the arms. "Wait. Give me a chance . . . I'll tell you everything."

"Keep your hands off me and I'll listen."

He flinched in the face of her contemptuous glare. "It's all a vendetta . . . the Beacon Tower . . . Please sit down while I tell you."

She did, suddenly very glad that she had come, glad she had decided to sign, glad for the champagne that had delayed her departure just long enough, glad even for her aunts' less than courteous telephone calls. They had precipitated the action that would now give her the answers she and Clif had sought.

Alex sat down across from her, a trembling hand clutching a glass of Scotch. "I meant every word I said to you about Alferic's. You must believe me. Alferic's was going to stay the same . . . just you and me and Alferic's. It was the second floor . . ." He gulped some of his drink.

"What about the second floor?" she demanded.

"Pop was going to turn it into an adult bookstore."

Jody closed her eyes and sank back into the chair. The rest of the building, she sighed. They had never given a thought to anything but Alferic's.

"Why?" she asked.

"To get back at your grandfather."

"To get back at my grandfather," she echoed, shaking her head in disbelief. "Why don't you start at the beginning and, Alex, I think I'd like another glass of champagne, if you don't mind."

He complied instantly. And then he began. "Pop is carrying on a vendetta against your family. It all started when the Beacon Tower was built. That was going to be my grandfather's claim to fame—the tallest building in Minneapolis, that North Star on top all lit up so you could see it for miles around. Well, to finance it, he incorporated and sold stock. Your grandfather bought some. Then, when the venture started to crumble, the board of directors began manipulating the stock, and your grandfather exposed their misconduct. It was the end of the dream."

Jody waited for him to continue, but he just sipped his drink and stared into his glass. "Is that all? Your father has gone to all this trouble because of that?"

"No, there's more. The publicity wouldn't stop and my grandfather was openly disgraced. Some of the men went to jail, but he escaped that fate for some reason. My grandparents just left town with their tails between their legs. Pop was a small boy then—six, I think—but old enough to be jeered at by playmates, hear his father branded a criminal and see his mother cut from every part of society. They wound up in New York, where my grandmother did nothing but weep hysterically in her room, and my grandfather turned to drink. For four years Pop watched his mother deteriorate until she had to be institutionalized, and his father become a drunken bum. Pop supported his sisters and himself while all this was happening."

"Supported? How? He was too young."

"I know. After-school jobs mostly. Not much support, but the best he could do. One of his sisters became a prostitute. She's dead now."

Jody pressed a hand against her eyes, appalled and sick at heart. "No wonder he hates us."

"Right. He vowed to get even no matter how much time it took. Well, to get to the end of this, Pop got into the adult-book trade by chance, and built up a money-making chain, all of it fronted by the discount business. And all the while he kept tabs on the Jensons of Minneapolis. His chance finally came when your uncles played into his hands with their ill-timed expansion. Pop decided he'd buy the building and turn the elegant Alferic's into a front for porno—change the name to Alfy's or Feric's. He figured it would be a fitting revenge on the high and mighty Jensons. I think he had some equally unsavory plans for the rest of the building—massage parlor, escort service, adult videos. All very discreet, of course."

Jody thought she might be sick. "And then I proved to be stubborn."

"Right again. That's why he sent me here with a somewhat altered plan. In fact he liked the new one better. Leave Alferic's as is, the porno up above... smut crowning literature, classy Miss Jenson right underneath. For as long as he chose to leave you there, that is. The important thing was to get the building and use it for peddling trash. There was another equally important consideration—avoid a court confrontation. Warren would surely have dug up the old scandal and Pop couldn't have that."

"Why did you go along with his sick scheme?"

"What did I have to lose? It was the first time Pop had ever considered letting me do my own thing, and I hadn't met you yet. All I had to do was come out, meet this unknown female and...ah...persuade you. The method didn't matter, just as long as you signed. Of course, a slight problem arose. You didn't turn out to be the corn-fed country bumpkin I was expecting. On the contrary, you were so wonderful that I..." He shrugged. "Anyway, my father saw the handwriting on the wall, knew I was having second thoughts and hauled me back to New York for a spine-stiffening lecture or two.''

''Which were successful,'' Jody mumbled, her voice dull and flat.

Alex leaned forward, elbows on his knees, his expression both earnest and pleading. ''Yes and no. Yes, I came back to finish the job, but, no—I hadn't the remotest intention of ever letting him carry out the porno stuff. I would have owned the Jenson Building don't forget. I've just been stringing him along until the deal was closed and we—you and I—were safely in charge of it all. You must believe that!''

''I do believe you,'' she said, thinking that regardless of his intentions, he'd been running scared for too many years to change the habit. He was conditioned to obey his father's commands. ''What will happen to you now?''

Alex polished off his drink before answering. ''I don't know. And frankly, I don't really care....''

Jody left him staring morosely into his empty glass. She was almost buoyant with relief. At last her path was clear and straight. At last she could do precisely what she'd wanted to do from the very start—say no— knowing it was the only course to take. When her uncles heard about the Renards' deceit and the merchandise they dealt in, they would refuse to deal with them at any price. And, if for some unforeseen reason they ever got to court, no judge would hold for a party guilty of intent to defraud. She was free of the burden; though, for tonight, she would tell only her mother and Alf. Let Alf wake his father up if he chose.

When Jody arrived home, she headed straight for her mother's room. Mrs. Jenson turned pale as Jody recounted the evening's revelations.

"Pornography? Massage parlors? Why it's…it's…I can't even find a word!"

Alf's reaction was almost identical when Jody telephoned him with the news. But his shock quickly became an intense fury. He wanted to dash right down to the hotel, collar Alex and throw him on the next plane for New York. But he settled for calling his father first thing in the morning.

Jody settled for some time alone by the kitchen hearth. She tried to clear her mind of the day's events by speculating on the gift Clif had mentioned. It was the one positive thing that had happened all day. . . .

CHAPTER SIXTEEN

LONG BEFORE the sun was up, Jody was awake and alert, anxious to be on the move, and wishing Clif hadn't decided to wait until noon to call. It was only six o'clock and still dark outside, yet it seemed silly to prolong the farce of sleeping. She would go to the store. Her family would be cross if they knew, but they needn't be aware of her seminocturnal outing until after she was safe in her office. It would be at least seven-thirty before her mother would awaken to read her note, and what could happen to her on a dawning Sunday morning?

Unlocking the door to Alferic's, Jody felt a deep sense of peace. Thoughts of Alex were behind her; indecision was in the past. She made a pot of coffee, and cradling a hot cup in her hands, she began a loving trip through her store. It gave her a feeling of contentment to touch familiar volumes, run a hand over leather chairs and polished wood, straighten a lamp here, a painting there. She wished it weren't Sunday. Any other day she could have dropped into the florist in a few hours' time to buy flowers to fill the beautiful vases her grandmother and mother had collected over the years. Never mind, she was here, and Alferic's was in Jenson hands. Still at peace, she mounted the stairs to her office to catch up on neglected work.

The early morning silence was pleasant to work in, and she had just congratulated herself on the quantity of paperwork she was clearing from her desk, when the sound of breaking glass intruded. Rather distant, she thought, probably a dog or cat in the alley foraging through the discards of some Saturday-night revelers. Shrugging it off, Jody pulled a pile of letters toward her and began making notations. However, she could not seem to shake off a sense of unease. There had been no further noise, but the stillness in the building was bothering her. She decided to make a quick tour of the store, to put her mind at rest.

A rapid check of the offices proved reassuring and she started down the stairs, only to halt at the sound of a thump, the sort of sound a pile of books would make if dropped. Her tread changed from careless to cautious, and she paused for a quick scan of the sales floor when it came into view. There was enough daylight now to show her that nothing was amiss there. The stockroom then. On the bottom step, she leaned over the banister toward the stockroom door, located underneath the staircase. It was ajar, so she tiptoed over to listen.

Muted voices reached her ear, and occasionally a laugh that was hushed instantly by a companion. She detected noises, which sounded like shuffling, more thumps and several shushing attempts. Puzzled, she frowned at the door. Putting her ear to the crack between door and jamb, she heard the sound of paper being crunched into a ball and then, distinctly, "Put the gas can up there." Jody stepped back in horror, rooted momentarily to the spot, before rage galvanized her into action and she barged through the door.

Alex and his father stood amidst a jumble of wadded-up paper and ripped books, a gasoline can perched on a ladder. The tableau resulting from mutual shock was but momentary. A quick movement and Jody was facing the snout of a pistol held by Renard Senior, a smile of pure malice shaping his face.

"No, Pop, No!" Alex put a restraining hand on his father's arm, attempting to get the gun.

"Outta my way, boy," he commanded, flinging his son aside like a broken toy. "Well, well, well, if it isn't Miss Jenson herself, the old bastard's granddaughter." His shrill escalating laugh rang out, bouncing off the walls, reverberating in Jody's ears, adding to the horror engulfing her. He kept talking, all the while waving the weapon about, pointing it at various parts of her body, as if trying to decide where to begin firing.

"How perfect. How absolutely perfect. One match, one lousy kitchen match and I get fancy store and bitchy granddaughter both."

Think! Jody commanded herself, but her brain seemed sluggish, her thoughts struggling against some watery current. There must be something she could do. Knock the phone off the hook? A dial tone would be no help. The alarm button then. She had to reach under the desk. But how?

As if reading her mind, the elder Renard leveled the barrel in a direct line with her chest. "Don't do it, Miss Jenson, whatever it is you're thinking about. I'll have a hole through you before you can shift your weight."

He jerked his head in Alex's direction. "Tie her in the chair, boy. Go on! Move it! No more screwups. Just do as you're told!"

"Her wrist, Pop, can't you see the bandage? She sprained...*I* sprained her wrist yesterday; it'll hurt to tie—"

"So make it loose. She's not going anywhere. Go on, hurry it up."

Alex snipped some rope from a carton, pulled the desk chair out and held it for her. Jody thought the courteous gesture almost worthy of a chuckle except that amusement was the furthest thing from her mind.

She could hear him mumbling as he ineffectually looped the light rope around her wrists.

"Pop's lost his mind...gone berserk...flew himself out here in a rage...I love you...won't let him hurt you...oh God, I'll never get away from him...."

Jody paid no attention, intent upon devising a way to reach the buzzer beneath the desk drawer. "Push me up to the desk," she whispered, "so I have something to lean on."

"What are you doing?" Renard Senior queried sharply as he heard the casters roll.

"Something for her to rest against."

"Hmph, you're going soft, boy. Grab that box of excelsior and start dumping it in the corners."

Wiggling her hands behind the chair back, Jody realized that the rope had gotten hooked on the lever that raised and lowered the seat height. A wave of panic hit her. Tugging at the rope only succeeded in chafing her painfully and sending a stab of agony through her wrist. She closed her eyes, willing calmness, but her thoughts flew to Clif.

She was going to die here, never having told him how much she loved him and wanted him. A sob escaped her, and the cry reached Renard's ears.

"Shut up," he snarled, walking over and poking the pistol barrel at her temple—hard. "One more sound and you're through. Got that?"

She nodded her understanding, forcibly quelling the continuing sobs that threatened to tear her apart. *Clif, I need you! There are so many things I need to tell you. I'll die here and... Stop! Stop thinking about dying, think about living! Think about telling him exactly how you feel and how much you love him—commitment or no commitment.*

"Start pouring gas, boy."

The harsh words were all the catalyst Jody needed, and she did the first thing that came to mind to distract them—talk.

"Mr. Renard, you realize that you'll be caught, don't you?"

He came to stand in front of her again and, too late, she realized that she'd make a mistake. Now his attention was focused directly on her. There would be no more trying to free her hands.

"Doesn't bother me in the least, Miss Jenson. It'll be the end of Alferic's and my life's work is done. Mission accomplished, you might say."

"Have you considered your son? I doubt that destroying my bookstore is *his* life's work."

Renard's eyes, which had been glittering in madness, filmed over. He blinked and swung his head slowly in Alex's direction. "She's right. Mustn't get you mixed up in this... your mother will need you... you must carry on. Go back to the hotel and get ready to go home. You can be on a plane while this pile of junk is still burning."

"I'm not leaving Jody here. I won't let you kill her," Alex retorted defiantly.

"You can't stop me, so don't try. Just get moving. Go on, do as you're told."

Alex shook his head and held his ground.

"Have it your way, then. Start pouring that gas." He turned back to Jody. "Maybe you'd like me to shoot you before we torch the place?"

She ignored his question. "Before you burn the place down, you might look in the safe for some of my grandfather's old papers. The safe won't burn, you know, and there might be some incriminating letters or documents in there."

"What's the combination, and hurry it up," Renard snapped, then gestured to Alex to assist him.

She gave him the numbers and both men turned their backs to her as they fiddled with the dial. Now she had another chance to attempt freeing herself, and she suddenly knew exactly what to do. It was so simple—if she'd been thinking clearly all along. Relaxing her arms, she dangled her hands as far toward the floor as she could. Her upward tugging had merely served to tighten Alex's loose knots; relaxing should result in enough slack to slip the rope off the hindering lever. It worked. Her bonds were no longer caught on the chair, but now she had to wiggle her hands free, and what if the rope dropped? Would they hear it or see her motion when she reached for the button?

A wild shriek of laughter interrupted her thoughts. Renard was in front of her, waving a picture in her face and yelling at her. "Take a look at this. Look! Pride! Pride all over the old bastard's face, your snooty grandma beaming. Take a good look at what I'm about to turn into a smoldering ruin. Take a good look."

The picture was a twin of the one she had loved all of her life, the one hanging in the library at home. Jody could have wept, but she forced herself to concentrate on her next action. Renard had returned to the safe and was scrabbling his way through more papers. Now was her chance to reach under the desk. As one hand slipped free she swallowed a gasp of relief and then, in a sudden roar of rage, Renard spun to face her. "It's all here. The newspaper clippings accusing my father of being a criminal...all the dirty gossip..." He leveled the gun at her.

Alex moved to stop him. His father's arm whipped back and caught him in the head, knocking him against the safe and dazing him. Renard fired. A corner of the desk splintered. He fired again, and a bullet hit the floor at Jody's feet, imbedding itself in the old wooden floor.

Jody tightened her face, refusing to show her terror. *He's toying with me, wants to scare me witless. I won't give him the satisfaction. Dear Lord, help me stay calm.*

"Stop!" Alex commanded, and to Jody's amazement, it was truly a command.

Renard turned in disbelief to face his son and Jody acted. She pressed the signal that would alert the police. The response was seemingly instantaneous. All three of them heard Alferic's front door crash open.

What happened next would always be remembered by Jody as a blur, a macabre dance in slow motion. She saw Renard's free hand move to steady the gun as Alex darted in front of him, his mouth wide in a scream of protest. She heard a shot, and then Alex crumpled slowly to the floor.

"Jody!" Clif's anguished cry was followed by the sound of toppling fixtures and flying books as he tore through the store, shouting her name in rising terror.

She stood, clutching the desk to steady a swaying she couldn't seem to control, and gaping at the grotesque scene. Renard simply stared in mute astonishment at the body of his son, prostrate and bleeding in front of him.

Clif erupted through the door. With a choking sob, he swept her into the safety of his arms, spinning around to put himself between her and the still-smoking gun. Alf ran in and halted in an attitude of bewilderment, trying to comprehend the meaning of what surrounded him—wadded paper, ripped books scattered around, a gasoline can, a body on the floor, the stench of gunpowder.

"My son, are you all right? Boy, say something!" Renard's voice was dazed with disbelief, heavy with dread. "He . . . he stepped in front of the gun." Renard's pleading gaze met the appalled expressions of the onlookers. "I have killed my son. I have . . ."

Alex moaned. One hand began groping toward a shoulder, and he rolled onto his side. The gun clattered to the floor as Renard knelt in relief. An arm still firmly around Jody, Clif kicked the weapon into a far corner, and Alf grabbed the gas can and capped it. The sound of approaching sirens swiveled all gazes toward the door. The answer to Jody's call was on its way.

She slipped from Clif's arm and knelt beside Alex, lifting his wrist to feel for a pulse. "Strong but erratic," she said.

Renard Senior suddenly turned ashen, his skin clammy. He began clawing at his shirt pocket. His breath was coming in great gulps, but he managed to utter, "Heart ... Pills ..." Jody reached for the small box of tablets and gave him the nitroglycerin he needed, then sat back on her heels, feeling too dizzy to stand.

"Come on, darling." Clif scooped her from the floor and held her tight against his chest. "Alf, I'm going to take her home—out the back way before the police get in here. Tell them I'll contact them after I've got her settled. On no account are they to call her. You and I can handle the questioning, for today at least. You know where to find me if you need me."

Once in the car, Jody gave way to a brief bout of weeping, replaced when the tears dried, by a dull torpor, a sense of unreality. The events she'd just been a party to only happened to other people or on TV, didn't they?

"At least he's not dead," she said.

"Renard can thank the Lord for that! He won't be facing a murder charge, just attempted murder, assault and battery, false imprisonment, breaking and entering, and attempted arson, for openers. Ought to get him out of the way for quite a while."

"I think he's gotten himself out of the way. He looked a broken man, even before the heart attack or whatever he was having."

"You're probably right. Are you okay?"

She nodded, unseeing eyes fixed on her lap. "How did you and Alf know we were there?"

"A chain of events set in motion by Alf, to whom I intend to erect a statue for saving your life. Fortunately, your cousin is an early riser and has no compunctions about disturbing the Sunday-morning slumbers of others." He placed a hand on her knee. "Just put your head back and try to relax while I jabber on. Don't try to talk yourself, let me do that. Anyway, first thing this morning, Alf began a series of phone calls, beginning with his father, who was understandably incensed at the news. Neither of your uncles had the remotest inkling of foul play of any sort, much less anything involving adult books. Alf then called Clark...same answer, no inkling. I was, thank God, the next one to get a wake-up call. I told Alf about our suspicions and he provided me with the missing pieces of the puzzle. As he was talking, I remembered you saying you'd club Alex over the head if he were involved in laying a trap for you, so I asked Alf where you were. The most unpleasant visions of you storming back to the hotel and swinging at Alex with an umbrella, or some such thing, kept going through my head.

Jody smiled slightly at his sally, but didn't comment.

Clif continued. "We're almost home, my love, and I'm almost done with this tale. Alf agreed that you might take matters into your own hands, so he called your house and woke your mother. She read the note you'd left and Alf called me back saying, nothing to worry about, you were at the store. However, he also said that he was so mad at Alex on your account that he was going to the hotel and punch the devious fellow out himself. Sounded like a capital idea to me and we met in the lobby. There was no answer at Alex's suite, but the night desk clerk was still on, and he told us that an older man—'a crazy old bird' were his words—had charged in during the wee hours and dragged their guest out the door shouting about revenge and that damn bookstore. I've never moved so fast in my life as I did getting out of that hotel and over to Alferic's. End of tale, and here we are."

"What a nightmare," she murmured. "If only Alex is all right. He tried, Clif, he tried to save me."

"I know he did and for that I could almost love the filthy... Never mind. We'll get it all squared away later. For now I want you to let me take care of everything, okay?"

She smiled her gratitude, happy to let Clif handle the situation for the time being.

TRUE TO HIS WORD, Clif had indeed taken care of everything. Quietly and competently, he had spoken with Mrs. Jenson, Anna and the chief of police—reassuring the first, giving instructions to the second and making arrangements with the third for a meeting later in the day.

Jody, meanwhile, had taken a hot bath after she had seen her mother, and had wrapped herself in the warmest pajamas and robe she possessed. Now she was in the library, ensconced on the couch, in front of a blazing fire, and sniffing the aroma of the fresh coffee that Anna had just set down. As ordered by Clif, there was also a bottle of brandy on the tray.

Although she was warm and her tension was beginning to seep away, there still seemed an unreality about the time of day. She was surprised to hear church bells chiming in the distance. How could it still be morning, still be Sunday even? It was so quiet that she wondered if Clif had left, but he couldn't have. He had been closeted with her mother when she came downstairs, and she would have heard him leave.

"Jody?" Clif called softly from the door.

She propped herself up. "Hi, I'm here. How's Mom?"

"Fine. Calm and comfortable. Anna's with her."

"Good," Jody said, settling back on the cushions.

She heard Clif lock the library door, and pull the drapes shut. Then he was beside her, urging her to sip the hot coffee laced with brandy.

"Why is brandy so good in a crisis?" she asked, relishing the heat traveling down her throat and chest.

"I don't know, but it's a time-honored remedy. Even the St. Bernards clamber through the snow with it to revive the hapless injured."

As they laughed together, Clif's expression was one she couldn't fathom. He wandered to the fireplace, rearranged some of the candlesticks on it and finally came to stand over her.

"Do you love him, Jody?"

She blinked at the unexpected question. "Alex? No, of course I don't. Whatever made you ask that?"

"Because of what he did today . . . I thought maybe something else had happened between you two last night. Something you hadn't told Alf."

"Nothing else at all, nothing could have. You see, it just so happens that I'm quite madly in love with you."

An inarticulate sound came from Clif's throat as he dropped to his knees beside her, burying his head against her. His words were muffled, but she had no trouble understanding them.

"Thank God! My love . . . Jody. When I thought . . . the shot . . . if anything had . . . my love, will you marry me?"

She wanted to answer, yet her throat was clogging with tears, and unaccountably, she began sobbing. All she could muster was a choked "Oh, yes" as she clung to him fiercely.

The tears were running down her cheeks faster than Clif could kiss them away. "I'm such a fool," he was saying. "Such a damn fool.... This morning didn't need to happen. I wanted the ring and a romantic setting before I asked you. I should have asked you yesterday. Then you'd have been with me..."

"You're not a fool. I love you for wanting it that way. I love you for everything you think, or do, or say." Her tears stopped as abruptly as they'd begun. She was now free to love Clif with the whole of her being, and she laughed at the joy of it.

"My love," she said, savoring the sound and feel of it.

In his happiness, Clif clasped her convulsively in his arms as if he was afraid she'd vanish any moment. His lips swept her brow, her cheeks, her chin, and then claimed her mouth in a starving passion that seemed insatiable. When his hands began traveling over her body, it was an act of reassuring himself that she was truly there for him. Then he lay down beside her, simply holding her, lips pressed to her hair.

"I never knew it was possible to be so utterly scared and so completely happy all in the same few hours. The sight of a gun, never mind the sound, after this will...my God! The ring! I've forgotten the ring."

He jumped to his feet, went to his jacket pocket and brought back a worn velvet ring box.

Jody pressed the tiny release button. The lid sprang up and she gazed at the most beautiful star sapphire she'd ever seen.

"It was my great-grandmother's. I didn't know if it was in the bank vault or in my parents' safe. That's why I said I hoped to have a gift for you." Then, as Jody continued to stare in silence, he added, "If you don't like it, I'll get something else for you."

"Rosemary leaves," she whispered, as if she hadn't heard a word he'd said. "The gold is all etched with rosemary leaves."

"For remembrance, so you'll always remember how much I adore you. You do like it then?"

She pressed the little box against herself defensively. It was a far more telling gesture than words could have expressed.

He chuckled and took her left hand in his. "I'm not going to take it back, my love, but I would like to put it on your finger." The lovely ring slipped on as if it had found its proper home, though its sparkle may have been slightly dimmed by the shine in Jody's eyes.

Clif started to lie down again but changed his mind almost immediately and stood up. "No," he said, "we're not going to make love here. Frantic as I am for you, this is emphatically neither the time nor the place. I want it to be perfect for you, and that can't happen on a narrow couch, where someone can come knocking any minute."

Jody's faced showed her disappointment, though she knew he was right. "So, what's next on the agenda?"

"A few loose ends to tie up." Clif grinned at her and straightened his tie. "A frantic rush from police chief to hospital, back here . . . and then to my place."

"I'm going to miss you. I've come to the conclusion that you are *the* most exciting, wonderful man on

the planet! I absolutely adore you and I'm in a frenzy
to get to that last stop!''

He moved to kiss her again and thought better of it.
Instead he blew her a kiss, gave a last pat to the knot
of his tie and picked up his jacket.

"Clif, shouldn't I be going with you? I mean, won't
the police want to see me? And the hospital, I should
at least go there.''

"Not today, darling. I'll get the chief to come over
some time tomorrow, and as for the hospital, you can
make up your own mind about that, also tomorrow.
For now, you just stay right here and wait for your
husband-to-be. By the way, your mother will be interested in hearing about this latest development.''

"Mom? Is that what you were talking about with
her?''

"Yep. Got the requisite parental approval before
popping the question. Aren't you proud of me?''

"I love you more every minute. That was such a
marvelous thing to do. You are the most fabulous...''

"Hush, woman! You start in again and I won't be
able to leave at all.''

"My lips are sealed.''

"Good. Though I much prefer them open under
other circum...never mind, I'm off to zip through my
rounds and clear the decks for us. Back as soon as
possible.''

As soon as possible turned out be several hours later
and it was early evening before Clif returned. He
walked into a veritable swarm of Jensons, all of them
in varying stages of shock over the happenings and
revelations of the morning. Kirsten and Hulda were

red-eyed, having cried at length over their parts in forcing Jody's hand. Cousins and their offspring were either stunned or thought it the most exciting adventure ever, depending upon their ages. And the uncles had declared that they'd gladly accept their niece's offer.

"Nils and I have been talking things over, Jody," said Eric. "We'll cut back the North Dakota operation and rotate the employees on shorter shifts so no one's out of work. And there's some fat right here in the Minneapolis plant that can stand some trimming. We'll finagle around, take a look at our whole layout, figure something out. I'm ashamed to say that we might have been a trifle greedy. Your offer is fair and we'll keep Jenson & Sons in business with a minimum of trouble—and some ruthless cost analysis."

Clif's announcement that both Renards would recover was greeted with relief. Now they could tell Warren to initiate the processes that would mete out formal punishment to "those scoundrels."

Alf posed the question that was on the tip of every adult tongue. "Do the police want to question any of us?"

Clif signaled a negative. "They obtained full confessions from the two men, including the fact that old Renard planted that loan officer here. He's some big shot in the bank's hierarchy, so no one dared countermand his decision. Just might be that the guy's in for some criminal charges of his own. Be that as it may, the fight's just gone out of the Renards. And Alex said the strangest thing to me. He said, 'Prison will make a man of me.' Made it sound as if he's glad he was caught."

Every face showed bewilderment, except Jody's. She knew what Alex meant and thought he was probably right. In fact his statement led her to believe he'd already begun his uphill climb.

Nils tapped his brother's arm. "Eric, I've been racking my brain, trying to remember if I ever heard anything about the Beacon Tower and a scandal. I came up with nothing."

"I've been digging around in the memory bank, too, but I can't come up with much—just that there was trouble. Nils, you were too young, and there were so many names being bandied about, so many people involved. We were all too young, only interested in getting dinner over with and leaving the boring old folks to talk, while we went outside to play. Who would have thought of this?"

Mrs. Jenson caught Clif's attention. "Would you please take Jody for some fresh air? A long drive, I think."

Clif jumped up and helped a trembling Jody from her chair. All the hideous events of the morning had come flooding back to her. She felt dizzy again, suffocating almost. She stumbled a bit as he led her from the room.

Clif helped Jody on with her coat and assisted her down the front steps. "Better, darling?"

Jody nodded, sinking gratefully into his car. "Sorry, the whole scene was just suddenly there again."

"Nothing to be sorry about." He eased the car out of the driveway. "I think you should probably expect that sort of thing for a while. Trauma like that doesn't just fade from thought once it's over. I just hope I'm around when the recalls come."

"So do I!" Jody wanted to hug Clif right there and then, but the sporty design of the car and the confines of their seat belts kept them apart. "Clif, I hate bucket seats. I want to be next to you and these fool things make it impossible."

"I know. Designed by a eunuch. Here—" he placed her hand on his thigh "—that's about the best we can do for now. Twenty minutes and we'll be in seclusion."

CLIF'S APARTMENT overlooked the Mississippi, though Jody got only a passing glimpse of the picture window and the swiftest impression of leather furniture, brass and glass tables, all buried in books and papers, before she was folded close against him.

She sighed contentedly, raising her face to welcome the tender lips whispering over her features. Quickly then, his voice thickened, his mouth became urgent and she clung to him, returning the hard pressure of his body. Without relinquishing her lips Clif lifted her and carried her into his bedroom.

What began as a leisurely undressing of each other, soon changed to haste, with clothes dropped and flung to land where they might and bedding whipped off to fall to the floor.

Deftly Clif's hands and mouth moved over her— now delicate and savoring, now powerful and hungry, traveling in lazy patterns and lingering in intimacy. Jody luxuriated in the absolute rightness of this loving as her body unfurled beneath his caresses. When at last he brought them together, they became a single, soaring harmony that reached a zenith to the cry of their names. And both of them knew that those were the only names they'd ever need to know.

Clif rolled onto his back, carrying her with him, still saying her name over and over again, stroking her love-damp hair, murmuring against her brow as he waited for her breathing to slow.

Once her senses felt comfortably back on terra firma, Jody began molding the hard muscles of his arms and shoulders with her hands, exploring the dark mat of his chest, tracing the clean lines of his face, testing the feel of him. As she outlined his lips, he caught her finger in his mouth and nipped it lightly.

"The splendor of you," she said.

"To complement the splendor of you. So sensuous . . . although I knew you would be. I knew it."

Jody blinked in surprise. "You did? How?" She frowned slightly in concentration, trying to remember. "They way I kissed you in the office?"

"That, of course, but I had you pegged twenty-four hours before that."

"Clifton McClelland, are you saying I go around advertising myself? Beast!" Her playful accusation was accompanied by a light clip on his chin.

"That's exactly what I'm saying, Miss Jenson," Clif teased back, as she punched him again, harder this time. "But, not to worry, darling, you're a role model for a lady, and there are very, very few out there as perceptive as your future husband."

Jody slid down next to him, rested on her elbows and glared at him in mock anger. "So tell me how you knew the very first time you saw me," she commanded.

He let his fingers rove through her hair and said, "This, for one thing. You wear it loose and free, just inviting me to do precisely what I'm doing. Your expressive face, for another, tells me that you're not afraid to let go with your feelings. Your behavior with your customers was a dead giveaway. You touched every single one of them, except me, of course. Then there's the way you eat—sniffing each new scent, savoring each bite. And once we got past the board-meeting phase, there are the clothes you wear, the warm colors, the soft, silky fabrics that want stroking...just like your exquisite satin skin. Jody, I'll never stop wanting you, never stop..." His words trailed off, lost in the renewal of passion.

Before the night was over Jody crested the waves of fulfillment over and over and over. She knew what it was to take the initiative with the man of her heart, pleasuring him in ways that seemed born in the tissue of her female body. She experienced love in the frenzy of need and the tranquility of time. She learned that loving could be tumultuous or languid, intense or playful, and she knew the unparalleled joy of awakening to a look of adoration and renewed longing.

"I'm a wanton," she announced over scrambled eggs at eight the next morning.

"Nothing wrong with that, as long as it's me you're wantin'."

Jody nearly choked her food. "Clif, that was awful! The worst pun I've ever..." And then she was off in peels of laughter at his feigned look of hurt.

"Easy for you to say," he grumbled. "I thought it was quite good, considering how exhausted I am.

"Oh-ho, exhausted, are you! Well, you poor man, if that was the effect I had when my stomach was growling in empty indignation, just wait until I get these eggs inside. Fresh fuel, renewed energy and all that."

Clif shook his head. "The mind reels, contemplating what you'll be wantin' once you're stoked up."

Later, fitting herself against a contentedly sleeping Clif, Jody was sure that there had never been such a love as theirs. She knew absolutely that she had never expected to be adored as Clif adored her. His words, his eyes, his hands and body all told her that she was the most precious part of his now complete world. He was pleased to call her a miracle, but as far as she was concerned, the word applied just as much to him, and to the glory of their oneness.

Clif stirred and turned over to hold her. "I will never, ever let anything hurtful happen to you again," he said, and promptly fell asleep once more.

Jody smiled against his shoulder. It was a beautiful promise and one she would always treasure, whether he was able to keep it or not. With Clif at her side, she was sure that nothing could daunt her now. She'd found the mate she'd longed for, and their partnership would be long and rich. Jody knew this beyond all doubt. Her woman's wisdom told her so.

**SIZZLING ROMANCE
IN THIS ACTION-PACKED SEQUEL!**

If you're one of the many Sharon Brondos fans who enjoyed reading about Kyle and Charity's adventures in *Give and Take*, Superromance #228, you'll love meeting them again in

SEARCH FOR
THE RAINBOW

This time, though, it's their dear friend, Bill Woburn, who takes the spotlight.

The burly police lieutenant isn't looking for romance when he meets Julie Chandlar, but he finds that—and much more—in this mysterious lady with a shady past.

Watch for *Search for the Rainbow*, Superromance #266. Coming to you next month!

IF GEORGIA BOCKOVEN CAPTURED YOU ONCE, SHE'LL DO IT AGAIN!

In Superromance #246, *Love Songs*, Amy had to protect her friend, Jo, from all the Brad Tylers of the world. Now in Temptation #161, *Tomorrow's Love Song*, Amy has her own troubles brewing....

She assumes a false identity and sets out to right a few wrongs. She's got everything to gain—millions of dollars. And everything to lose—the one man who belongs in her future....

Look for Temptation #161, *Tomorrow's Love Song*. Coming to you in July!

Take 4 best-selling love stories FREE
Plus get a FREE surprise gift!

For the millions who can't read
Give the Gift of Literacy

One out of five adults in North America
cannot read or write well enough
to fill out a job application
or understand the directions on a bottle of medicine.

**You can change all this by joining the fight
against illiteracy.**

For more information write to:
Contact, Box 81826, Lincoln, Neb. 68501
In the United States, call toll free: 800-228-3225

**The only degree you need
is a degree of caring**